Rich Man's Blood

ALSO BY JOHN C. BOLAND

Easy Money

Brokered Death

The Seventh Bearer

JOHN C. BOLAND

Rich Man's
BLOOD

ST. MARTIN'S PRESS
NEW YORK

Design by Basha Zapatka

Library of Congress Cataloging-in-Publication Data
Boland, John C.
      Rich man's blood / John C. Boland.
            p.   cm.
      "A Thomas Dunne book."
      ISBN 0-312-09371-3
      I. Title.
      PS3552.0575R5   1993
      813'.54—dc20   93-1110
                                                                    CIP

First edition: July 1993

10 9 8 7 6 5 4 3 2 1

FOR ED AND RHODA

1

I dropped onto the boat's aft deck in the hammering rain. My light wool suit, never intended for the Gulf Coast in August, clung like steaming burlap. The raincoat I'd picked up the day before had become soaked thirty seconds after I stepped out of the boat yard's shelter. Water splashed off the brim of my hat and streamed down my chest. The wind drove the rain almost sideways, pushing it up the river from the Gulf of Mexico like a hot tidal wall. Underfoot the boat thrashed in the river's current, pounded against the fenders that shielded the hull and the pier from mutual destruction. From where I had boarded on the long, flat rear deck, the bow's flat triangle thirty feet upstream looked like a gray sketch that faded suddenly as the rain thickened. I moved forward, stepping over loose pipe casings and lines. Reaching the deckhouse brought me out of the direct line of the downpour, but the drumming of water on steel overhead smothered all other sound.

The superstructure bulged ahead of me. Following its contour, the rail left a passage about three feet wide. Two white-painted steel doors led into the boat. Both were closed. My destination, the pilothouse, was perched directly overhead, reaching back about half the length of the main structure. There were two ways to reach it: either from the ladder on the foredeck, which would put me outside the windows, or by an interior companionway, which would come up inside the bridge.

The outside ladder exposed me to more than raw weather.

My hand slipped on the oily bar of the door. I gripped it harder and twisted. The door was bolted. I continued down the deck and tried the second door. It refused to give.

That left the outside route.

Stepping around the curving bulkhead earned me a massive slap in the body from the wind and rain. The force seemed to have doubled in the past half minute. Out from under the metal, I could hear a little bit again, and the lines to the pier whipped high and banged the railing. The boat swayed, trying to tear loose from the mooring and surrender itself to the river. A roll caught me unprepared. As the deck dipped, my feet slipped. I crashed to my knees and was promptly flung backward against the railing, then dumped forward onto my knees again. I grabbed the ladder to the upper deck and clung to it. The violent pitching went on. Looking up, I saw eight steps, a climb of less than six feet. Beyond the ladder loomed the rain-blurred nose of the pilothouse. Its gray windows looked as opaque as steel plate. I braced a shoulder against one of the ladder's handrails and clutched a metal tread. One step at a time, I hauled myself up.

From the upper deck, I should have been able to see most of the yard, its administrative and refitting buildings, the lashed-down canvases, and three other boats tied along the wharf. The nearest tug, which had a bright red stack, was a colorless shadow. Thirty yards of rain hid any trace of the shipyard. Even the office lights had vanished. It would have felt lonely if I had imagined I was alone.

No sound escaped from the pilothouse. Poking my head above the bottom of a window, I tried to peer inside. Runnels cloaked the glass, turning it into a distorting lens. Nothing seemed to move in the darkened room. I duck-walked around to the side and tried a door. It opened with a muffled squeal. I scuttled into the deeper gloom. When I pulled the door shut, the vessel tilted and steel slammed against steel with a clamor that must have been felt throughout the boat.

Another sound answered. A thud.

I couldn't tell what it was, only that it came from below. For a minute I waited, but there was no repetition of the noise. The weather's sounds repeated.

Whoever shared my shelter was waiting and listening. I had an advantage in that I was certain of his existence. He could only speculate on mine.

If I tried to move around, the scrape and clatter would be unmistakable and we would be equal. In fact, he would gain the advantage. He would know what had brought him here, and that he had been discovered. I knew only that I had seen movement on the foredeck of the *Brangus* five minutes earlier from the office building.

I had come out thoughtlessly, just as the storm resumed its day-long assault. Curious whether the trespasser had been friend or foe of Stu Harris. Not curious enough, it seemed to me now, about what he might be like if he fit the foe category.

Creeping ahead, I hunkered at the opening of the companionway that led down to the main deck. It was even darker down there than in the deep dusk of the pilothouse.

Then I heard the sound again, a rhythmic clanging that rose hollowly like tapping from a well bottom. Not from the main deck but from farther down. How deep was the engine compartment? It had been ten months since I had toured this boat and others with Stu, their proud proprietor. I seemed to remember a third deck, below the waterline, where a giant diesel engine had gleamed spotlessly in factory-fresh red paint.

I eased myself into the opening, shoulder to the wall for support, and slid down the ladder on my backside. It was a quiet way of descending, and steady. The companionway opened onto a hall that traversed the boat. On either side were doors leading to the narrow walkway on the deck. In front of me was another door going forward. Behind me a door led to what I recalled were bunk quarters and a galley for the crew.

I went forward.

The passage fed into more living quarters, with narrow closets, narrow bunks, a portable television that would be bolted to the dresser it stood on. At the end of the corridor a ladder reached down to the engine compartment. Light seeped up the companionway. I crept to the opening and could see nothing except a section of mammoth diesel power plant. Enough muscle lay dormant in those engines to pull a thousand-ton drilling rig across an unfriendly Gulf. From below, breathing came raggedly, little explosions that accompanied a methodical scraping, the sound of a man working hard and fast. An impatient mutter, then the scraping resumed.

Then it stopped. He cursed softly. Not in frustration but in satisfaction. After a minute, the light went out. The top of a head appeared, a scalp scratched by sparse black hair, then a heavy brow, a pixie's nose, rubbery pitted cheeks, a tan jacket. Both hands were occupied, one with a blue-and-white-striped canvas bag, the other with a long pipe fitter's wrench. He paused, shifted the wrench to the hand with the bag, and grabbed the railing.

He was starting to look up when I drew back, searching for cover.

The forward door was the closest retreat, but opening it couldn't be done silently. I took the passage toward the bow and slipped into the tiny galley, crowded with stowage cabinets, a refrigerator, a sink and a counter full of hot plates. I hugged the wall beside the doorway.

He was a trespasser, clearly. Not one of Stu's men come back for some gear. Not a mechanic working even though last week's paycheck was late. A trespasser who had picked a stormy morning when he was unlikely to be disturbed in his prowling.

I wished I hadn't left Tom Avery in the business office and wandered upstairs to the soda machines, passing windows in the dispatching room that looked down onto the yard and the wharf, where a figure I could barely discern was scampering across the deck of the *Brangus.*

At the top of the ladder, the intruder paused. There was no sign that he had heard my escape. But I could imagine his muscles bunching as some primitive part of his brain noted the smell in the air of human hair, sweat, damp wool. The evidence might be too faint for the rational brain to recognize, but the subrational part bristled.

His feet fell heavily on the steel decking, headed down the hall to the left. That way lay one of the doors to the outside deck. A metal groan reached me, and suddenly the storm was louder. An instant later the door slammed.

I breathed easier. There would be a car in the employees' lot or just outside the gate. From a reasonable distance I might get a license number for the police.

When I reached the passageway where he had hesitated, I knew I had been lucky. My shoes were soaked, and water lay in the grooved steel deck. Either he hadn't seen the evidence or had chosen retreat over confrontation. Since he had held the only heavy wrench, I approved the choice.

Confrontation as such I could stand, could deliberately provoke when it suited me. But the ensuing violence occurred only in numbers flashed on computer screens. Brutal in their coldness, sometimes deadly to a rival's financial plan, they were not nearly as primitive as a swinging wrench.

Not as final, anyway.

I opened the door and stepped into the rain. Scanning the yard, I expected to see a retreating tan jacket. There was nobody.

I leaned against the railing and stared along the wharf. He might have gone down the line for a look inside another boat.

He wasn't in sight.

A puff of rain caught my face as I turned for a survey of the river side. The river was called the Atchafalaya and emptied into Atchafalaya Bay and the Gulf of Mexico thirty winding miles south of Stu Harris's headquarters. The churning water was heavy and brown with silt, stirred to a frothy chop by the wind, and moving fast with the weight of billions of gallons behind it. The opposite shore, a hundred yards distant and barely visible, was a dense pine forest.

No flicker of movement alerted me, no scrape of shoe. His feet, as he swung from the pilothouse deck, struck my back and I went sprawling. My knees caught the edge of the gunwale, and my cheek hit a tire fender.

As I tried to straighten, he sprang down. Hands as hard as vises grabbed my arm. His expression was concentrated, businesslike. A little bit like a certain chief executive I knew confronting a problem.

He didn't snarl that I shouldn't nose around. Didn't threaten.

The wrench swung up, and I twisted, arms tangling around my head. There were coat sleeves, muscle and bone, and a poplin hat between my skull and the steel. The blow landed with crunching ferocity.

My face was on the deck. Getting rained on. Then it left the deck, as he lifted me.

The next impact was muddy water that first resisted, then pulled and spun me downward.

2

By any reasonable standard, Patrick Welles, Sr. was a bastard. Not from parental neglect, nor from harsh circumstances, nor because of bad-tempered genes. He had gotten there by struggle, determination, conviction. Every bit a self-made man.

By his own judgment, he was demanding but fair. He mentioned his fairness when meting out harsh and undeserved punishments. Through the distorting lens of his ego, which looked coldly and critically in every direction but one, his temper tantrums, pettiness and outrages against the people around him became acts of love. Harshness was kindness if it made a man stronger.

And if it made a man weak? That we didn't discuss.

By being born third, ten years behind a brother and two years behind a sister, I had escaped the brunt of our father's attention. Seeing the stammering coward that had been crafted of her eldest son, our mother sheltered me with her first successful defiance of Patrick senior's will in their two decades of marriage. I was pampered, shielded, coddled, cooed over—spoiled relentlessly to earn my father's contempt, his pity, and, most important, his neglect. *You've made a mess of this one,* was his attitude toward my mother, *and since I can't repair the damage, you may continue with the disaster.*

Partly my escape was due to my brother's bad luck. When I came along, Father was still making a man out of him—molding him, and discovering much later to his bitter disappointment that the clay couldn't hold a shape.

Out of deference to the old man, my brother scorned me for the first fifteen years of my life, then began to seek me out for advice when his world crumbled, which was quite often. By the time I entered college—in New Mexico, which seemed a safe distance from home—Pat had accumulated a failed marriage, co-respondent standing in a junior partner's divorce, a revoked driver's license, and the benign contempt of even the office boys at the firm. He was indifferent. In movies, layabouts are portrayed as charming rogues, but Pat cultivated charm only when it served an immediate goal. He was affable when he approached me for practical advice. How much did the old man know about this or that screwup? Could I cover for him on the paperwork for the Bendheim account? He was charming when he invited a new secretary to lunch. He was agreeable when he sought my opinion of a high-flying stock he wanted to buy. Absent such a purpose, Pat was surly. Life may have been a party, but he didn't have to pretend to enjoy it.

For my part, I felt grateful that I hadn't been the one crippled.

"You're in trouble," he had confided on Monday, commandeering a corner of my desk. His features were settling into the family shape, heavy and blunt, so incongruous without accompanying authority. He was neither grumpy nor chummy that morning. The pendulum had paused in midswing, and Pat would behave as a normal adult until something upset him. He was wearing a maize foulard bow tie and a double-breasted linen suit, French cuffs, blue pindot socks, and cordovan slip-ons. He could step out the front door and be recognized anywhere as one of the town's gentleman investment bankers.

It was early in the week for anyone to be in trouble. "Aren't you exaggerating a little?" I asked.

"If anything, understating the case. The grand dragon himself was breathing fire at breakfast." He spread some analysts' reports with casual fingers, smiled. "As you'd know if you'd been there."

Missing the Monday morning breakfast at the firm was definitely a bad way to begin a week. Mr. Patrick, as the senior waiter in our dining room called him, hadn't missed presiding over a breakfast and strategy session in twenty years.

"I overslept," I admitted.

"Contemptible rake. Who was it?"

"No such luck. The Feldmans took me sailing. We went over to St. Michaels and didn't get back to Annapolis until after midnight. We slept on the boat, and I drove up this morning."

Pat listened with an inquisitor's judicial smirk. "I don't think I've ever heard a more feeble story, and I've concocted some hopeless ones. Anyway, the old bastard was going on about substantive matters. And I fear that where you're concerned, he had Harvey's ear."

At sixty-eight, Patrick Welles, Sr. would have mismanaged the firm with the same foul temper in which he presided over his family except that the partners had elevated him to chairman of the executive committee—a new position with vaguely defined authority—three years earlier and had installed a managing partner to oversee operations. The usurpation had probably saved the firm. The brokerage and investment banking businesses had become fiercely competitive, and Ambrose & Welles, the second oldest house in Baltimore, struggled as a regional firm to survive among national financial companies that were many times our size. We needed to keep all the professional staff we could attract, and Harvey Breton, the managing partner, made that task feasible. He was unfailingly cordial and unflappable, a combination that enabled him to disarm even old Patrick on a rant. Fortified behind a clerkish air, mildly curious about any complaint,

Harvey could respond to my father's expletives with a businesslike, "We'll work this out." After the first year, the senior Welles had ceased lunging at so unresponsive a target. He hadn't ceased trying to discredit Harvey with the other partners, but they understood; and the backbiting submerged into the background, as part of the status quo, almost comforting in its predictability. A monthly partners' meeting in which Father failed to launch an ingenious attack on Harvey Breton's management would have left the partners picking over the agenda in puzzlement, searching for a piece of forgotten business.

Harvey weathered it all. He was fifty-three, spent two hours a week on the handball court, and looked as if he could comfortably thwart the old man for another twenty years.

If there was a complaint against me that Harvey had endorsed, it was likely that I deserved blame. For whatever the sin might be.

And what was the sin?

Pat refused to say.

He strode off with a sunny look in the direction of his desk in the trading department. A big desk, loaded with decisions to be made, none of which affected the routine of the department or its traders. They took in shares of stock that came to us, bid for shares of companies we wanted positions in, sold shares from inventory when the price was right. They fastened their attention on a few dozen of our pet stocks and kept a peripheral watch on the market's averages, the way a sailor makes it his business to know what the barometer is doing. Would we have a breezy day for prices? Or was pressure falling? The game was obsessively entertaining and challenging to my mind. Ephemeral to Pat's.

I watched him go and wondered why he hadn't hit me up lately for any stocks to buy. His approach to investing was like his approach to charm. There had to be an end clearly in sight or the effort wasn't justified. His view of the future had its horizon about three months ahead, beyond which lay a blackness of uncertainty. So if he yearned to celebrate spring by buying a boat, he would show up at my desk in February wearing an affable mask and inquire, "Is Honeywell good for a few points?" If I said I didn't know, there would be a pause because I always had a stock I liked, or a bond of a company in bankruptcy, the name of which could be wrung loose with patience. Once Pat had his lead, he would laugh disparagingly. "Is this one of your long-term things, or can I expect a payoff in this decade?" And then he would borrow money to buy several times as many shares or bonds as I owned, ride them for two or three points if I was right, and get off. If my idea failed him, he turned surly for weeks.

What else were brothers for?

For half the morning I kept an apprehensive watch out for Harvey Breton, until I got absorbed in looking over one of our analysts' reports. The document was meant to tell our retail, stock-buying customers about recent developments at Pharm-Tek, a small medical testing laboratory that had its headquarters in a Washington suburb. Two years earlier we had managed the original sale of PharmTek's stock to the public, and the three chemists who ran the firm had made good use of the money the stock sale had raised. The company's revenues had doubled in the past eighteen months, according to the report, and the net income was rising almost as fast. The founders were in their forties and were finally making it big. While we were getting their company ready to go public, I had drunk with them, slept on their couches, met their wives, patted their dogs, and looked their business over like a surgeon inspecting for a hidden cancer. That was part of the job, making certain that Ambrose & Welles knew what it was backing. Our rival investment banking house across town, which did three times our business in a year, often missed problems. Their clients changed, ours stayed. Customers who bought the stock we underwrote trusted us to find all the warts, sprains and lesions on a company, and they would never forgive us if the president had a drinking problem that I hadn't uncovered. Sometimes my job was like a family counselor's instead of a corporate financial adviser's. If a chief executive had a problem that would hurt his company, it would also hurt any investors we had recruited. So I recommended drying-out clinics, psychologists, speech therapists, public relations experts, auditors and private detectives. And

I made a pest of myself talking to our clients' customers, suppliers, friends and enemies. Was the product or service better than average? Did bills get paid on time? Did invoices go out promptly? We had a rule of thumb in the corporate finance department: If a client was still talking to me a week before the financing became final, I had probably overlooked something.

The reward for this midwifing, for both me and for Ambrose & Welles, came when a company prospered as Pharm-Tek seemed to be doing. A. & W. held warrants to buy stock at a vanishing fraction of the current market price, and I owned a one-quarter-percent interest at a similar cost. A couple of my tweedy, fortyish colleagues in the corporate finance department had become wealthy on quarter-percent interests.

Pat ambled out at eleven-thirty, glancing over the desks that separated us. He seemed disappointed that I hadn't been thrown onto the street.

When twelve-fifteen came and Harvey Breton hadn't rung down, I stacked my papers. Except for traders who ate lunch at their desks, the partitioned cubbyholes on our floor had emptied promptly at eleven-fifty. That was normal.

Nobody had stopped at my desk with an invitation to join a group. That was normal, too.

I walked two blocks south and ate a Chinese lunch under a Cinzano umbrella near the harbor. The restaurants and boutiques were clustered there because Ambrose & Welles had backed a developer in convincing a dozen banks and insurance companies that a waterfront slum could look like old Boston, given twenty million dollars. Our cut, devised by my father, had included a large fee plus a tiny royalty on the project's management income, which guaranteed the firm payments into our next century.

That knowledge didn't improve the view of lazing sailboats. Instead it made me wonder whether I was wearing the tiny, smug smile that shaped so many faces at the office: comfortably bland, comfortably comfortable, ever so proud of both. There was no trace of closet Bolshevik in my temperament, but I recognized that I was prospering not entirely on my merit. People at other tables worked hard. Most could claim fair intelligence. All they lacked was a hereditary link to the town's second-best-connected investment banker.

That I ate lunch alone bothered me less. At twenty-nine I had settled into bachelorhood too insistently, my mother said. *You can't blame your father for everything, and—please!—I hope you don't blame me!* I didn't blame anyone. I didn't see solitary habits as penance. Just as relief from family life. There were bullies and those bullied, and I wanted to be neither.

Harvey's secretary caught me on my way out of the office at four-thirty. "Have you seen Mr. Breton?" she said suspiciously.

"No," I smiled, "have you lost him?"

"If you'll wait, I think he's free now."

Harvey had studied being gray and unthreatening. As you noticed the pale blue eyes, the withdrawn chin, the wrinkled forehead—creased from eyebrows lifting in polite inquiry, never frowns—you assumed that given his position, Harvey must be tougher than he looked. I had known him for three years and wasn't sure. He understood finance, markets, people, and office dynamics. He dealt with all of them quietly. I couldn't remember seeing Harvey lose his temper, though the temptation must have been fairly common. His avoidance of confrontation was both a useful tactic and a frozen habit.

He wore a white silk shirt with a stiff plain collar, a navy blue necktie with a motif of flying ducks that reappeared on blue suspenders. Once or twice a year he went gunning on the Eastern Shore. When he came back with an empty bag, according to office lore, he bought a necktie. He had filled his office with hunting oils, Audubon prints, bouillotte lamps and old leather furniture, the trappings that people like Patrick Welles, who were born to them, didn't bother with.

Harvey looked up with a worried smile. "Richard, how long has it been since you talked to Stuart Harris?"

The name was the furthest thing from my mind. "Three months, give or take," I stumbled. Trying to remember. Stu had phoned to announce that Noël had given birth. In the midst of another company's finances and personalities, I'd had a tough time pulling her face from my memory. A dark, plump girl who doted on a two-year-old daughter. Obviously a second little Harris was a happy event.

He had bought an extra workboat from a distressed owner, and I had congratulated him. That had been his strategy when he had come to us for financing eighteen months earlier. The Gulf was a big traffic snarl of excess commercial boats, as falling prices discouraged oil drilling. Weaker service companies, which owned the boats that ferried supplies to the diminishing fleet of offshore drilling rigs, were in trouble. We raised twelve million for Stu to build Harris Marine Company so it could expand its fleet at rock bottom prices and be ready to handle more customers when business picked up. I had put together the financing: bonds paying twelve percent a year, which we sold to a few big customers.

Harvey's smile trembled. "He's going to miss his interest payment. We were notified by express letter on Friday—uhm, after you'd left."

He held out the letter, and I took it. Addressed to our payments chief, it was straightforward to the point of brusqueness.

Dear Mr. Levy:

I regret that circumstances make it impossible for Harris Marine Company to submit the debenture interest payment which falls due on August 18. The trustee for the bonds is also being notified. This arrears will be corrected as soon as it becomes feasible.

Thomas H. Avery, Asst. Treasurer

I looked at Harvey in disbelief. "This is all? No explanation? No phone call?"

"Aaron Levy took the initiative of calling Harris Marine immediately. Stuart Harris was not in the office. Mr. Avery said he had been ordered not to disclose any more than he already had told us. Aaron tried again over the weekend to reach Stuart Harris, but he wasn't home. Mr. Avery said that Harris wanted to talk to you, personally."

"What about Ellis Samuels, the chief financial officer? Did Aaron try him?"

"I believe someone of that name was on vacation. Mr. Avery disclosed that much in explaining why he, instead of the financial officer, signed the letter to us." Harvey hemmed, embarrassed, and opened a folder. "I had Miss Perry pull the file from your cabinet. We discussed the situation at the morning meeting today. Our chairman suggested that you had been derelict in inspecting Harris Marine's finances and proposed—in keeping with his views on nepotism—that we fire you. Let's see. The debentures are secured by Harris Marine's assets, so our investors should get their money, eventually. If there's a market for used drilling supply boats. Is there?"

"A weak market."

"So it would be better if we can avoid having Mr. Harris go into default." He extended the file folder, eyebrows rising pessimistically. "Could you?"

I crept back to my desk. Default was about the worst word in our business. It set off series of repercussions—all of them bad. A debtor's note like Harris Marine's had a market value based on several considerations. One was its face amount, the size of the debt that was scheduled to be repaid. Another was the size of the interest payments investors got in the meantime. And finally, and most important, was how much faith the trading world had that the interest payments would continue and the principal would be paid off. If investors lost faith, the note lost most of its market value. In that event, banks and insurance companies that held the paper would have to mark down its value on their books and report the loss on the next earnings statement. The loss would make shareholders unhappy with management. Management would remember who sold them the Harris Marine bonds.

Anne Hargrave, the only other person still in the department, looked up from her quotation terminal. "So now you know," she said.

"Everyone else knew?"

She nodded. "Sort of." She was thin and pretty, brown-haired and green-eyed. Beneath the desk, her stockinged toes crossed atop a pair of cordovan pumps. She wore a gray-striped business suit, an open-necked pink shirt, a string of small pearls that were probably the best she could afford. She had gone to a local college, worked at a bank in New York, and moved back home a year or so ago. She had an apartment in the old Floyd building, according to Pat.

"Why no tip-off?" I asked. Normally the department was chatty to the point of distraction.

"No one wanted to be a bearer of bad news."

I almost laughed and said that I didn't shoot messengers—wasn't authorized to even if I got the urge. But she seemed serious. Even the chairman's unfavored son was still a chairman's son.

"How bad is it?" she asked. She had a tentative smile, prepared to be sympathetic. In the thirteen or fourteen months that she had sat nearby I had developed little impression of her. Anne Hargrave performed her work without flash, with methodical competence, and with evident pleasure. What made her happy or sad outside the office I had no idea. Our conversations never veered into personal territory.

Now I shrugged, turning away from eyes that seemed to be friendly. "I don't know how serious," I said. "In any event, it's my problem."

3

It was an hour earlier in New Orleans, so I tried phoning Stu. The headquarters of Harris Marine was actually a hundred miles farther down the delta, in Morgan City, a roughneck town whose fortunes bobbed in perfect harmony with the Gulf of Mexico's oil-drilling economy. It was Stu's birthplace, and he had lived through a half-dozen booms and busts for the drillers and the small businesses that served them. As a high-school boy, he had hired onto shrimp boats in summers when only a handful of drilling rigs worked the region. In those days the squat little drilling platforms stuck to the shallow waters near shore. The deep-water platforms that cost a hundred million dollars each and stood tall as skyscrapers had come along when Stu was getting out of college and casting around for a career. There was nothing to be made in fishing. He was too lame from football to take up diving. Yet the vast emptiness of the Gulf drew him as nothing on land ever had.

He settled for ferrying pipe, tools and supplies out to the offshore drillers. After paying off his first supply boat, he built

Harris Marine cautiously, never again owing a dollar to a bank. It wasn't only what he'd picked up as a finance major at Baton Rouge that told him to be careful. More powerful was a deep distrust of giving anybody a leash that might someday be yanked. A few of his competitors had borrowed to buy boats and hire crews when there was profitable work for every vessel they could put on the water. When the booms died, the banks foreclosed on the boats and the companies. Stu's competitors returned to gigging frogs.

When we got together, Harris Marine Company had a net worth of slightly under six million dollars and no debt. Business was awful all along the coast. Oil prices had been falling for three years. Drillers were sinking into bankruptcy, scuttling rigs now and then to claim insurance rather than let creditors have them. Harris Marine was breaking even in some months and turning a small profit others. All Stu's boats were working, though at prices that were ruinous to rivals who had to meet interest payments. All that Stu Harris had to meet was a payroll, which he had cut drastically, and a small overhead.

When things get that bad, he explained, you begin to think they're going to stay rotten permanently. But of course they don't. So maybe—he was thinking—it was time to expand. Time, in fact, to borrow some money for the first time in twelve years so he could buy out the weakest of his competitors. He saw five-year-old supply boats sell at auction for scrap value. People were giving away businesses, he said, and he couldn't see passing up a bargain.

He said it all confidently, a crewcut, sun-darkened working man with a cigar burning close to his fingers. He admitted later that he was nervous. He didn't like asking for money. You were supposed to go to bankers with your hat off, like they were gentlemen. Then hope they didn't find an excuse to steal your *cojones*. A friend of his who owned a small regional airline in Nashville had referred Stu to us, testifying that Ambrose & Welles was trustworthy. That allayed part of his suspicion. That and the fact that we weren't really bankers, not like the Citizens & Planters National.

"Mr. Harris is out in the ya-ard, sir," a soft, far-off voice on the phone apologized. "Could he call you back?"

I left my number and hung up. She had promised to send someone out to find Mr. Harris, but the yard covered four acres so it might take a while. If I didn't hear back in twenty minutes, I decided, I would phone Ellis Samuels, Stu's treasurer. If I couldn't reach either of them at the office, I would bug them at home till I got answers.

There was empty time, so I filled it browsing through the back pages of the *Wall Street Journal*. Depending on how the market had done, the gray statistical tables could be as forbidding as death notices or as cheering as a list of lottery winners. My favorite stock, a small American Exchange company called Midwest Carriers, had climbed another half-point on Friday, giving me a sixty percent profit in five months. I had never mentioned it to Pat.

The phone rang, and a gravelly, familiar voice bawled over the miles: "Richard, how are ya?"

"I'm healthy. What's going on down there?"

"Looks like a little problem." He cleared his throat, tried to chuckle. "Say a pretty big problem."

"Which is?"

"We ain't gonna pay the debenture interest for starters." His voice shook, and I couldn't tell whether he was angry or about to cry. "We've run out of cash, just about."

Hearing it from Stu himself was a jolt. I stared at an oatmeal-colored partition and wondered, in profane detail, how he could have blown so much cash in so short a time. All I said was, "What happened?"

"We got hoodwinked, that's it. Bright boy from Texas sold us a fleet of supply boats for less than salvage value. We bought and ended up with one rusty, sunken tug."

"How?"

"This *banker* swooped in and attached everything except the tug, which in truth ain't worth raisin'. The boy who sold us was long gone with our money. That check cleared faster than hay out of a mule's ass."

"How much?"

"Eight point four million. I guess you wanta say holy shit."

"I want to understand this. You're saying the seller lacked clear title to the boats. That a bank had a lien."

"That's about it."

"Why didn't you check his title?"

"We did, Ellis did, and it came through with this seller boy owning the boats almost clear. There was just this tiny little bank mortgage, and we figured on paying it off. Then the bank came back and said the guy only had an option or was agentin' and, ah hell. . . ." His voice sputtered out like an exhausted motor.

"What the blazes did the bank tell Ellis Samuels the first time?"

"That our Texas boy—Charlie Fentress is his name, or what he called himself—that he owned the boats except for about a quarter-million dollars owed to the bank. Ellis wouldn't *not* talk to the bank, if you know what I mean."

"So the bank says now that it make a mistake?"

"Naw. The bank says Ellis made a mistake, or just lied. He never met anyone over there, that's what the bank says."

"Let's get Ellis Samuels on the line, Stu."

"As for Ellis, this was eatin' at him," the gravelly voice said. "I made him get out of here for a couple of days last Thursday. That was another mistake. Ellis had an accident down in St. Martin Parish. Sheriff called me about it Sunday. Somebody mistook poor Ellis for a bear, or a deer, or a goddamned moose and put two bolts in his back."

I wasn't keeping up with him. "Bolts?"

"Arrers. A few boys down here hunt that way, bows 'n arrers. These come from a crossbow, sheriff said."

I took Stu up on his earlier suggestion, thought *Holy shit,* and almost missed what he said.

"Ellis, he's lucky he's alive."

I went back to see Harvey. "It looks simple. Ellis Samuels can give a deposition. He'll swear he got confirmation from the Gulf Helmsmen's Bank that Charlie Fentress was a part owner of the fleet. Then we depose the fellow at the bank he talked to. If we're lucky the bank antes up a lion's share of the eight million to avoid being named party to a fraud."

"If I ran the Gulf Helmsmen's Bank, I would be closing ranks right now, getting my stories straight," Harvey said. "I wouldn't roll over for eight million just because you showed me a deposition."

"They're in a bad position. They cleared Harris Marine's check the same day Fentress deposited it. You could suspect Fentress had an accomplice at the bank."

"Or at Harris Marine," Harvey said. "Ellis Samuels seems to have made the game easy for Fentress."

"Either way, given the amount we're in for," I said, "I think I should go down."

Harvey smiled, too polite to ask if I planned an extended vacation. "You would be out of the line of fire there, which is good."

"Am I authorized to negotiate terms with Gulf Helmsmen's?"

"Negotiate all you like. Just remember that any deal giving Harris—and the people we sold the bonds to—less than a hundred cents on the dollar will have to be approved by the partners, not to mention the bond indenture trustee. And you can count on one 'no' vote."

As I headed out, the "no" bore down the hall, resplendent in navy pinstripes and a maroon necktie, black town shoes buffed to a mirror gloss. Smooth gray hair swept back from a forehead that looked as solid as pink marble. The heavy black eyebrows knitted as he saw me. Mr. Welles was on his way to torment Harvey and didn't break stride as he spared me a cursory glance. The thin Scottish lip twisted up, his burlesque of a smile, and he said cheerfully, "Good afternoon, Richard. Are you satisfied with yourself?"

4

From the front seat of Stu Harris's car, acres of parched delta lowland stretched in every direction. Mountains of cloud rolled up the delta, pulling a line of shadow like a flattening blade across canals and fields and clusters of low-rise apartment buildings. Almost a year ago, I had expected a countryside of shanties and tobacco patches and had found Burger Kings and strip shopping centers. As the storm neared, the shopping strips and the carryouts looked decrepit. Some of the apartment courts had put up signs offering discounts on short-term rentals.

Every few minutes we ran into a wall of rain, and Stu flicked on the headlights and wipers to gain ten percent visibility. He had the air conditioning running full blast, chilling our sweat.

"We're having it a little warm," he half apologized. "Not too bad, though."

"Baltimore gets steamy," I said.

He glanced at me. "You oughtta stay with us. You're

denying Noel the chance to be hospitable. She gripes at me that all she gets to see are baby butts."

"I would have, but you're down in Morgan City. That's a hundred miles from the people I've got to see in New Orleans. I booked in at the waterfront Hilton."

"You won't eat there like you would at Noey's table." He swung across a bridge and down a curving ramp. Without my noticing we'd reached the city by the back door and were driving through a shabby neighborhood where rickety iron balconies hung from warped storefronts.

"I've got to drop in on Ellis in a little bit," he said.

"I'd like to come along."

Stu Harris stared gloomily ahead as a traffic light caught us. "I can't believe we were so dumb, Richard. I've met a hundred con men of all sorts, from guys like you—I mean boys in the finance business, well dressed and smooth who talk twice as good as they deliver, not that you folks didn't deliver, damn I get myself in trouble!—and I've met the little liars who got bounced from their last three jobs but think I'll be too slow to check. Most of 'em I spot. Something about the way they look me straight in the eye. But this Charlie Fentress could have sold us the moon."

"Have you gotten a lead on him?"

"He is *gone.*" He relaxed his grip on the wheel and ran blunt fingers through his hair. "I'll tell you, they aren't being too friendly at the bank. Saying if we got a problem it's with Mr. Fentress, that the boy just plain didn't have title to the boats. They say he came to the bank as a broker who could move the fleet for 'em. Yesterday I had this guy at Gulf Helmsmen's staring at me like *I* might be trying to con him!"

"If Fentress was acting for them, surely they've got his address?"

"What they've got is a fancy printed letterhead for a post office box in Dallas. If they're beginning to suspect that ain't worth much, they didn't let on to me."

"Was Fentress staying in New Orleans when you negotiated?"

"Yessir, at the Hyatt we passed a ways back. He had me and Ellis Samuels up for a drink. Nice layout probably costing him three or four bills a day. Had his secretary there, a leggy blond dish named Missy something. That was the first time, last day of June. She interrupted him once to take a call that was supposed to be from Alaska. In the livin' room he was plugged in with one of them attaché-case computers and his own printin' machine. Had a stack of paper from it. Said the thing was tied into his home port in Dallas and he could keep track of every boat for sale anywhere along the Gulf. Told me they kept updating every four hours when any of the oil companies changed a drilling schedule. All real low-key, like only a hick wouldn't be doing things that way."

"Impressive."

"Aw, yeah. Fentress said he figured we had already seen the bottom of the drill cycle. The companies adding drill work were more than making up from those cutting back. So as soon as people saw that the worst was past, they would start buying boats. You take that one step further and it meant I was getting a heck of a deal. Two months from now, I was goin' to wish I could have done it twice."

He swung into the driveway of the Hilton, threw the keys to a soaked kid, and followed me upstairs. The room faced downtown, where clouds darkened the buildings that had gone up during the boom. Tops of palms shook in the wind. A trolley made its way down one of the main streets, its roof invisible under the spume of rain. Stu sat in a blue vinyl chair and stared at the flickers of lightning while I washed up.

"Have we got time for lunch?" I said.

He glanced indifferently at his watch. "Not really. Told Ellis I'd be around. Ellis was saying yesterday how dumb I was. I want to hear it again. Everything I got is tied up in the company, and I let some asshole take it from me. All those years of work and saving. Maybe it's just as good you ain't coming home with me. I ain't let on to Noey how deep I got us in. If she took one look at your sour puss, she'd guess for sure."

5

No one had ever tried to kill Ellis Samuels before. The event had been not only traumatic for him but profound. "Ellis says it's a serious philosophical decision, to kill a man, which shows how naive the boy is," Stu said. He joked fondly about his financial executive, who had joined the company straight out of college. "Ellis is lookin' for deeper meanings in a plate of soup. Hasn't shut up about his insights since coming off the anesthesia. It's driving Marsha crazy. His missus has been hanging around the hospital since they brought him in."

His missus was perched on the edge of the bed, a bird-boned woman who was squinting as she hemmed a skirt. She had black hair that was cut to the same length all around, leaving bangs to brush the tops of her glasses. Without looking up, she intoned, "Hel-*lo* Stu," as if she knew that Little Stu had broken a school window.

"Hello, Marsh. This is Richard Welles, who's down from Baltimore." He leaned past her. "How *you* feeling, bub?"

Marsha wasn't ready to be ignored. "I know all Ellis's

friends, Richard Welles. And most of his business acquaintances."

Stu said, "Richard is our investment banker. Ellis, if you don't feel up to it, we can come back."

"I'm up to it," said the small man in the bed. His speech was slurred. Partly regional accent, partly painkiller. He had light skin with large pale freckles along with thinning orange hair that was pitched forward to camouflage a horseshoe-shaped bald patch. He looked younger than I had remembered, in his late twenties. He stretched out a tiny hand, and I reached forward. The hand was cool and weak. He met my eyes intently. "If the Lord gives us a second life, we have an obligation to accept. Don't you agree?"

"You got no obligations, least not right now," Stu said.

"Oh yes I have. Somebody tried to murder me, and I've got an obligation to see them brought to justice. There's no vengeance in my heart, you know that, Stuart, but you also know I believe in what's right."

Stu sucked in his bottom lip, quelling a smile. "That's for sure, bub. You don't let me get away with nothin' on the accounting side."

Ellis Samuels didn't smile.

"Stu said you were out fishing when you were shot," I said.

Ellis nodded, stretched his shoulders uncomfortably. "Yes suh, that's right. Got a little catboat, eight foot, that I can load on the roof of our car. Stu said take some time off, and I needed it, so I went down to Scarlet River. That meanders down through St. Martin Parish and crosses Route 9. Not bad river bass. I've fished it since my dad first took me twenty years ago. Never had anybody shoot me before. . . ."

His voice dimmed, and his lips pursed as though he wanted to cry. "So I took the boat out for a few hours, and when I was pulling it back on the land there was this kick, like I'd been hit with a tree, didn't hurt any but I looked and saw this point sticking out of my chest. First thing I thought was I'd been speared by a buck and I looked around and there wasn't any deer—and they got me again. That one went right through on this side, came out under the collarbone."

He had a pillow at the base of his spine, keeping him from lying back on the wounds. Leaning forward, he craned his neck at the gauze pads taped over each shoulder. "I'm not supposed to do any arm wrestling."

"You're too skinny for arm wrestling," Stu said.

Ellis ignored the older man. "So anyway, Sheriff Baliou says they were shooting downhill and aimed too high. The second bolt knocked me off my feet, right into the boat, and it must have looked like I was a goner. I sure thought I was. I couldn't move, and blood was dripping into the water in the bottom right under my nose. But the bolts sort of filled the holes they'd made, so I wasn't bleeding all that much."

He wound down, his forehead pale under the freckles.

Stu patted his arm. "Ellis was right next to the road. They must've been waiting."

"Shooting a boater twice isn't much of a hunting accident," I said.

"If you want someone dead enough, maybe how it looks is secondary," Stu said. "Ellis is the only one who can say first hand that a Gulf Helmsmen's Bank officer vouched for Charlie Fentress."

"Ellis didn't see who shot him?"

"I don't even know for sure there was more than one person. I just feel it was," Ellis said. "Can't even swear they were from a car. I wasn't awake enough to hear anything drive away. Guess I'd have gone to sleep for good if those other fishermen hadn't come along."

"Tell me about your contact with the Gulf Helmsmen's Bank," I said.

He tried to shrug but couldn't move enough. "It was routine. They were listed as holding a small note, with the boats as collateral. The gentleman I spoke with, Mr. Edwards, confirmed that and said the bank had no objection to the sale. Mr. Edwards said that Charles Fentress had done business with them before."

"How often did you speak to Edwards?"

"Twice—no, three times if you count a thirty-second call, which was occasioned when I needed to check a tax aspect."

"Did you meet him or do it all by phone?"

"By telephone," Ellis said meekly. "As I indicated, suh, it was al-to-gether routine. I don't mean that I had bought a fleet of boats before, no suh, but ones and twos here and there. You find out who has a lien, and there almost *always* is a lien, and you clear the sale with that party so's they'll release the title. An' this was just like that."

Stu Harris touched my arm. "Richard, let's leave this man get some rest."

"I'm okay, Stuart."

"No, you surely ain't."

I said, "Ellis, did Charles Fentress give you the names of both Gulf Helmsmen's Bank and Mr. Edwards?"

"Yes suh, that he did. So I just called Mr. Edwards direct." He sighed and said he was ready for a nap.

We went into the hall. "Ellis is a virtuous fellow," I said.

My tone annoyed him. "Well, he's got a little too much church in him. But he's for real. His missus is the holy roller."

His wide face was set, but it looked angry and sad and naive.

"How long has he worked for you?"

"Six years."

"Are you buddies?"

"Wa-ell, I like Ellis."

"So you don't think he'd screw you."

He gave me a bleak look.

I asked, "How are the police treating this?"

"They figure somebody tried to murder Ellis. I didn't tell 'em much about the weenie at Gulf Helmsmen's Bank. What do you figure is goin' happen there?"

"I doubt that they're going to accept liability for your loss gracefully," I said. "Nobody in their position would."

"The way our check cleared so fast, the way the money went out. . . ."

"It's a point that would help us in court," I said. "And it would help if we could prove somebody at the bank was working with Fentress."

"The guy Ellis talked to, this Alexander Edwards, surely got his pockets filled. He just sat there yesterday and *lied,* claimin' he never talked to Ellis."

"Do you know of a reliable private investigation firm down here?"

"You could use whoever you had check me out," he said.

"We had a Baltimore firm do that. Somebody in Louisiana might have had connections to you."

He laughed. "There's an outfit that handles commercial stuff, people stealing from the boats, payrolls. They're in Metairie. That's right up the road."

"Okay. You hire them and get them going on Fentress and Edwards. And since there's an interstate fraud here, you should talk to the FBI. They'll want copies of all the records of the transaction. They'll do a better job of talking to the bank and looking for Fentress than we could."

"I was hoping, till Thursday, that this was all a mistake. That's when my general counsel sits on his big butt and says the bank's got all the rights. Two weeks earlier, he was impressing himself with how good he was working on the papers with Fentress. Just not letting anything slip by him. We had two guys that drove up to Galveston, that's where the fleet was, and spent a week going through those boats. My big-ass lawyer sat there and haggled with Fentress over the number of hours on an engine and when they were last certified. He read every line of the papers Fentress showed us on how he'd come to own the boats. Just like a bunch of god-damn hicks."

We rode down with a load of nurses, who left us floor by floor, and Stu drove me back to the Hilton. In my room, we got on the phone with Tom Avery at Harris Marine's head-quarters and reviewed the company's immediate financial plight. The $8.4 million check had used up all but $200,000 of the treasured cash hoard. They still had receivables that brought a slow stream of cash. Tom said there would be no trouble meeting the previous week's payroll, which had been held up in the financial department's panic. He could slow down other payments without alarming Harris Marine's suppliers. That would leave about $150,000 in the till. The quarterly interest payment on the bonds was $780,000.

I asked them, "Before finding you'd been swindled, how

did you plan to make the interest payment? You still had used up your cash."

Stu sighed. "Aw, shit. We were getting such a good price, I'd already resold two of the boats at a million and a half profit. We were getting ready to close on that Wednesday morning when the bank grabbed the fleet. That would have tided us over on cash. We were thinking of selling one or two more in the next six months—heck, I would turn 'em over for a profit all day long. And we've been running so close to the bone that enough of the other boats coulda been put to work to carry the ones that stayed berthed. It was a real nice opportunity, Richard."

He asked Tom to have the company's chief lawyer call him. Waiting for the phone, he paced silently. When he caught himself cutting tracks in the carpet he sat down. His face was slack, tired, heading for resignation. For years he probably hadn't faced a problem that defied his driving determination for more than a couple of days. He had gotten used to going to bed knowing Harris Marine was prosperous.

The phone rang, and I let him get it. "Yaw, Willie. I'm with Rich Welles. I want you to make an appointment for us with the FBI, then get up here with as much paperwork as you can. Have Jan make copies. We'll keep the originals. Well, tell 'em it's an eight-million theft"—he glanced at me—"using interstate devices. You should make it up here by four o'clock."

He broke the connection, dialed again. "How are the yippins treating you?"

He listened, putting in a couple of "Yaws," and looked almost happy. "Look, skeedunkus, my business up here is stretching out. It's nothing major, just that as long as I'm here I may as well get it squared away. So I won't make supper, and don't be surprised if you don't see me before nine or ten. There's one meeting that may take a while."

The person on the other end said something, and his tanned face cracked into a wide grin. "Yaw, you caught me. She's got hips like two Bertram cruisers tied together, and she revs up to one-twenty horses at full throttle. An', oh!—she's half-Cuban and hates kids. Yaw, I'll have a swell time. If it's gonna be later than ten, I'll call."

He hung up, stuffed his paws into the pockets of his tan suit. "You wanna have lunch?"

We settled for the Polynesian room on the main floor. At the end of the feeding hour, the jungle clearing was packed with casually dressed couples in their fifties and sixties, healthy and unhurried-looking. Comfortable but not wealthy, which meant that any millions scattered through the room didn't get above the low single digits. The sums got them into the better neighborhoods in most of their hometowns, excluded from only a few dozen of the priciest enclaves around the country. Distributed among these older folks were sleekly combed, brightly smiling, expensively clothed young men and women with a distinctly hungrier look. Both groups wore name badges. The oldsters' were blue on white, the young smiling people's black on gold. It was easy to guess that gold badges marked the sales crew, white badges the prospective customers.

The adjacent table was close enough that the white-haired man's complaint was audible. "You guys were telling me gold was going to the moon last year and it didn't. I'd've done better in real estate or orange juice."

His young saleswoman's response was fervent and whispered, advice too precious to be spread among the other tables, where somebody who listened might get the jump on her favorite white-haired old man.

Stu tilted his head. "Financial convention, all the folks from up north worried about inflation. A guy here runs quite an operation. Folks pay their own way down, pony up about a thousand a couple for registration, which gets 'em a few eats and Dixieland bands, pay a hundred-twenty a night special rate for their hotels, and sit around three or four days being hammered by guys and gals telling them the world's a goin' end—and how they can be survivors if they put a couple hundred grand into gold, or Vancouver mining stocks, or platinum or little old postage stamps, or freeze-dried dates and shotgun shells. Je-sus, Rich. Can you imagine running a business where people pay to hear your sales pitch?" He glanced derisively at the nearby table, then looked down at his menu. "I could tell this guy he coulda done a lot worsen gold."

He checked in with his company's lawyer after lunch and announced he had business around town and there was no point dragging me along.

I bought a light raincoat and hat at the hotel men's shop and took the elevator upstairs. Sitting at the phone table in my room, I debated whom to call back in Baltimore. Despite six years under Ambrose & Welles's roof, I lacked any confidant at the firm. My relations with everybody were cordial, a source of comfortable pride to me, and my relations with nobody were more than that. I felt a stirring of dissatisfaction that wouldn't have occurred a month ago. It felt a little too neat and even-keeled, like sailing across the bay with a politely level deck all the way. Coffee cups didn't get tossed about, and you didn't get your face wet. It could be a pleasant, tranquil no-risk day. My ideal seemed to be a succession of such days.

I finally asked for Anne Hargrave. She picked up with a cheerful "Hello?"

"It's Richard," I said, adding, "Welles."

"Yes, Richard Welles. Your desk is next to mine. You seem to be missing from it."

"I'm in New Orleans." I was surprised the office grapevine was so slow. Richard Welles's location might not be an item of lively interest. Perhaps, if the man vanished altogether, they might wonder after a couple of weeks. Or there might be a short discussion over whether he had ever occupied the space that now seemed only slightly more vacant.

"So how is the jambalaya?" she said.

"I'll let you know. So far I've had a steak sandwich Polynesian style. That means a slice of kiwi on the side. Look, I wanted to ask somebody up there to do some digging. How jammed are you?"

Investment banking has its own summer doldrums, which had taken hold on the department. We were looking at a half-dozen prospective clients who wanted, with various degrees of justification, to raise money in the next twelve months. But the effort was a shadow of the lunatic frenzy that gripped everybody when a deal was making its way over the last hurdles.

"My services are available," she said.

"Thanks. There's a holding company called the Gulf Helmsmen's Bank Corporation. They were used, wittingly or otherwise, to help snooker our favorite marine services company. Any documents they've filed with the Securities and Exchange Commission, plus anything you can find on them in Dow Jones News Retrieval could be helpful. If you can put together a bundle this evening, have it expressed down to me care of Harris Marine's headquarters in Morgan City. I'll be there tomorrow."

"I'll send what I can get. So the trouble isn't your fault?"

We wouldn't have the last word on that, I thought. "Stu Harris got his pocket picked. If I had stayed in closer touch, I might have been able to warn him." Or ended up hip-deep myself. I asked, "What should I eat besides jambalaya?"

"Beignets, absolutely. And crayfish at the Sonesta."

"Forget that one."

"And Dixie beer."

"All right. How long since you've been down here?"

"Easter break in college, many many years ago. And stay away from the tacky stripper bars, though I imagine you will."

I heard a voice in the background inquiring about tacky stripper bars. There was a laugh and my brother came on the phone. "You never know who will be calling in for tips on decadence. Listen, Richard, there's a little place two blocks from Preservation Hall where they do things you wouldn't *believe.* Uh, wait—Anne says you shouldn't go there, either. As long as you're on, where would you recommend I take the prettiest investment banker in Baltimore for dinner? She has consented after the feeblest of protests."

There was a struggle, and Anne Hargrave came back on. Her voice was flustered, trying to be businesslike. "I'll get what you need on Gulf Helmsmen's in an overnight envelope. Enjoy your trip, Richard."

She hung up before Pat could take the receiver again.

The conversation had left a sour aftertaste, not all of it due to her confidence that I would not drop by a stripper bar. Nor could it be news of an impending dinner in Baltimore. I understood Pat too well for the prospect of his racking up another office conquest to matter.

The fact that he was evidently aiming for the girl I sat next to but didn't know—that queasy thought I thrust away before it was fully shaped. Contemplating the disappearance of $8.4 million was less disturbing.

6

Gulf Helmsmen's Bank Corporation occupied a skyscraper on Canal Street, four blocks from the river. When I phoned, Mr. Alexander Edwards, an assistant treasurer, did not expect to be available that afternoon. Passing on the bad news, his secretary did not sound particularly regretful. Twenty minutes later, I showed up at the windowless reception area outside his office, the walls and floors of which were identical apple-green tweed, and told a deeply tanned young woman whose lipstick and nails were a deeper, nautical green that I had an appointment with Mr. Edwards.

She picked up a phone, announced me in bird chirrups, then lost a month's color and put the receiver down very quickly. She said, in a deadly neutral tone that covered shock, "Mr. Edwards will not be able to see you."

I was already seated in a chrome and green vinyl armchair. I picked up a copy of *Oil Weekly,* smiled across her glass-topped play area. "That's okay. I've got nothing to do but wait."

Her shallow blue eyes shifted to the door that led back to this level of executive habitat. She looked at her phone with a new distrust. When the set purred, she lifted the receiver, used her chirrupy voice, and gratefully switched the caller back to Miss Holmes, who was yes-sir-expecting the call.

The set purred again almost immediately. She picked up, looking unhappy. The other end was slightly audible because she held the handset a half inch from her spray of blond hair, farther from her ear. She stared at me and finally said one meek word:

"Yes."

Yes, he's still here. Or perhaps, *Yes, he's really digging into our* Oil Weekly *issues.*

I made a finger motion suggesting she could hold the receiver farther from her face. She was only too happy to comply. I announced: "Mr. Edwards *could* call security. They could throw me out. But that would be a bad show of professional courtesy."

She frowned, then smiled. "Mr. Edwards asks who is it you are with?"

"Ambrose & Welles, in Baltimore."

She reported back. "And what would your visit concern?"

I had gone through all this with his secretary. "The situation at Harris Marine."

He came out two minutes later, a tall, short-haired man in tortoiseshell glasses, red suspenders and a bow tie. He managed a smile as he came over and offered a long hand. His cuff links were gold doubloons. "Alex Edwards. Sorry to have kept you waiting, Mr. Welles. We're closing a financing and it's a little harried." His accent was a shock, Back Bay Boston.

In a loping gait, he led me back to a conference room, slammed the door and threw himself into another apple-green chair. "This Harris Marine thing has gotten out of hand, Mr. Welles. Stuart Harris came to see me and just about accused me of stealing his company. I can tell you, Gulf Helmsmen's Bank has served this area too long for anyone to put any store in such allegations, but they're unwelcome nonetheless."

"I don't think he's saying anything in public," I said. "But we've got a problem. Ellis Samuels——"

"I've bucked this up the line to our vice chairman. We want to make sure we *aren't* somehow exposed. Apart from holding a note on the fleet of boats that exceeds the price Harris Marine says they paid, we had no connection to your client's transaction. We were the original lender when the boats' owner, a company over in Corpus Christi, was building its fleet. Not a happy decision—one of my predecessor's deals. I came down here a year ago to take over the bad-loan portfolio. Along the Gulf, you can imagine the kinds of problems we're finding."

"Your borrowers have big payments coming due and not much business?"

"That's right. Some of the business that they find is at such low rates it amounts to less than the cash cost of operating the boat. Every dollar in revenue they get leaves them twenty cents deeper in the hole."

"Who was the owner?"

"Corpus Christi Tug & Barge. We hadn't quite decided what to do about them when this broke. They missed two interest payments, but did Gulf Helmsmen's want to own a bunch of docked supply boats? Apparently Charles Fentress, who sounds like a prototypical swindler, approached C. C. Tug and us saying he had a possible buyer. We said fine—we would have to sign off on any deal because the bank stood first in line to get its money. Anything above what was owed would go to Corpus Christi. Frankly, I was skeptical that anybody would pay the amount of our note. That's thirteen point five million. Apparently, Fentress went to your people posing as majority owner and offered the vessels at about their scrap value. A slick deception."

"And Harris Marine's check cleared the day it was deposited."

"Yes, I looked into that. It was a certified check drawn on the Royal Bank, right across the street. Our proof department cleared it by telephone at the client's request. There was no reason not to. They had no way of knowing that this confidence man had sold an asset against which we had the senior claim."

He spread his hands. "Candidly, it's embarrassing as hell."

"It's quite a coincidence that Fentress chose to run the check through the bank that had the claim."

He pursed his small mouth. "I would say, Mr. Welles, that it is no coincidence at all. Fentress clearly set up the fraud so that the injured parties would go for each other's throats while he vanished."

His candor was overpowering. And to a point convincing. He was worried about Harris's allegations hurting the bank. Not worried about the allegations concerning himself. He was harried because a financing was closing. But he would take the time to walk an out-of-town investment banker through a fiasco.

"Then there is Ellis Samuels," I said.

"Oh, God! Don't mention his name. Mr. Welles, I assure you, I never spoke to the man. *Never.* Not once. Mr. Harris said that Samuels had been shot. Could the wounds have been self-inflicted?"

"No."

"Then—have you considered the possibility that the architect of this scheme was trying to eliminate his accomplice?"

"Yes, I've considered it. But have you?"

He hesitated. "I don't understand."

"This fraud wasn't put together to last," I said. "It was put together so Charlie Fentress could get the money and run. He needed an accomplice somewhere, either at Harris Marine or here. But the accomplice was left behind. An obvious target for investigation. A very weak link. Abandoned. It makes me wonder two things. What did the accomplice—Ellis Samuels, let's say—get out of this? And why didn't he hightail it away?"

"Those are intelligent questions, Mr. Welles." His Brahmin voice was barely audible. "Perhaps Mr. Samuels felt that he had no choice."

"But think about his predicament. His story had to run flatly counter to what the man at the bank said. So he knew the authorities would look him over from top to bottom. They would press him, ask questions, press some more, come back time and again. He wasn't a professional liar. He knew that sooner or later he would break. So why stay on the scene to face that ordeal?"

Alexander Edwards shook his narrow head silently, eyes lingering on mine.

"Why didn't he run?" I said. It was an interview, I thought with a moment of distracted pain, that Patrick Welles, Sr. would have rejoiced in conducting. We both knew how to tear skin off an inch at a time. "Samuels must know a lot about Fentress. They both would know he would break under pressure. Wouldn't it occur to Ellis Samuels that Fentress might see him as a risk to be removed?"

He stared at me but was looking inward. It was the introspection I had seen a half-dozen times from clients lying to me, hiding a problem. Peel away the skin of deception, and what remained was raw and shivering. I had never stopped hating the sadistic skill.

"And even after being shot, he sticks to that stupid story. Insists he talked to you several times, knowing you can paint him a liar. You would think he would spill everything he knows about Charlie Fentress."

"You would," Alexander Edwards agreed.

"Charlie Fentress must have fooled Ellis, told him he could have the banker fixed so he couldn't talk. But instead of having *you* killed, he goes for his accomplice. There's an intriguing question: Looking at it from Fentress's vantage, are you better off murdering your accomplice or murdering the man who can contradict your accomplice's story? Your perspective might change, don't you think, Mr. Edwards? One day, the accomplice looks like the liability. Another day the banker. If you're Fentress, you're probably nervous about how much your accomplice knows, how close he can point the police or the FBI to your home base, to your real identity."

Edwards got to his feet like an old man afraid of falling.

"It just wasn't set up to protect the accomplice," I said. "Though I suppose there might have been a few precautions. Ellis Samuels says he spoke to you by telephone. So I would bet he'll have a record of long-distance calls placed from Harris Marine's headquarters down in Morgan City to the bank's switchboard. Or maybe even direct calls to your line. Do you recall anyone hanging up when you answered?"

When he shook his head mutely, I stood up. "Well, thanks for your time, Mr. Edwards. Just personally, I would like to know what the accomplice gets out of this. Or what Fentress promised. The FBI can ask Ellis Samuels."

I opened the door, stepped into the corridor. "I'll find my way out."

From the end of the corridor I glanced back once. He hadn't emerged. Turning left would get me back to the reception area. I turned right and walked as though I were a minute late. I circled the suite, stopped at a water fountain, washed my hands in a men's room, then stopped a pert little black woman. "I seem to have taken a wrong turn," I said. "How do I get back to Alex Edwards's office?"

"You certainly did. Straight down this corridor, then left."

"Thank you." I went the way she said. Edwards had had not quite five minutes to pull himself together. His office was marked by a small nameplate beside the door. I turned the knob, held it tight and pushed the door as he said into the telephone, ". . . never mind, just pick up the kids at the goddamn pool and meet me—"

He looked up. His jaw sagged.

He took a deep breath.

He said quietly into the phone, "Pick up the kids, darling. Go where I said, and I'll meet you. I love you." He put the receiver down and looked away from me. His office was cluttered with family mementos, lucite-clad pictures, a trophy, an oil painting of a sailboat reefing over against what looked like a Boston skyline. He didn't look at them. As if words were heavy things, he said, "I've known you less than an hour, Mr. Welles, and I wish I didn't."

"The FBI would have had you in handcuffs by now," I said. "I didn't bring any. You can still volunteer your cooperation."

He removed the tortoiseshell glasses, rubbed his eyes. "Volunteer, huh? This reminds me of the way a banker volunteers for Charlie Fentress's little project. Are you going to throw a dog's head at me?"

"What?"

"That's what Fentress did. Out of the blue. Tillie was our English sheepdog, more Cathy's than mine, nine years old. I went down to the garage here a few months ago and found Tillie's head under a blanket on the driver's seat. I lost it— really lost it. Wouldn't you?"

"Yes."

"I was sort of hanging on the edge of the door when this guy came up. He walked right up behind me, and I didn't hear until he scraped his feet a couple of times. You know the curly-haired, big grin go-getter type? The Texas boy who wears boots under his poplin suit, maybe pearl snaps on his shirt? I used to expect them to drive pickup trucks with rifles in the back window, but down here you get them in Cadillacs and BMWs. They hustle cheap deals. If they try to hit on the Gulf Helmsmen's Bank, they don't get past the lobby. This guy—he was like that, but different. Cool pale eyes. I couldn't tell the color in the garage but I wondered—light green or gray. He pointed into the car and said, 'Sorry about the puppy, but I wanted you and me to have a business discussion an' talkin' won't be productive if you don't understand something. You gotta believe—*really, truly believe,* like a religious man, deep in your soul—that this little trophy coulda been your wife's head. Or a kid's. All the same to old Charlie, just about. I actually like dogs.' When he stared at me with that boyish face, curly hair, mouth used to grinning, I had no doubt he was for real. That's something which has never happened to me before, Mr. Welles. A banker meets a fair number of people who might be killers at heart, who do their deals so it hurts someone. But I had never stood face-to-face with anyone who seemed capable of more cool brutality than Charlie Fentress."

"What did you have to do?"

"He didn't make that clear at first. Said there would have to be some token of trust, some little thing I could give him. I assumed he was going to ask for money from the bank, and I shuddered thinking he wouldn't believe I couldn't get money. He outlined things only sketchily. Said there was a business deal he needed my help on. I wouldn't have to do much, that if I was lucky I wouldn't be implicated. The details weren't important just then, he said. What mattered was that when I was home that night, feeling safe and thinking of calling the police, I should focus on Tillie. And if any little object wasn't lying around the house—a portable television or something—I should especially focus on what happened to Tillie. . . . I knew it wouldn't be a television set missing."

He wiped his forehead as his bowels rumbled loudly. Without a word, he sprang out of the chair and bolted from the office. His face was set in a tight, desperate grimace.

He returned in twenty minutes, shaken, damp-faced. "I apologize, I haven't been feeling well."

"Who had he taken?"

"Alex junior. From a swing set in the backyard. When I got home Cathy was calling around the neighborhood, not terribly alarmed. He's seven and might have gone over to a friend's house. From the timing, I knew it must have happened about the time Charlie Fentress was talking to me in the garage. It was all I could do to keep her from calling the police. I had to tell her about Tillie."

"When did Fentress tell you he had your son?"

"He let us sit and stew until about four in the morning. Then he called and said my son was visiting with a nice woman who liked boys. He was being well cared for. We had no reason to be alarmed. He said if we were good for the next few days, he would call again. Do you have any children?"

I shook my head.

"You probably can't imagine how vulnerable you feel. Alex isn't a lawn ornament in our lives, he's a little person we've loved and watched develop since his first day. We went over what we should do a dozen times each hour, twenty-two hours a day for four days. It always came out the same way. Fentress would know if we brought in the police. We wouldn't hear from him again. We wouldn't see our son again. By the time he called, his request seemed modest. I'd have done anything. But all he wanted was for me to give a reference. When he described it, it was a little more than that. I didn't care. Someone would contact me, almost certainly by telephone, to confirm that Fentress held the major interest in a fleet of boats. I might have to write a letter, he said. This was very routine. But it wasn't likely. I almost certainly wouldn't have to meet anyone face-to-face. Just talk on the phone. With luck, I could deny the conversation ever occurred. Because he had a way of protecting me. The person would be given a phone number in an empty office with the same exchange. A device there would forward the call to my private line. There would be no record of our ever having spoken. So I could see that the risk of cooperating was minimal. He was being a friendly businessman then, making me understand that the arrangement was attractive to both of us."

"When did this part happen?"

"About three weeks ago. The bastard really played me, just right every time. I thought bankers had to be good psychologists." He tried a smile, reasserting his expertise in financial matters. He could still be the upscale-and-climbing young banker with the jolly suspenders and optimistic bow tie. He could be that as soon as he forgot how much Charles Fentress had scared him.

"What did you think when you heard that Ellis Samuels had been left for dead with crossbow bolts in him?"

"Hoped it was unrelated," Alex Edwards said quietly. "Knew better. It wasn't done to help me. That I'm sure of. Fentress must have decided to muddy the waters."

"What about your son?" I said.

He slipped his glasses back on, looked critically at me.

"Nice of you to think of him, you chilly son of a bitch. He's been home since Fentress got his money."

Stu Harris and a weary, heavyset man I recognized faintly as his lawyer, Willie Dreyfus, were slumped in the anteroom of the FBI's office suite. When I opened the door, Stu was staring at his beefy folded arms. The heavyset man was reading the top sheet of a thick document. Alex Edwards stepped in and Stu's chin came up.

"Je-*sus!*" Stu bounced off the plaid sofa. "Richard, what in hell is this guy—"

"He's here to help. Alex is just as much a victim as we are." I was hewing to Alex's view, not wanting to shake his confidence in the future. In the taxi crossing town, he had talked about needing protection from Fentress so he could concentrate on his bad loans. If he realized that his confession put the Gulf Helmsmen's Bank and its insurers on the hook for more than eight million dollars, or suspected that fact might have an impact on his career, he gave no sign.

"I should call my wife," Alex said. "She'll be at our rendezvous by now. . . ."

"She won't expect you for a while. Sit down and relax." He was right. Richard Welles really was a chilly son of a bitch. Ready to pat a shoulder and say: *Don't worry about your future, old buddy. Banks love guys who cost them a year's profits.* His self-hypnosis wouldn't last forever. When it wore off, he would begin to suspect that no matter how sympathetic his bosses were, they were going to adopt the corporate version of triage. Here's a career shot through the guts with its neck broken and an arm missing. If we don't waste time on this one, there will be more gauze and wrappings for ourselves. So a plaintive smile and spread hands. *Jeez, Alex, if only you'd called the police—or clued us in.* When he realized that much, if he had any brains, he would demand a lawyer and shut up.

A young woman with short, gray-flecked hair walked into the room, leaving ajar a door that had looked like standard office suite veneer but had drawn a grunt as she pushed it open. She had light freckles, a pug nose and a no-nonsense frown. She wore a navy poplin suit and low-heeled black pumps. "I'm Special Agent Fertig. Is one of you Stuart Harris?"

When we got it established that all four of us were there on the same business, she led us back to a small conference room. We took seats around a scarred laminate table. Before she could set the agenda, I said, "It will help if you hear Alex Edwards's account first."

He had gotten barely twenty words out when she asked him to wait. She left the room, came back five minutes later with a tape recorder and a huge blond man whom she introduced as Special Agent Wosocki. She put the tape recorder in the center of the table, started it turning, and said to Edwards, "Do you understand that you're giving a voluntary statement?

That you have certain rights, which include not speaking or having an attorney present?"

He was still coasting on optimism. He nodded, giving her an earnest smile. "This needs to come out in the open, like a cancer needs daylight."

"Go ahead then," Fertig said.

As he repeated most of what he had told me, I caught the old lawyer's eye and he clamped a hand on Stu's arm. Alex Edwards's story took about fifteen minutes. When he tried to add ornamentation, Fertig cut in with a clipped, "Never mind, we'll come back to that" and pushed him ahead. He finally slumped in his chair, hands flat on the table. He yawned and looked surprised. Carefully, Agent Fertig led him back over several points. Could someone else in his department have provided the same corroboration to Ellis Samuels? What had led Fentress to Alex? She left that and skipped around. What small things had he noticed about Fentress? Did the details support a background in Texas? Had Alex been able to contact Fentress? How many people did Fentress have working for him? Did Alex's son know where he had been kept? Had anyone in Alex's department, perhaps someone known to be stubborn, suffered a serious accident in recent months? When was the last contact? Did Fentress ever indicate he might dispose of Samuels? Had Alex's son ever seen Fentress?

Half an hour into the grilling, I excused myself and went looking for a water fountain. Edwards's composure was fraying, which would be what Fertig wanted. From now, the investigating mechanism would grind along on its own power.

When I came back into the suite, I sat on the couch and stared at my watch. Somehow it had gotten to be six-fifteen. The anteroom had the bland, timeless lack of character common to places where nobody expects to find any pleasure. The secretaries didn't bother to put a plant on the lamp table. The agent in charge didn't order subscriptions to *Popular Mechanics*. I sat and stared and thought about flying home. In Baltimore it was seven-fifteen, and my brother would be acting surly to a young waiter at L'Auberge. Demanding deference to his position was his clumsy substitute for earning respect for an achievement. Pat had gotten his way when we were kids because he was bigger, and when I had grown enough that he had no clear physical advantage, he had gotten his way by speaking with our father's authority. And when that no longer worked, he had never forgiven me, the subordinate who scorned lawful commands.

If he had ever found something that engaged his attention past the easy surface, he might have grown into a different man. No telling whether better or worse, but authentically sure of himself. Our father treated waiters kindly. But Pat's interests never lasted more than a few weeks. An early fascination with oceanography melted into resentment, then indifference, after he glimpsed the effort that lay between the daydream and a degree and career.

The door opened and Stu Harris and Willie Dreyfus emerged. Stu dragged himself as though he were on his last mile. He squeezed a palm over a yawn. "Little Joanne says we're not needed no more."

"Joanne?"

"Special Agent Fertig," Willie said to me. "You, sir, did quite a job on Alex Edwards. Congratulations."

"Richard can charm the bark off a tree when it suits him," Stu said. "He charmed every fact out of Ellis and me before selling our bonds. An' when charm didn't work, he used wristlocks. Ol' Alex Edwards prolly confided his mother's maiden name and whether she was a virgin when his dad married up."

"Has Edwards remembered anything useful about Charles Fentress?" I asked.

"Fentress is beginning to look like the man who wasn't there," Willie Dreyfus said. "An amazingly controlled man. Neither Stu nor I nor Ellis nor Edwards saw anything beyond what Fentress offered of himself. A different picture for Edwards's consumption than for ours, of course. But remarkably consistent within each context. No little falters that we've recalled. If I had to guess, I would say that Edwards saw the portrait that is closest to reality, though perhaps even there he was distorting the truth. Edwards observed an insensitively brutal man. Stu and I perceived an insensitively crude but affable deal maker. It may be that Fentress is a more cultivated brutal man."

Stu said, "Willie would psychoanalyze a cockroach if it sat still. I better call Noey and tell her we're headin' outta here. Don't look like that li'l shit Edwards will be gettin' loose for a while. Can we drop you at the hotel?"

"Actually, you can wait ten minutes while I check out of the hotel. Is there someplace in Morgan City I can stay?"

"I told you, stay with Noey and me, same as before."

"All right. Thanks." I didn't want to intrude on their love-filled nest. Contrasting the noisy, cluttered rooms with my immaculate and silent apartment meant I would have to recite all the reasons why silence was better.

"Good, good," Stu chuckled. "Noey'll add five pounds to you by noon tomorrow."

7

We rolled into Morgan City in the late dusk, sharing the road with pipe-laden semis and an occasional pickup truck. Front Street was a long, bleary stretch of workboat yards, mom-and-pop supply shops, lunch counters and taverns. We turned left at a dead end only a hundred yards from the river, passed under a rail embankment in axle-deep water, and drove through a stretch of run-down houses before hitting the shore road. Harris Marine owned four acres with almost a thousand feet of river frontage.

It was after eight o'clock, but there were twenty or more cars in the parking lot. "You work your people late," I said.

"Office staff goes home at five, but we got people round the clock in operations and maintenance. Our boats are going in and out all the time."

"I thought business was slow."

"Well it is, but this is just the way the job works. If you got a load of pipe for a drilling rig that's twelve hours out onto the Gulf, we might shove off at midnight to get there during daytime. Off-loading is dangerous enough in ideal light and weather."

"What are you doing in this weather?"

"If it gets any worse, we're going to lay up. We haven't sent anything out since yesterday except for emergencies. One of our copters took a sick man off Delta 48—that's a Belo Consortium platform almost a hundred miles out. The water wasn't as rough east of here, but that may have changed by now."

He waved to a half-seen man in the guard booth and parked next to a brick stairway leading into the main building. Dim light bled through a wire-mesh window at the top of the steps, where Stu jangled a key chain and opened the steel door. The hallways and office cubicles had emptied out three hours ago, and as we headed for the accounting department Stu flicked on lights. If you can walk through a building, saying nothing and making only practical motions, and still exude pride of ownership, then Stu showed his pride and fondness for every concrete block in the walls. He could have personally troweled down every layer of mortar in the construction, so clearly did his walk say, *I did this—I built it.*

He thumbed through his keys and opened a door with ELLIS SAMUELS, TREASURER on the glass.

"Here—these file cabinets—here's the computer—can you operate it? I'll call Tom Avery and tell him to come back and help."

"Thank you."

"Don't thank me. You'd do better with Ellis here to explain things." While I set my bag in a corner and peeled off a damp suit coat, Stu phoned Tom Avery with the news his evening was ruined and then Noel Harris with orders to make up the guest room. He wandered down the maze of halls and came back in five minutes with paper cups full of strong coffee. "I'm gonna check in with operations," he announced.

I followed along.

Stu lumbered through the administrative office, picking a clipboard off the wall, and read the afternoon's reports. Chewing his lip, he headed down a short hallway and up a flight of stairs. We ended up at a broadly windowed room at the back of the main building. From there Ginnie Miller had a view of the boat yard and the churning river that carried Harris Marine's boats out to the Gulf. More important, the south wall's battery of radios and receivers enabled her to maintain contact with all the work vessels and tugs while they were away from home. When I had first met her ten months earlier, she had dispatched a helicopter carrying a doctor to a site ninety miles out on the Gulf where one of Stuart's deckhands had been injured.

She was a tiny, frail woman of at least sixty-five dressed in blue jeans and a faded tank top. As we came in, she stubbed out a cigarette and cut off a radio conversation with "Gotta work, sweet—the old goat rolled in." She flung a small hand my way, shook vigorously. "Heard you was back causing us trouble. How're you, Mr. Stu?"

"Jes' fine, Ginnie. Sorry I interrupted your love play. What's this about the *Precious?* That damn engine ain't a year old."

"You'll have t' ask Cap'n Boone, and he got his hands full."

"When did he report in last?" He glanced at the clipboard.

" 'Bout two hours ago. I hadn't got a chance to run the sheet downstairs. Oil pressure fell and she just overheated. Read for yourself." As she retrieved a page from the desk in front of the long bank of radios, I went over and peered from Ginnie Miller's roost. Floodlights caught reflections in the yard. Rain was spattering lightly on the windows.

Stu folded the paper, tucked it under the clip. "I'll be in for a couple hours. Keep me posted—tell Raoul the same when he gets here. If Boone decides he needs a tow, who've we got that's closest?"

"*Down About* is delivering pipe to the Mobil Nine."

"Okay. You alert them to stand by."

Tom Avery arrived at eight forty-five looking as if his mother and best friend both had gotten reprieves from death. He was limp-haired and had a spreading waist that stretched his old knit shirt. We shook hands, drank coffee, and sorted through Harris Marine's current financial status. Avery kept picking at his buttons. The skimpiness of the company's cash had him uneasy. "I keep thinking there's a bill coming in that I've forgot about—and that we can't pay," he complained. "We're going to need some bridge financing till we can squeeze money out of that bank."

I shook my head. "The bank and its insurers are going to be very cooperative. They won't want Harris Marine or its noteholders to claim any incidental losses."

"I want 'em to pay for repairin' that spot over on the wall where Stu and me've been banging our heads."

"They'll hang chintz curtains in the bathrooms if you ask."

"Stu would never go for that."

We ate a late supper on a screened patio at Stu's house, while crickets and frogs argued in the blackened yard. As we carried dishes inside, a warm wind brought another shower sighing across the trees—audible on the water, then on the lawn, then drumming on the fiberglass awnings.

Noey's kitchen was cheerful, all copper pans and ceramic tiles. She was still round of face and body, dark-eyed and placid, deeply content under the burden of two young children. Dinner had been taken up with talk of budding jealousy. The two-year-old, Molly, had announced that her favorite doll didn't like the new sister—though Molly guessed she was okay.

The comfortable domestic patter was my favorite kind of home life, somebody else's, to which I could listen with detachment. If Stu and Noel Harris brawled like two cats in a bag, it was when I was gone. If there were domineering silences or affection bitterly withheld, the anger occupied hours that were left safely empty in my own life.

We set plates and saucers on counters, and Noey's jangled. Turning away from her husband, she said to me, "I sure wish Stu hadn't borrowed that money from you." She was crying.

He mumbled, "It's okay, sweetie."

"No it isn't! We could lose everything! An' it's just money to him."

He soothed her, told her the company was in safe hands with ol' Rich. "I tol' you, he even caught one of the rats today."

She dried her eyes and gave me a fleeting, embarrassed look. Not friendly—nor quite as wary as the look she might reserve for child stealers. She couldn't pretend much friendship for a stranger who had the power to wreck her life, never mind whether the power would be used.

"Well," she said practically, "I still wish he hadn't borrowed the money. It's more trouble'n it's worth."

Stu squeezed her narrow shoulder and laughed. "I'll bet ol' Rich has heard that before."

"I'll bet he has," she said.

We resumed work early the next day. When it was eight o'clock in Baltimore, I went over to a corner and phoned Harvey Breton. I had expected my good news to earn the same diplomatic uh-hum that would have greeted a disaster. Instead, our managing partner surprised me with warm enthusiasm. He was delighted. He had known his confidence in me was well placed. It was a pleasure hearing from such a valued member of the team. Hanging up, I felt more than a little disbelieving.

A little after ten my express package arrived from Baltimore. On top of photocopied pages of Gulf Helmsmen's financial history, Anne Hargrave had scrawled a bold note: *A Senior Executive is still after your scalp. Best of luck.*

Sitting at my empty desk, I read through the file. The bank's managers had been pretty nimble. As business turned soggy along the Gulf, they had dumped some of their vulnerable loans onto workout syndicates. Others they foreclosed before asset values trickled away. Somebody had clung to the old dictum that the best distress sale is the first one. The lending window had come down fast and tight. Alex Edwards's binful of soured deals wasn't as full as a lot of bankers'. The bank's file didn't promise to cast any light on Charlie Fentress, so I set it aside and concentrated on getting caught up on Harris Marine's fortunes. Tom Avery patiently went to the file cabinets and pulled what I needed. It was hard to see any sign that business was improving. Oil prices kept clicking down a few cents on world markets, and that kept the companies that should have been drilling in the Gulf nervous about whether the wells they brought in would justify the exploration costs. If Stu hadn't operated scared all his life, he wouldn't have survived. As it was, nothing I found would make Harvey Breton flinch.

At eleven-thirty, I got up and stretched. The office had filled without my noticing. Around me were desks occupied by unfamiliar faces. Tom Avery had gone off on some mission. Stu was at the far end of the room, on the telephone. Numbers still marched behind my eyes, sinking into a cranial stuffing of damp cotton.

Upstairs I found soda and candy machines tucked into an alcove beside the stairwell. I bought a Coke and glanced into Ginnie Miller's domain. She wasn't there, and neither was anyone who looked like Raoul. A young, curly-haired man wearing earphones sat at the radio bank, talking feverishly into a mouthpiece.

The day hadn't gotten any brighter in four hours. Mounds of heavy cloud swirled upriver, trailing shadowy arms of rain. The concrete yard was deserted except for a dingy confetti of gulls standing in their reflections. At the bulkhead, four of Stu's boats rocked on the river's chop. Two were in port for a couple of days waiting for equipment, and the two closest to the crane at the yard's south end were due for engine overhauls. Another squall blew through and the boats vanished behind a gray shade.

By tonight I could bid the subtropical weather good-bye. Stu and his lawyers could bird-dog the bank. I'd gotten as much of a view of Harris Marine's operations as I needed. With a clear conscience I planned to be on the 8:20 flight to Baltimore.

Going home seldom inspired me. I had done little to make the prospect inviting. The apartment was a place to sleep and, only when it couldn't be avoided, a place to eat. The office was a ritual to attend, like a funeral or a wedding for somebody I didn't know well. The day was a thing to occupy until it ended.

The work itself, coping with the perversity of clients and markets, I adored. But most of my memorably good times had come in the field, where the booby traps weren't of friend's or family's devising.

As I turned from the window, the wind tore a hole in the

shade and I saw a man moving in a crouch across the deck of the nearest boat. His posture was an eloquent announcement that he didn't belong on that long bare aft deck. The stealth could mean anything: a lazy machine-shop worker looking for a secluded place to steal a nap, a thief looking in the rain for tools. . . .

The radio operator was still intent on his business.

I looked back to the boat and couldn't spot my stalker. He must have been on the far side of the crew quarters. Leaning close enough to feel the glass's warm vibration, I watched intently without picking up another flicker of movement in the rain. He had been wearing a tan jacket, dark slacks. No cap or hard hat.

I went downstairs, saw neither Avery nor Stu. A young man with a tall brush cut looked around in surprise when I asked for them. "Mr. Stu said he was gonna go out to the shop."

If I raised an alarm over someone ducking off for a smoke, I would survive the embarrassment. And Stu could enjoy a laugh at Rich's paranoia.

It wasn't someone going for a nap or a smoke.

I donned the light raincoat and broad-brimmed hat I had bought in New Orleans. The machine shop lay down a tortuous path of corridors at the west end of the compound. It was reachable from the business office if you knew the route. I struck off blindly, opened a door that seemed familiar and ended up standing with warm rain blowing in my face. I turned and spotted a low flat structure of concrete block jutting from the main building fifty yards into the wind.

I sprinted that way.

Stu Harris had left the shop floor. I'd met Eric Devalier, the foreman, ten months ago. I remembered the big redhead, and when I took my hat off he recognized me. "You just missed him, Mr.—uh, don't recall your name."

"Have you got a man out working on the boats?"

"What boats—"

"The ones tied up here."

"Naw—we gotta wait for parts on the *Brangus*."

"I think you might have a prowler. I'm going out to have a look. Will you call Mr. Harris?"

"No offense, but you better let our security boys do the lookin'. I'll call Stu."

He went over to a wall phone, and I walked back into the rain. The hot wind almost knocked me off my feet. I huddled near a cinderblock wall. No need to go out to the boat. Stu and a guard could indeed do the lookin'. A gust of rain swept across me. Richard Welles had too much sense to board a boat where a trespasser lurked. Reliable, predictable Richard.

So I walked down to where the *Brangus* was thrashing at its lines and climbed onto the deck.

8

And got thrown overboard for my trouble.

There was a moment of blackness when the water closed over my head. Black shot with bolts of color and sensation— black tracks of hair across a bronze head, a rubbery face concentrating on violence, bone-bruising pain of the hands— and warm water like molasses, churning over arms that felt too heavy to move.

Trying to breathe, I got a mouthful of muddy water. I tried to swim. The arms didn't respond. I was drowning in the raincoat.

The skirts were up over my head. I scissored my feet, broke to the surface. Struggled out of the raincoat. My suit jacket followed, and I rolled sideways, trying to figure which way the shore lay.

I slipped past the bow of the *Brangus* and kicked to the right. Then realized that the bulkhead loomed six feet over me without a handhold. A foot offshore I could drown as surely as at midchannel. I let the current carry me, keeping my mouth above the chop for a hundred feet. At the next boat in line, I grabbed a tire fender and clung.

For the longest time I didn't bother trying to climb out. The Atchafalaya no longer was lethal. Just a seething warm stew. More comfortable staying with it than struggling to change my situation.

Back to being practical Richard. Already I regretted ditching the suit coat that held my wallet.

I was looking at the *Brangus* when the sides blew out in gouts of red flame. The explosion lifted the pilothouse clear off the deck like a tin can, opening its seams as it rose. A ball of fire jutted from the ship's lower decks, throwing greasy black smoke toward the clouds. Burning fragments of unidentifiable wreckage hit the roiling water and sizzled. A wall of blistering heat reached me a moment after the shock wave. The entire length of the *Brangus* was ablaze in a furious squirming pyre, undiminished by the rain.

I turned away from the heat.

Hooking a foot in the tire, I levered myself over the gunwale onto the *Lil Puss*. From the cluttered rear deck I could see figures running across the yard. Stu, in the lead, decelerated into a loose-jointed walk. He looked as if all his tendons had been cut.

I climbed onto the pier. He barely noticed me when I reached out and shook his shoulder. "Stu——"

He glanced reluctantly my way. "Yeah, buddy?"

The intruder would be long gone from the lot. My description wouldn't help the police unless someone else could link the man to a car. I started to explain this to Stu, then saw a man in a guard's uniform and gave it to him. The guard radioed the front gate, from which a broken voice responded that nobody had left the parking lot on foot or by automobile.

A couple of the workers who had pounded across the yard stood muttering to each other. Uneasy glances flicked at the *Brangus*. It was becoming obvious that Stu Harris had enemies. The burning hulk of the boat was an eloquent warning that the boss's problems could have unhealthy implications for his men.

"Jesus," Stu choked. "What the hell's going on, Richard?"

"Brangus was bombed."

"Sons of bitches . . . she was my first goddamned boat."

The complaint was barely out of his mouth when the rear deck of the *Lil Puss* where I had stood sixty seconds earlier lifted like a handkerchief on a gust of wind. The blast's shock sent me sprawling into Stu. We hit the concrete under a wave of heat.

When I sat up, something whimpered beside me. The security guard was holding both hands to stanch a flow of blood from his hairline. I could see glints between his fingers and pulled his hands away. A shard of metal the size of a dinner plate was lodged under his scalp. Rain kept it shiny, washing the blood away. Leaning between us, Stu Harris pulled the fragment out of the man's scalp. He pressed a handkerchief over the wound and brought the man's hands back. "Hold it there, Billy."

He found the radio and called for an ambulance.

Men had gotten to their feet, running uselessly to watch the *Lil Puss* burn. Stu couldn't help himself. He clapped my hand on Billy's shoulder and lumbered over to join them.

Both vessels burned to the waterline and sank before fire trucks arrived. By that time the yard was crowded, and the buildings were empty. I found Stu pacing along the waterfront and suggested he post men at Harris Marine's entrances. He gave the orders. Back at the edge of the pier, rain streaking down from his hair, he glared defiantly at the two remaining boats. An hour later, he led two volunteers aboard and searched both vessels without finding explosive charges.

Twenty minutes after Stu came off the boats, Special Agent Fertig showed up. She said Willie Dreyfus had called her.

She wrinkled her freckled nose at the smoldering bits and pieces of wreckage that littered the pier. One quite large section, which appeared to belong to a diesel stack, had come down fifty feet from the water. No one was quite sure which boat it had risen from. The relic's arrival had caused no casualties, unlike smaller projectiles that had found soft flesh here and there.

Fists on her hips, she stepped to the water's edge. She studied the oily water, then the bulkhead where charred lengths of rope trailed down to the water. "How long did it take your boats to sink?" she asked Stu.

"Not very long at all, ma'am. One of the explosions tore open the *Brangus*'s side below the waterline, and she was a goner. The other—five minutes."

"Mr. Dreyfus said there was a witness."

"Rich here saw the fellow and got dunked."

Her glance held a trace of friendly recognition. "Can you provide a description, Mr. Welles?"

"Yes." I had been thinking about something. "He may have had a small boat tied up somewhere along here. If the police could be notified—there probably aren't a lot of small craft on the water today."

"Why do you think he had a boat?"

"The guard out front didn't see anybody walking or driving out."

"The police can't stop every boat within a ten-mile radius," she said.

"They could stop the ones carrying a stocky man without much hair wearing a tan jacket."

"Probably not all of those either. But we can get the word out."

We went back to the office. I phoned Baltimore and convinced Harvey that I should stay over. He was instantly agreeable. Trench warfare echoed dimly in his tone. He asked if Mr. Harris had kept up insurance payments on the fleet and "uh-hummed" contentedly when I said yes. I spent the next twenty minutes talking to credit card companies and arranging with a banker friend in Baltimore to clear a cash advance at a local bank. When I told my friend that I had lost my wallet, he demonstrated that he shared my brother's perspective. "I hope you got laid before you got rolled," he said.

When I got off the phone, Agent Fertig was still sitting on the edge of a desk with a receiver pressed against her ear. I hunted up a motel chain and booked a room. Stu's Noey had her hands full without a lingering guest.

Stu ambled between desks. "You going home tonight?"

"I thought I might stay. I took a room at the Coral Reef."

"Aw, that's not necessary." His heavy face sagged. He was

too tired to offer more than a passing protest. "Willie's got our security firm sending more people around. Nobody's getting on this property again that I don't want here."

"That's good. You might want to do the same thing at your home."

He thought about it. "Jesus, you're a scary man. Where's their profit in hitting me there?"

"Where's the profit in what happened today?"

"I'll do it." He swung around heavily, like one of his tugs pushing too much of a load, and lumbered back to a desk.

I was a real bringer of good cheer.

"Mr. Harris seems to value your advice." The FBI woman stood with her hands in her pockets. There was no trace of a smile on her pale lips. "I'm not sure I understand your relationship with Harris Marine Company. Can you fill me in?"

"I work for Harris Marine's investment banker. The name is Ambrose & Welles, in Baltimore."

"And you're Mr. Welles."

"One of several. The most junior of several."

To avoid smiling, she frowned. "Has your firm lent money to Harris?"

"Not exactly. We've raised money for them from other investors—banks, pension funds, individuals. We sold about twelve million worth of bonds for Harris Marine last winter. So you could say I'm down here looking out for the bondholders."

"I see. . . . Do you normally give out security advice?"

"Not normally. But sometimes a client isn't careful enough."

"Why do you think Mr. Harris's boats were destroyed?"

"Retaliation. Why do you think?"

"Our investigation is just beginning. From your conversation with Alex Edwards, do you think Charles Fentress would bother with property destruction?"

"I'm not sure he would stop at it. What bothers me is the 'why' of it. The thing was set up to come apart with Alex Edwards telling his feeble story. That's happened. Fentress has his money. Why strike again at Harris Marine?"

"What answer can you think of?"

I shook my head. "We don't know enough about Fentress. Who is he really? Is he the mastermind or hired talent? When your people track him down, everything may make sense."

"I can tell you this," she said. "Charles Fentress isn't known by that name in Dallas. The telephone numbers he called from his hotel connected to an empty office that may have been a sort of electronic mail drop. There were signs that somebody had call-forwarding equipment there, bits of left-over wire, evidence the connection box had been worked on. We don't know where those devices kicked the calls."

"You did all that this morning?"

"Last night. The bureau takes eight-point-four-million-dollar crimes seriously. If we move quickly, we usually pick up a trail." She walked off to meet a squad of explosives technicians. She returned in fifteen minutes with Agent Wosocki and Stu Harris in tow.

Stu leaned close to me. "I took care of that thing you suggested. Thanks, buddy."

Agent Fertig looked annoyed.

He said, "I'm a mite peckish. You wanna come along to lunch, Rich?"

"Actually, we have more questions," Agent Fertig said.

"Good, good, we'll talk over catfish." He wanted to take his station wagon, but the agents prevailed and we rode in a white sedan equipped with a radio. The parking lot beside the Riverfront Cafe was only beginning to fill. We went inside to a broad room where scuffed linoleum covered both the steel-rimmed tables and the floor. The customers were a mix of local shopkeepers and blue-collar workers, several of whom Stu greeted with a nod or a "hi-yah."

We sat at a window table that gave us a view of nothing but a muddy ditch. Stu ordered a beer, the rest of us soft drinks. Agent Wosocki asked questions with perfect phrasing, as if Fertig might be grading his special-agent skills. The inquiries all came around to whether Charlie Fentress could have had an inside man or woman helping him at the company.

Stu didn't like the idea of betrayal and acted stubborn. I thought it was possible and rated Ellis Samuels as the number one prospect, Tom Avery as number two. But given the experience of Alex Edwards, I didn't think any traitor at Harris Marine would be able to tell us much about Fentress.

Joanne Fertig relaxed marginally during lunch. Wosocki asked reasonable questions and didn't put a spoon up his nose. Whatever list she kept in her mind had been satisfied with "X's" entered in the appropriate columns, proving that so far the investigation was being run according to Hoyle.

When Stu asked how she had become an FBI agent, she responded coolly that she had always had an interest in law enforcement work. He said, "Y'mean that when other girls was playing with dollies, you had a six-shooter?"

I had a feeling that almost anyone else who asked the question would have been maced. But Stu Harris's good nature was too apparent for his clumsiness to offend. She gave a twisted smile. "Something like that." She thought for a moment, weighed the pros and cons and added, "Actually, I had the whole set. G-man buzzer, handcuffs, fingerprint powder."

Stu guffawed. "Betchu were hell on the little boys."

"On a couple of them."

We drove back along the river to the boat yard, and Fertig and Wosocki took Tom Avery into a cubbyhole. I parked myself with the cash ledgers and understood after about ninety minutes why Stu had been optimistic enough to buy more boats. If you looked at the business according to accountants' rules, which required Stu to charge off depreciation on everything from the workboats and shop equipment to the headquarters building, Harris Marine was losing money. If you forgot about all of that and looked at the flow of cash in and out the door, the company was taking in a little more money than it was spending. It was the test of viability, no different from a weakened man's ability to hold nourishment above the body's daily expenditures—no different from the older Welles brother's ability to balance an intractably out-of-balance checkbook or life.

As I finished up, Tom Avery emerged from his interview with a soggy collar and a look of despair. Fertig came past five minutes later, her square, pleasant face giving away nothing.

9

Joanne Fertig knocked at my motel door the next morning. It was six forty-five. I was awake and showered, dressed except for a necktie. From the balcony she nodded down to the parking lot. "Since you're the only witness, it might help if you came along."

Two tan cruisers with light bars on top sat at angles beside Fertig's white sedan. Looking over her shoulder, I could see Wosocki's blond head between a couple of trooper hats.

"You've found somebody," I said.

"A good possibility," she said briskly. "Do you have to go to the bathroom?"

"I don't think so."

"Let's hit the road. We should have been out of here before daybreak; in that case I wouldn't have woken you. We've got enough to place this person under arrest, and I'd have opted for that," she explained as I locked the door. "But Sheriff Berteau wasn't ready till twenty minutes ago. So we go in by daylight. But having you along gives me an option. I'll explain in the car."

We went down the outside stairway, and she introduced me to a rawboned, mahogany-tanned man with a face so weather-checked he could have been thirty or sixty. Sheriff Bebe Berteau didn't smile or offer to shake my hand. He just pointed his horn-rimmed lenses at me and said, "You keep out of the way of any shootin'."

"The sheriff and the bureau intend, of course, that there won't be any shooting," Fertig said.

"Lorie Menard won't come easy," the sheriff said. It was clear he didn't dread the thought of taking Menard the hard way.

Fertig forced home the point of who was in charge. "The government hasn't decided yet whether Mr. Menard will be taken into custody."

Wearing no expression, Berteau looked at his car, which was spanking clean, consulted his watch, glanced up at his hat brim. He tightened his lips, straining, and farted. He said, " 'Scuse me, ma'am."

"Grits do that to me, too," she said.

He took a shotgun from the backseat rack and worked the slide, while a deputy scowled at us. Wosocki and another officer consulted a map spread on the hood of the federal car. Fertig went over and eavesdropped. I stood hands in pockets and watched the interplay of men who thought they might kill somebody within the next hour. There were six sheriff's department men besides Berteau, of ages ranging from early twenties to what could have been late sixties or older. The eldest deputy, who bore some physical resemblance to Sheriff Berteau, did and said the least. Backside planted against a cruiser's trunk, bare forearms folded, he stood with his back to us, staring at the highway. Two overweight, middle-aged men traded Vietnam memories loudly, like schoolboys reciting magic spells.

We got into the cars and headed out of town in a high-speed convoy with Sheriff Berteau's cruiser in front, challenging Wosocki to keep pace. The young agent ducked his head and stepped on the gas. Fertig threw an arm over her seat back, ignoring the road, and asked me, "Did Alex Edwards mention the name Loren Menard to you?"

"No."

"And you didn't hear the name at Harris Marine?"

I shook my head. "What makes Menard a suspect?"

"He had a fight yesterday afternoon with a man at the Berwick town dock. The policeman who broke it up got to thinking—later, of course. Menard fitted the description you gave, and he had just brought a small boat in. So the officer called the Morgan City department."

"We got lucky," Wosocki said without looking around. The sheriff's car was a hundred feet ahead on a winding road that had a narrow channel of water snaking alongside. Wosocki said, "Menard learned demolition with a diving company, and he did eighteen months up at Angola for burglary."

"Angola?"

"State prison," Fertig said, adding with satisfaction, "at hard labor."

"Louisiana likes to make its criminals tougher?" I said.

"That may not be the purpose," Wosocki said.

"Do you have opinions on penal reform, too, Mr. Welles?" Fertig asked. In addition to my meddlesome opinions on security measures, she meant.

"No."

"Let me explain what you can do for us," she said.

I listened nodding at every third word and was back in her good graces a few minutes later. Ahead, the sheriff's cruiser turned onto a side road, crossed a small concrete bridge and slowed to a stop on a stretch of built-up shoulder that looked like a fishing spot. Wosocki got off the road, backed and filled a little as the other sheriff's department cruiser stopped in the middle of the road. Sheriff Berteau got out and walked back to our car. "I'd be in favor we send Eugene and Roddy cross by boat, and we can walk."

"That sounds good," Fertig said. "This is Bayou Boeuf?"

"That's right. You look through them trees ahead, see that trailer park? Lorie Menard's house is a quarter mile on down the road from there."

"All right. We will try to give Mr. Welles a chance to make an identification of Menard. If that works, you and your men will do a quiet fade. If we can surveil Menard, he may lead us to an associate."

"Lorie'll know he's bein' watched," Berteau said. "He's got the instinct of a woods boy."

Two deputies were unloading a small, shallow punt from the trunk of their cruiser. They sidestepped down the grassy bank and set the boat half into the water. One of the men went back to the car and collected a lightweight outboard engine.

"Roddy, take your rifle," Berteau said, slapping the younger man's shoulder. "We'll give you ten minutes."

"Yessir." The deputy threw his hat into the trunk, and when Eugene's followed he slammed the lid.

Berteau leaned toward Roddy. "If you get a target that's bein' a threat to public safety this mornin', you do your job." He accompanied the men down to the water and stood by as they clambered aboard the boat. The early light hit the ridge of Berteau's forehead and cheeks, washing silver on top of brown. Shadows sprang from his lashes and brows.

Joanne Fertig watched him, her arms folded, a small oval watch peeking from beneath the navy sleeve of her jacket. Her feet were planted firmly, slightly apart. She said to Wosocki, "Don't get between a deputy and a target. You either, Mr. Welles."

Berteau had the two cruisers driven as far as the trailer court, left a deputy in charge of each car and brought his oldest deputy along as he climbed into the back seat with me. Wosocki drove the unmarked car almost a quarter mile down the blacktop before spotting the turnoff. It was either an unnamed and unnumbered road or a long driveway serving several properties. Menard's house was right on the water, a flat one story with broken asbestos shingles and a yard strewn with bicycle parts, the shell of a Volkswagen and wooden crates. Just off the rutted drive a showroom-bright sports car sat in the weeds with a skim of mud on its skirts. The road curved on past the lot to reach a couple of other places. Wosocki stopped beside a scrim of trees and bushes.

"Just like I told you," Berteau said.

"Can you see the front stoop?" Fertig asked me.

I turned around in the narrow quarters. The back window gave me a hazy but adequate view of most of the house. "It's okay."

"Good. Then you stay in the car."

She climbed out, closed the door silently, went around to Wosocki's side. Beside me, Sheriff Berteau and his parched deputy stepped out, bent low.

Wosocki removed his suit coat and necktie, rolled up his sleeves, pulled his shirttail out over the holster at the back of his belt. He rumpled his blond hair, put on a pair of horn-rimmed glasses. He glanced at himself in the side mirror, announced, "Revenge of the nerds." Stooping beside the open door, he scuffed his palms over the sides of a rear tire, came up dirty. He looked suitably rumpled for an unhappy motorist who was knocking to ask a homeowner to call a tow truck. When Loren Menard opened the door, or better yet stepped out to chat with his visitor, I would nod to Fertig if I recognized the man from the *Brangus*. If Wosocki's shtick seemed to be working, we would leave and the bureau would put the house under surveillance. If Menard seemed to have doubts, Wosocki would arrest him on the spot. Embarrassing if I didn't recognize him. But we couldn't get around that problem while having Menard off balance.

"Be seeing you," Wosocki said. He sauntered around the back of the car, tramped down to a bow-backed culvert that he walked across into the yard. He approached the house with slump-shouldered resignation, a grimy hand wiping his neck. I looked down at Joanne Fertig, who was crouched beside the door. Tiny teeth held her lower lip, which was trembling. Without taking her eyes off Wosocki, she said, "Watch the house—you may not get much chance."

"Does he have a bullet-proof vest under that shirt?" I asked.

"We both do," she said.

Wosocki mounted the two steps to the cement stoop, knocked on the aluminum screen door. The inner door was barely visible drawing back, and then the screen exploded and Wosocki hurled himself sideways off the platform and landed in the grass and rolled, clutching at his back. He huddled against the foundation blocks and, holding his revolver with both hands, fired two or three shots at the door.

A voice near me whispered urgently, "Fuck, fuck, fuck," as hands pushed my feet away from the seat well. She reached under the driver's seat and pulled out a machine pistol with a long clip, whirled out of the car pushing Berteau aside. "Tell your deputies to lay down some fire back there, get this guy's attention."

She headed toward the house as Berteau talked to his radio. Climbing out of the car, I could see Wosocki still on his back, aiming the gun alternately at a window above his head and at the empty doorway. Fragments of the metal door hung from the frame. Menard must have used a shotgun, but I didn't remember hearing the blast.

There was plenty of shooting from the back. "Told her he wouldn't come easy," Berteau said to no one. Certainly not to me, and his deputy was closing in on Fertig, shotgun seeking a target at the windows. Berteau called out, "Nack, you watch yourself!" and went after them.

She was already across the culvert, moving in a crouch for a tree. The grass was knee-high, and I thought she had tripped until the sound of the shot registered, crisp and clear. She went down and the machine pistol flew off like a black bird.

The old deputy crouched behind the sports car and blew every window out of the front of the house, then lowered his aim and tried tearing away at the walls. The sheriff ran across the culvert, head bending to his radio, and called, "He's goin' out the back! Hey, Eugene—talk to me!"

Berteau went to the right, Nack to the left. As I crossed the culvert, I noticed that after a burst of shots there was silence from the back of the house. Wosocki ran past me in the opposite direction, his face stricken.

I reached the rear of the property, a jungle of industrial scrap that ranged from water heaters to cinder blocks. On a muddy bank tangled with tree roots, Loren Menard lay on his side, knees up, hands pressed against his abdomen. His face was clenched, his bald head wet. His belly and hands were red.

"He's had it," Nack said.

Tilting his hat back, Berteau looked from the deputy to Menard. His expression was readable. For so early in the morning the day had gone rotten stinking sorry. He bumped his foot against Menard. "Cut your groaning, you dumb shit." He thumbed back the hammer of his revolver, bent near the bare head with his intent clear.

I didn't have time to do anything but grab his arm. The gun discharged into the mud. Berteau whirled on me, bringing up the pistol. I didn't see Nack except peripherally as he stepped close and backhanded his shotgun into my face.

As I rolled over, spitting blood, the old man looked down with disapproval. "You shouldn't done that to the sheriff."

I found a handkerchief to put under my nose. Bebe Berteau was heading down to the deputies in the boat with a fast, stiff-legged gait. When the sheriff was out of earshot, Nack said, "He'd have shot you. My nephew Bebe ain't bright."

I tried to get up, found my knees were jelly. "Menard has information."

"He won't tell you. Ever one of them Menards is shit."

Lorie Menard was on his back, rocking side to side, breathing raggedly between locked teeth. His face was deeply pocked, his nose tiny, his brows almost as hairless as the crown of his head. I sagged beside him, shook his shoulder. "Tell me about Charlie Fentress."

His eyes opened in slits. "You—you fingered me. . . . Thought I'd drowned you. . . . Who was the woman? Did I get her?"

"You missed."

"Shit—I know I didn't." His rocking slowed as he gasped in pain, and his eyes rolled back.

I said, "You planted the charges for Fentress. Tell me about him."

"Huh? Oh . . . sure . . . Charlie . . . but . . . you gotta do something for me. . . ."

"What do you want?"

His eyelids fluttered. The eyes were gray and remorseless. "You gotta promise . . . promise after I'm dead you'll suck my cock." He smiled around clenched teeth. "Shoulda hit you harder. . . ."

I stood up and left him. In the house, Deputy Nack held a rifle with a scope. He set it down on a blond boxwood table laden with handguns and cartridge boxes. Two of Menard's shotguns had gone out the back door with him, but there were three others, two handguns, and a broken-down machine gun. The house was a collection bin of unwrapped garbage, empty beer cans, pornographic magazines, filthy sheets, armaments. Only the air coming through the empty door and window frames made the stench endurable. In the bedroom, on a broken-legged dresser, lay a crossbow that I knew had been used on Ellis Samuels.

When we went out, Berteau was stomping around the side of the house. Wosocki planted himself in the path to where his senior agent lay. His shirt covered her head.

"Get away from here," he said.

10

I got back to Baltimore twenty-six hours later. Harvey Breton was in splendid cheer. He came bounding up the curving stairs from our retail office, red hunter's necktie flapping over pink stripes, cheekbones rosy, thin hair freshly barbered and brushed. He looked me up and down. "A week gone, a problem solved," he said, a careful man's motto. "So we got you back in one piece."

I nodded. "No damage."

"Your lip is swollen. Well—our client is on the road to solvency. You did a fine job. But I don't think we want to raise any more money for Mr. Harris, do we?"

"There are probably better risks," I conceded. Turning over eight point four million to a con man made Stu a very poor risk, even if we had retrieved the money. His next misjudgment might not be repaired.

"But—I suppose you'll keep in touch with him, do what you can?" His narrow brows lifted, his forehead wrinkled in concern. He didn't want to imply a rebuke for my previous inattention.

"I'll talk to him twice a month," I promised.

"That's just fine."

He hurried off, and I tried to count the number of times in the preceding three years that I had seen Harvey striding through the building in shirtsleeves. I couldn't think of one occasion. Harvey's domain was his tradition-festooned office or the board room, less so the executive dining room with its ancient black attendants whose lot seemed to embarrass him—though they were a tradition more authentic than his hunting prints.

I turned a corner and saw Anne Hargrave in the hallway, heading back to the investment banking department. She had on a navy skirt that came a sensible inch below the knee and low-heeled pumps. She was leggy and thin rather than small and compact, but I felt a jolt and had a vivid memory of blue-clad hips motionless on wet grass.

I followed her along to our desks, threw my jacket on to a stack of unopened mail. I had been back a little less than five hours, and the office still seemed only half-familiar. "I saw Harvey Breton," I said, "without his jacket on."

She looked up, considered the information, shook her head and didn't answer.

"Is Mr. Welles still chairman?" I said.

"Welles père. The other is trying out and finding it dull."

She understood Pat. I had seen my father and his most promising son an hour earlier, flanking a client as they returned from lunch. Pat's elongated stride had Center Club written all over it.

She leaned her chin on a fist. "While you were playing cops and robbers, Mr. Breton brought in our biggest client. Would you believe Ambrose & Welles is now an investment banker for Consolidated Illuminating? They want us to sell stock this fall."

It explained why Harvey was chipper. Consolidated Illuminating—known with probably little fondness as Con-Ill to rate payers in four southeastern states—was a blue-chip electric power consortium in Atlanta that normally took its business to the larger underwriting houses in New York. Bringing them in as clients was a coup by Harvey that my father would have a hard time dismissing at the next partners' meeting. Thinking of the broad glare of satisfaction I had seen Patrick senior wearing, I wondered if somehow he had failed to hear of Harvey's success. It was unprecedented that both men were in good spirits at the same time.

"Is it true you were involved in a shoot-out?" Anne Hargrave asked.

"Sort of, as a bystander." I contrived to smile, didn't feel it. If word had gotten around, I would have to answer a lot of *What happeneds?* before my colleagues' interest wore off. The picture of what had happened remained too sharp for the prospect to be anything but depressing. Harvey and I had had our gloomy debriefing by telephone. He asked about the agent's family, which consisted of a sister and parents, and sounded relieved that he didn't have to wrestle with an indirect and remote responsibility for a breadwinner's loss. Dreadful thing all the same, he said and seemed to mean it.

Charlie Fentress had done a lot of damage in pursuit of his millions. The thought stayed with me during the hours of explaining the little that I knew to other federal agents, and it was never far away on the flight home. A lot of damage for money that could buy only a handful of things that would make any difference in his life. The expenditures had been too big for the meager reward.

I was less angry than truly perplexed. In the isolation of a half-empty airliner, it was easy to imagine one had fastened on some truth about human brutality that could explain away Ellis Samuels and Joanne Fertig as costs of doing business, no more important than a bulldozed pasture or a filled-in pond. In the morning glare outside the airport, the insight thinned to vapor.

My perspective was wrong, I thought. I had never been hungry enough, either from deprivation or from greed, to understand an equation that put value only on the predator's fulfillment. I wouldn't understand a Charlie Fentress if he tried to explain himself any more than I really understood the obsessive money-makers who bought a hotel one Monday, a steel wire company at midweek, an airline the next week.

My lack of avarice might not be a virtue. Unless my father

disinherited me, I could afford to be indifferent to my financial prospects. Charlie Fentress might have grown up in rougher circumstances.

Anne Hargrave stretched, put a hand over a yawn, and interrupted my half-formed thought by saying, "I thought it was just possible that the shoot-out story was made up to cover your debauching on Bourbon Street. But I should have known—"

"Actually, you were right," I said. I kept my voice flat. "The debauching got out of hand. I ran out of credit cards and had to settle a bill at one dive by promising to bring them someone peachy-skinned, fresh and good with numbers to work the sailors."

She was unruffled. "Sometimes I could use a sailor or two."

"I think they expect more productivity than one or two."

"That's the trouble with belonging to the working class—the boss man is always speeding up the line." She looked at her watch and got back to doing some working-class drudgery, and out of a sense of obligation I tried deciphering a folder full of monthly profit-and-loss statements that a prospective client wanted us to believe.

The company had its headquarters just across the line in Delaware, and their directors knew our directors. So we were giving them polite consideration. The founder had built up a chain of twenty company-owned Lickety Lube Shops in Delaware and New Jersey, along with about fifty stores owned by other people who paid a monthly fee to use the Lickety Lube name and bought oil supplies from the company. The founder wanted to go regional, jumping in five years to more than a thousand shops, and needed twenty million dollars of someone's capital to pay for the first couple of steps. Getting to a thousand shops would cost about eighty million, the founder projected. I read through his recent years' results, his projections, and knew he was in a grow-or-die dilemma. The seventy existing stores weren't doing enough business to cover corporate overhead and advertising. If the chain were larger, the founder could spread the expenses over more stores and get discounts on bulk supplies. What bothered me was the numbers from individual Lickety Lube shops, most of which seemed to be losing money. If thirty cars a day rolled through Lickety's service bays for an oil change and whatever extras the staff could promote, a shop broke even. If forty cars came in, the business was nicely profitable. The problem was that a typical Lickety Lube was attracting only twenty cars a day. The founder had gotten along on two financings from venture capital groups that now owned forty percent of his company. He wanted us to take his stock public to try to hoist the company out of what appeared to be a lethal predicament. The strategy reminded me of a painful one-liner used by retailers: *We're losing money on every sale but we'll make it up on volume.* A worse bet, I thought, than well-intentioned Stu Harris, who pinched pennies and misplaced millions.

It wouldn't be politic to wrap the projections in brown paper and drop them into the mail for return to the company. Instead I would set up an appointment with the founder, chat with his financial people and go through a few other motions before telling Harvey we should turn them down. By then I would have a polite lie ready to soothe the founder—probably my standby, which was, *We would love to do this deal, but we haven't got the marketing system to do your stock justice.* Literally true in part. We couldn't do justice to a stock offering its buyers more risk than any possible reward. The founder would troop cheerfully over to Shearson or another firm with a national sales staff to spread the shares wide and thin, and Aunt Tillie in Des Moines would own two hundred Lickety Lubes in her retirement account.

Better on Shearson's head than ours.

At five-thirty, the nearest desk emptied out with a flash of mirror and the rustle of a shopping bag. At six, I put the top down and scooted up the JFX to the Ruxton Club and found the pool as deserted for the pre-dinner drinking hour as I had hoped. For twenty minutes I had the lanes to myself, except for a preteen game of water polo at the shallow end. I swam a few laps and then lay on my back staring at the sky. When I climbed out and toweled off, the game was still going strong, a girl of about ten and a slightly older brother bantering in English accents. Their father managed the sales effort of a

British cable equipment company that had opened an East Coast branch. When I came out of the changing room and brought a whiskey and water out to the patio, the game had attracted a couple of adults and the girl was complaining the pool was grotty.

It was a fairly safe place for a drink. My mother maintained the family membership, but the club was too down-at-the-heels comfortable for my father to bring clients by. The regulars were too settled in their social arrangements to give Pat many openings at other people's wives. Mother showed up solely for charitable functions. I could drink in the August evening with little risk of being caught up in disagreeable moments or, in Mother's case, tedious prying. When the poolside lights came on, it would be tempting to stay for a second or third round, after which "why not another?" sounded only reasonable.

I walked the empty glass into the paneled lounge just off the dining room and spotted my brother's seersucker jacket and tousled head as he guided a blond girl I didn't recognize into dinner. His left hand held a glass; the other hovered at the small of the woman's back like a thrush waiting for an opportunity to land. In profile, she was striking, with a high forehead, features that came somewhere between grace and strength, confident bearing, good clothes, not much jewelry. Mother wasn't the only one in the family who could price them on the hoof, but my habit had been acquired in the line of duty as I tried to size up clients. My fleeting judgment here was that Pat had stepped up in class, or overstepped, I thought, hoping I didn't feel envy.

I went down the winding hall toward the parking lot and met Hank and Wanda Grismore, whom Mother would have priced high on Hank's side of the family while dropping into what she took for delicate silence about Wanda's. On matters of character, one could give a slight edge to Wanda, who had possessed enough purpose in life to marry money. Hank Grismore drifted comfortably and without embarrassment. He seemed to have no strong likes or dislikes and was only mildly adamant about conservation of the state's estuaries, a cause a daughter had drawn him into. He made a frustrating dinner companion, unobnoxious yet utterly indifferent to the minor vanities and obsessions of his acquaintances. A cutting remark from a vicious person implied that the victim's feelings were worth wounding. Hank Grismore offended without meaning to or caring.

He stopped and shook my hand. "Haven't seen you for a while, Richard. Are you still with the firm?"

"Still. And you?"

"Oh, the usual." The usual meant nothing much. He was a couple of inches shorter than average, trim and muscular, going bald from the back so that a pair of thin bands of rusty hair crossed the scalp in front.

Hank had been tossing his key fob. He dropped it into a pocket and said, "Do you think you'll hang around after your father retires?"

I took his point. Why would one? Why would I, in particular, expect to? Wasn't it a little silly to pretend to be actually working at the family firm?

"I might, just for a while," I said.

"You haven't asked how I heard about your father," Hank said.

He was subtle enough that he could be checking a story he had heard, offering me a chance to knock it down. Almost anyone else would understand human nature well enough to know that Patrick Welles, Sr. meant to be taken out of the office feet first, preferably in his ninety-fourth year, and that "retirement" was synonymous with "surrendering power," which was something only a weakling second son might contemplate. A real Welles never surrendered anything.

If he was fishing, I didn't jerk the line. I said, "How you heard what?"

"That your father might be retiring."

"I didn't want to pry. Are you here for dinner?"

"Yes, what else?"

"I'd better let you get on with it. Nice seeing you, Wanda."

I got to the parking lot before smiling, wondering only a little where Hank had picked that one up. My reaction might have given him the impression that Patrick senior's retirement was common knowledge around town, in which case playing mum could come back to torment me if Hank repeated his story attaching "And Richard practically confirmed it" to someone who would pass the account along to my father. Harvey Breton would get an even more combative and perplexing visit than usual.

I got as far as the car before running into a rowdier group from a downtown brokerage house. Ulrich Lenz, who led the pack, was a sometime sailing friend who boasted he went ashore only to pick up new girlfriends. Sailing overnight with him on a small boat got crowded. When he was drunk enough to start wooing in his native German, it also could get noisy. He was tieless and flushed, dark suit rumpled, hair in spikes. Bernie Culverson and Mimi Kane, who swaggered in his wake, looked similarly scuffed-up. Either it had been a rough day in the market or they had taken their preppy charm on a tour of working-class bars.

"Ohh—Richard, Richard," Ulrich sang. "You are not going home?"

"Richard Richard's called it a day," Mimi sort of echoed.

"Have you had dinner?" Ulrich demanded.

"No."

"Then join us and lend an ear. The Dow fell one hundred forty points, recovered eighty, fell sixty—"

"Seventy," Bernie Culverson said.

"—bounced back forty, and not a single program trade to blame for it, just all these nervous nellies at the pension funds. And I heroically tried to keep up with them!"

"I thought you got beat up in a bar," I said.

"The average man knows we are parasites but does not understand the finer points of the parasitism," Ulrich pronounced slowly.

I went in to dinner with them, listened to their gleeful tales of woe at clients who had failed to get orders executed as prices jumped or dived away, of major trades that had been brazenly front-run on the options exchanges, of a small customer who had been wiped out in calls before his check arrived, of orders that got forgotten and then miraculously filled as a convulsive heave reversed the trend of prices for twenty minutes, and on and so on. They would tumble into their beds with ticker quotes flashing behind their eyes, thrash in nightmares of order avalanches, wake yearning for the overnight numbers on Tokyo's trading. I had never met anyone who had become obsessed with insurance or wholesale produce the way some brokers and traders ate and slept the stock market.

Our waiter, Gus, said to me, "I see your brother, Mr. Richard."

"And what's he having tonight?"

"The blonde," Ulrich said.

"Swordfish, Mr. Richard. It's a good choice, broiled or baked."

"Broiled, then."

Gus took the orders of the rowdies with impenetrable courtesy, and I asked Ulrich, "Do you know her?" We were on the other side of the room but the view was unobstructed.

"No," he said, drawing the word out to express regret. "Do you think she will jilt him?"

"Go over and introduce yourself," Mimi suggested. "Tell her you trade index futures and you've got stones."

"I could," he said. He looked at me. "But it wouldn't be nice to Richard."

"You're awfully confident," I said. "For all you know she doesn't like the visceral, muscular type."

"They all do," Ulrich said.

The Grismores came in from the bar, and Hank spared me a surprised scowl. Mimi and Bernie resumed an old argument about suburban restaurants. Ulrich suggested we charter a boat the next morning and try a hard run down to the mouth of the Chesapeake and back. Once or twice I glanced at Pat's table. The conversation there seemed friendly but not cozy; they leaned forward without reaching for nose-to-nose intimacy, business-minded diners. When they left forty minutes later, Pat noticed me but didn't bring her over for introductions. As Ulrich watched the snug hips in a cobalt knit dress, Mimi said, "I knew you were just talk." We had second coffees and dessert, and with Ulrich and Mimi competing on office romance stories of progressive vulgarity, we closed down the dining room.

In the parking lot, Ulrich said, "Are you game? Seven A.M. tomorrow at Bay Brokers? They've got a thirty-footer called *Dunuthin'* that cannot be sold." He spelled it, as if adding to the appeal.

It was either the bay, with its weak August breezes, or a weekend of reliving yesterday morning. No contest. I said, "I'm game."

11

"Con-Ill dumped us," Robby said, passing my desk on Tuesday. He was a junior analyst in the municipal bond department and a bubbling spring of gossip. He veered from desk to desk, sprinkling a few words, hoping to get a volunteer for full submersion. The news on Consolidated Illuminating, whether true or not, must have made his progress through the office satisfyingly slow. I pretended not to hear.

He jerked himself around and came back. "Hey, Rich. Some break, huh?"

"What break, Robby?"

"Con-Ill dumped us. That's one deal that didn't last long."

I wondered if he was sure, didn't ask. Too bad for Harvey Breton. "What spoiled it?"

"What I hear is Ambrose & Welles isn't big time enough for them."

"They must have known that before," I pointed out.

"Well, maybe there was disagreement at first and wiser heads prevailed." He went on his way, utterly delighted with his information, shamelessly disloyal to the creaky dynasty that paid his keep, infallibly aware of whom he could share his scorn with and whom not.

It wouldn't have been wiser heads, I thought; he was wrong about that. A regional firm like ours would do a better job at raising money than the boys in New York. The offering would get our department's full attention for weeks, while at Morgan Stanley it would just be one more stock sale jammed into a crowded pipeline. We would try to time the sale, price it right, place it well, which meant with long-term pension accounts so that shares didn't come spilling right back onto the market, knocking down the price and infuriating buyers and old stockholders alike. The big firm would concentrate on getting the shares out the door fast, with no time for a backward glance.

That was the pitch I made to wavering clients, at least. It was mostly true, though idealized. Ambrose & Welles and Morgan Stanley both lived on fees, and neither of us forgot that the fees came from doing deals. Good deals, if we were looking to the longer health of our business; or after a dry spell, any deal that wouldn't embarrass Harvey or Mr. Patrick in the next twelve months.

A piece of Consolidated Illuminating's business was like a Christmas present in August. Nice until the present was snatched back.

Ulrich rang up at eleven and said the yacht broker was complaining about rubbers jamming the head. As I set down the phone, Pat announced, "There's a partners' meeting this afternoon. I'm invited; you're not."

It wasn't the first of the month, when the firm's senior partners—at least those who were ambulatory—got together for lunch and the Welles-Breton monthly rematch. I asked, "What's the occasion? Is it true about Consolidated Illuminating?"

"It's true, but that's not the reason for the meeting. There's some caterwauling from a couple of people who want to take their capital out. Leviticus and Mortimer, per usual."

Jimmy Leviticus had to be eighty-five and had retired while I was still in high school. Walt Mortimer was in his early sixties and had been pushed out of an active role at the firm by Harvey. Perfectly reasonable that each would want his capital out of the partnership.

"Why does that require a special meeting?" I said, then caught myself. "Oh. How big is Leviticus's stake?"

"Bigger than ours, brother. And bigger than Ambrose & Welles can afford to cash out. Though if he insists, we haven't much choice."

"Maybe they'll assess the other partners," I suggested. A few had substantial money outside the firm; most didn't.

"They put him off six months ago," Pat said, "But I don't think that will work this time. How are your bank lines? Mine are tapped out. Otherwise, I would say you and I should pool our resources, buy out Leviticus, and we could vote one of us in as chairman."

Even with the extra shares, we couldn't muster enough votes. And both of us respected the value of slow change in a business so dependent on the confidence of other people. I asked Pat, "Which one of us?"

"I'm older."

"And presumably deeply loyal to the present chairman."

He laughed. "Actually, yes." His smile dropped away. "I couldn't do anything to hurt him. Could you?"

How would I hurt Patrick Welles, Sr.? He seemed as invulnerable as a bronze monument to anything I might do, as emotionally remote from my reach. If withdrawal of affection was the cruelest act, it was also an impotent one when no affection had ever been sought. But as Pat stared, I fumbled and shook my head. "Of course not."

He looked across the office, at windows offering an empty sky over the harbor. "No, me either. You can know someone's a prick and still be loyal. Why's that, do you think?"

"I don't know."

"Blood's thicker than judgment. That explains a lot."

"Why are you invited to the partners' meeting?"

"I told you. Blood's thicker than judgment. Why do you think the old man would do it?"

"It sounds like you're being groomed."

"God, that's a dreadful thought! Right now I've got most of

the perks of authority without the burdens. It's like I'm getting laid whenever I want without ever having to listen to some cow's morning-after mooing and moaning. I'd be a fool to give up that deal. So would you."

I wasn't that cynical about irresponsibility's advantages, I wanted to protest—but refrained. It was a matter of degree.

Half-hidden behind an armful of papers, Anne Hargrave returned to her desk. She glanced peevishly from Pat to me. "Don't you two ever work?"

"It would be bad for morale if we did," he said.

She shook her head and focused on a stack of monthly profit-and-loss statements. Pat quirked an eyebrow at me, gave an exaggerated sigh. "They do moo and moan."

He left and her eyes followed tentatively. Without looking around, she said, "Are you sure you two are related?"

"There's no question."

"What was that about 'mooing and moaning'?"

I thought about dissembling, decided not to. "It was my brother's way of saying he had slept with you."

Her face came around, wearing dismay, like a child discovering the adults have been told. Then she settled back, mouth shifting into a crooked smile. "He would."

"Sorry. You asked."

"If your brother turns up with a letter opener in his back, will you forget we had this conversation?"

"Gladly."

She shook her head, muttering, "In his dreams."

I spent an hour on the telephone with the treasurer of Lickety Lube, who imagined criticism in my blandest questions. He swung from bravado to evasion to wheedling, and by the time the interview was over we were both exhausted. A foolish man, too worried that I would detect the bad news at his company to let me glimpse any of the parts that were good.

Or, I thought tiredly, he knew the company too well to have any misplaced hopes.

A little after four, Harvey Breton rang my extension. "Could you spare a moment, Richard?"

I went down the hall, around two corners. He was sitting in his crisp blue pinstripes, presiding over a neat desk upon which a lacquered metal lamp cast a convincingly antique glow. He seemed preoccupied, forearms rising from the desk, chin propped on his fists. "Does the name Povane mean anything to you?"

"Not that I can think of."

"Very well. Thank you."

He must have wanted more than that. I said, "Should it?"

He had never quite looked at me directly, and for a moment he didn't answer. "Mr. Povane is a businessman; he seems to have offered to buy old Leviticus's partnership interest. And Mortimer's. Of course the partners would have to decide whether to approve the transfers. . . ."

If they didn't approve, they would have to buy Leviticus and Mortimer out themselves. A rock-or-the-hard-place dilemma if ever there was one.

"I presume you've heard of our . . . setback?"

I put my hands in my pockets. "Yes."

"It received mercifully brief treatment this afternoon. So I got away with being vague on Consolidated Illuminating's problem. You—uhm—play a part. It seems that somebody told Con-Ill's president about one of our young hotshot investment bankers who was beating up a nice group of southern bank executives, making threats, rushing to the Federal Bureau of Investigation—in short, trying to extort money from these gentlemen to cover a blunder of our making."

"A few facts seem to have been left out," I objected.

"And others distorted, but it doesn't matter. We no longer are the kind of nice, accommodating people that the light company chooses to do business with. We have the wrong image."

"Did they mention how they found out?"

"No. It could have been somebody they knew in New Orleans."

Or somebody in Baltimore, of course, if word had gotten out. It seemed like not many days for the town's grapevine to have picked up my adventures along the Gulf. And it was unlikely that anyone would think the Harris Marine fiasco, once repaired, was worth chatting about. The only ears eager for the story would be at our rival firms' shops.

"I haven't discussed it," I said.

"I'm certain of that. Getting a report out of you was like pulling teeth. It—ah—can't be pleasant to think about."

His gaze touched me lightly and drifted away as if expressing his hope I might slip out quietly, sparing him the formalities of ending a conversation. His favorite delicate push was "Well, let's talk later." I stayed put.

"Do you think the partners will approve?" I said.

"Old Leviticus rather sprang it on them, which didn't help. Apparently he's been talking to Povane for months."

His voice dropped off. Not much of an answer, all told. I said, "Ambrose & Welles tends to be wary of outsiders."

If he'd had a sense of humor, Harvey might have said, "So I understand." He was still an outsider—a regrettable necessity in the view of the pragmatists, a rectifiable mistake if my father were polled.

He sighed. "One can't pull up the drawbridge in today's world."

I hunted up Pat. "So who is Mr. Povane?"

He grinned lazily. "A bombshell in poor Harvey's lap."

"Beyond that."

"You must've seen him at the Center Club or Dominique's. Or in the newspaper? Englishman—bought Wood Chatwick early this year. Controls a commodity house of some sort in Chicago and a money management firm down at the harbor."

Wood Chatwick was a one-office, suburban stock brokerage that had been losing ground to the discount houses. Not a prized property, but probably a cheap way of entering the business.

"What money management firm?" I said.

"Overseas Asset Managers. They've got a suite at Harbour Court. The business pages have written them up. Their pitch is a broader, international perspective guiding money management," he said as if quoting, and added, "or some such bullshit. It seems to sell. They've got pieces of several large pension funds."

"How does our chairman feel about Leviticus selling?"

Pat folded his hands behind his head, assuming an air of openness. "Anything to get Harvey. All he did this afternoon was declare a dose of new blood commendable."

"Did he know it was coming, or just you?"

His face tightened. "What makes you think I knew?"

"Your air of anticipation. Also that blather about not hurting the old man. So he didn't know."

"You're too fucking clever. Ask him yourself." He was more the Pat I'd grown up with, body still frozen in that unlikely image of candor, eyes angry, cheating exposed. The Pat whose surly denials were never intended to convince, only reject. Had he taken the car?

"Fuck no!"

The grille is smashed.

"Why accuse me?"

Did you sleep with Becker's wife?

"Fuck no!"

I ignored my brother's anger and used a well-meaning grin that I usually tried on clients who were being difficult. "How did you beat the rest of us in hearing about Leviticus's plan?"

"Finding out things is my job, little brother." His gloating smile told me he would keep that secret at any cost.

"Congratulations then," I said. "How do you feel about new blood?"

He shrugged. "Anyone buying into this firm has more to worry about than the partners do. It's Povane's money. Suppose our chairman and Harvey manage to assassinate each other and take us all down with them?"

There were unmistakable signs that afternoon that regardless of Harvey's views on the futility of defense, drawbridges were being raised, moats filled, and castle loyalists identified. Wister Burns, a senior partner who ran the investment management wing, took aside his three assistants and assured them that if anything compromised the integrity of the department, they were welcome to join him in founding a new investment counseling firm.

Anne Hargrave reported the meeting with the gleeful smile of a person who loves intrigues. "You'd think Mr. Povane had just won a proxy fight and announced layoffs," she said. "He won't even be in control, will he?"

"Far from it. Jimmy Leviticus's partnership is about fifteen percent of the total." A datum that I had dug up that afternoon.

"Why the fuss?"

"The surprise, I guess. Povane isn't well known, hasn't talked to anybody but Leviticus, so he's viewed as a Hun."

"He seems to be a gentleman," she said.

"You know him?"

"Not *know*. But I've met him. He's on the symphony board and actually attends the concerts. Come along tomorrow night, if you want. I'll tell Mother I've got a live one. She won't mind."

"All right."

The phone was ringing as I got home a little before ten. Stu Harris had had the number since I worked on his bond issue. His voice was raspy, and he sounded as if he were trying for detachment. His news jolted me back to steamy Gulf mornings and the buzz of flies. "Thought you should know. My buddy Ellis came home from the hospital last night, an' someone broke into his house. Put a lamp cord around both him an' his wife's neck. The police say it could have been a burglar. The FBI don't think so."

He didn't want to talk but gave up details as I prodded. There weren't many. A sister-in-law had found the front door open a crack that morning. She stumbled across the yard minutes later screaming.

I said, "Are you being careful?"

"Yessir. Got the house guarded, and Noey's walking around with a thirty-two on her hip. Thing I don't understand is what's it matter now? Why blow up my boats—well, guess

I can understand a fellow's being pissed. But why hurt Ellis? He never did nobody harm."

Neither had Stu Harris, nor his boats, nor Alex Edwards's dog.

"Hey, Rich?" Stu said, when I didn't answer. "This is just me fussin', but maybe you oughta watch your own back. What do you think?"

"I will," I said.

12

Well, you cost us a bit," my father said.

He glared at me with the intimidating advantage that came from being an inch and a half taller and sixty pounds heavier. The face was as unyielding as polished stone, his dislike for the failed offspring by now a principle not to be bent. He never let his convictions change, because if one article of faith were undermined the rest might give way like an old brick wall. What would a stern man be without his convictions?

He corrected himself abruptly. "I should say your negligence *and Harvey's* has cost the firm dearly."

There was no point in debate. I couldn't change my father's mind, and I couldn't retrieve the Con-Ill business we had lost. He was close enough to being right in any case. I should have kept a closer eye on Harris Marine.

"Consolidated Illuminating got a twisted report on what happened," I said. "Don't you find that curious?"

"I find your behavior irresponsible," he said, and walked away.

I wondered if he could have steered the warped information to Con-Ill himself, hoping with righteous clarity that damaging the firm would damage Harvey. And thereby, in perverse circularity, rescue the firm by restoring its rightful ruler.

Simon Povane had gained entree to exalted social circles—at least as exalted as they came in Maryland—by a combination of good manners and an open checkbook. His contribution to the symphony orchestra had installed a new composer in residence, whose role, judging from that evening's performance, was to introduce either one of his own creations or that of another minimalist with ten minutes of cheerful erudition, as if that might excuse what followed. When the violas screamed and two popguns sounded the opening notes of the composer's "Caprice Baltic Avenue," Anne raised her program to muffle giggles. During the intermission, she said, "I think Mr. Povane has better taste than this. But you know what local orchestras are like. . . ."

"Actually, no."

"Donors' money is welcome but not their artistic opinions. That's the province of the professional staff."

I wondered what it must be like to be financially dependent and decided that self-respect required beneficiaries to feel scorn for the benefactors. The principle might apply equally to ungifted composers living off the largesse of businessmen or to women collecting child payments from the state. Dogs were grateful pets, humans ashamed and disloyal.

I said, "Suppose a donor puts some conditions on his gift—say that at least one Rachmaninoff concerto has to be performed each season?"

"Then the donor is interfering with the artistic freedom of the orchestra."

"The idea seems to be that one person pays for the soapbox, another declaims from it."

She nodded, smiling with mischief. "If they thought in economic terms, the orchestra members would say each side is an example of human capital finding its best use. The donor's best use is to be tapped for money. The artist's best use is to make music."

"A pig's best use is to become bacon," I said. "But nobody asks the pig's view."

"Fortunately donors can't be carved like pigs," she said. "Some people on the staff would be willing to try."

"Have you spotted Simon Povane?" I said.

"Not yet."

We were following a curving glass wall that looked onto a slightly rundown section of town. A few couples had drifted outdoors for a breath of the muggy evening. There wasn't much for them to do except turn their backs on the sun's hard red disk. Anne led the way to a bar, pushed my hand away. "My treat."

"A Coke, then."

She got a plastic cup of wine and a soda. "Come on. Five minutes outdoors won't kill us."

We stepped out into the suffocating dusk that could have been brought straight up from the bayous. The surrounding streets were empty of traffic. She stood with her arms folded, cup poised at her lip. "You must feel sometimes as though you own the town, after what your grandfather did."

I shook my head. "It's impersonal that far back. I feel I own Harris Marine's problems."

"But you'll inherit an interest in the firm?"

"Possibly."

She raised a questioning eyebrow.

"Disinheritance is still every father's prerogative," I said. *And nobby club,* if he could make it one, I thought. One more reason I disappointed him. The club never found a target that squealed.

"All right, you don't own the city. Do you feel any responsibility, a little sense of noblesse oblige?"

"None whatsoever," I said, laughing inwardly. "Grandpa Welles made his money the nineteenth-century way. There was nothing noble about it. It confers no privileges, no obligations either."

"So you're a free agent."

No, I thought. But it would be nice.

We went inside and Anne spotted Simon Povane. Pat was right. I had seen him around town. He stood near a carpeted stairway that led to the boxes, a man of about average height but wide enough to blot out much of the scene behind him. A striped navy double-breasted suit added to the appearance of bulk, as did a square head that seemed to rest more between the shoulders than on top of them. As a younger man, Povane might have been a formidable presence on a rugby field. His face was large-featured and humorous, with a bulbous nose, big pale cheeks, deeply lined forehead, jet black hair. Light gray eyes, stubby lashes—a brisk nod as he responded to a blond-haired man with his back to us. Simon Povane, like many successful men, projected confidence and energy. Beside him stood a woman with tightly drawn graying hair who seemed faded.

"That's the symphony board chairman with him. Do you want me to introduce you?" Anne volunteered. "I've given some time to one of the committees, and he may remember me."

"Let's see."

We approached them, and I was about to thrust a hand out and introduce myself when Povane's glance darted away from the blond man and his face brightened. "Why—I believe you're Richard Welles! I'd been hoping to meet you."

I shook the long strong hand that gripped mine.

The blond man said, "Excuse me, Simon—we'll chat tomorrow."

"Right, William. Darling," he said, only half-turning, "this is Richard Welles, an exceedingly talented young investment banker. Say hello to him."

The woman's face contracted into a smile that left her eyes sad. Her hand was the barest touch. "Good evening, Mr. Welles."

"And Miss—Miss Hargrave." He seemed puzzled, visibly sorting the pieces until they made sense. "You're with the Friends of the Symphony and . . . of course, you work with Ambrose & Welles."

"Another talented young investment banker," she said.

"So, Mr. Welles—perhaps you can tell me whether my

investment is in trouble?" His accent was subtle, a few inflections that he probably couldn't help. Sounding just off the plane from London would be an asset in Boston, I supposed, but not in insular Baltimore. If Povane was succeeding in his investment management business, it was a tribute to his selling a multinational outlook to listeners who were at heart homebodies. No small task.

"I'm not the one to tell you," I said. "Have the partners responded?"

"I really don't expect them to so soon. In truth, I'm afraid Jimmy Leviticus is more anxious than I. If someone local, who wouldn't be controversial among your partners, stepped forward to take over my offer, I might give them my blessing." He made a small throwing-away motion. "That's not to say I wouldn't be disappointed. Ambrose & Welles appears to be positioned to grow and prosper."

A bell sounded announcing that the intermission was over. Simon Povane exposed small, square teeth. "Guess we'd best get back to it. Are you enjoying the concert?"

"Tremendously," I lied. "A program should challenge the audience."

"Quite. One loves the old war-horses but—they do get tedious, don't they?"

We went back to our seats and endured a rapturous Brahms' Fourth, during which I wondered what Simon Povane would have said had I admitted the opening modernist serenade made my teeth ache. A tactful businessman found something to agree with in every statement.

"So what do you make of Mr. Povane?" Anne asked over a late supper. The restaurant was a few square meters of Left Bank bistro inconspicuously tucked into a row house on the town's West Side.

"He's intelligent," I said, ready to leave it at that. The man had given too many contradictory signals in a few words for me to have much opinion except that Simon Povane was bright and complex.

"You didn't like him," she said.

"How do you know that?"

"You lied about enjoying the concert. You normally tell the truth to people you like even when it isn't diplomatic."

"I didn't *dis*like him," I insisted. I thought hard, wanting to explain my reaction to both of us. "There are too many layers in him for me to know whether I should like him or dislike him."

"You seem to have gotten a lot out of a short conversation," she said.

"Professional habit—not all of our clients want to be understood," I said. "When he recognized me right away, even though we hadn't met before, what did you make of it?"

"He'd done a little research. That's not surprising."

"No, it's not surprising. But you wouldn't expect a certain kind of businessman to give the fact away like that. He would appreciate the advantage in knowing more than other people suspect he knows."

"A careless slip then."

"Or a deliberate slip. He comes off looking candid to a fault, even a little clumsy, not in the least Machiavellian. That isn't a bad idea, if he needs to allay suspicion among the partners."

"Should they be suspicious?"

"If they think a serious businessman would make a large investment without plans for influencing its fate, they're optimistic. None of *them* would." Mentally I amended that. One partner had frittered away much of his family's capital on negligently attended investments. The rest, even old Leviticus, would carry their hardheadedness to the grave.

She tapped the bottle of Beaujolais with her glass, which I refilled. She looked around the room with a puzzled smile, having noted the life-sized plaster bread lady, the tin walls and bric-a-brac. "This isn't on Ambrose & Welles' normal lunch circuit," she said.

"We'll have to come back in January for one of the owner's winter soups," I said.

"Okay. And the summer soups again next week."

"All right. There's more, by the way, about Povane. He asked me whether his investment was going to be rejected—

'in trouble,' I think he said. He couldn't really have expected me to become his confidant, passing on the views of the partners if I knew them. When I declined to help, he dropped the matter. He had clumsily solicited indiscretion and been embarrassed. More buffoonery from Simon Povane."

"You don't think he expected an answer?"

"He probably would have been happy if I had answered. But this way he has built up my confidence that he's a simple-minded source of capital for the firm."

"He could claim to have made a smart move," she said, "if you had a lot of influence at the firm. As it is. . . ."

I finished for her: "Povane is just a Simple Simon who was cultivating the wrong Welles."

13

My mother called on Thursday morning with a ten-day collection of family news followed by an inevitable complaint about how little time she had for really important matters. My sister was pregnant again. A cousin I hadn't seen since childhood was recovering nicely from surgery. And my energetic mother, Elizabeth Welles, a youthful sixty-four, was co-chairing an endowment campaign for a local music conservatory but still expected to see Pat and me at dinner Sunday. She explained, "We have six co-chairs, so everybody's burden is doubled. Hattie will do a rib roast, so please don't find you can't make it." Life occurred in unlikely syllogisms for her—circumstance A leading "so" to B, and C going on to D—and only she understood the connections that she so often implied between As and Ds, or fairly often, vice versa. If her day had encompassed four or five activities, a report could be as complicated as a teleological proof, with a similarly misplaced reverence for cause and effect. Patrick senior had no patience with her. My brother's eyes glazed if he had not been a player in the events, and I delighted in following the turns of a mind that had become a little harebrained only because reality, erected and guarded by her husband, was intolerably empty. For protecting me from Patrick Welles's cold certainties I owed her more than I could repay. She had protected herself as well, so I couldn't even return the favor.

Which meant I went to dinners at home when invited.

The old house had never felt oppressive. Even when its master was making some rooms dangerous, there was an abundance of secure places in a less-used wing, which had its own slate-floored kitchen, guest rooms and a second-story porch. If one really had to go to ground, there were two acres of trees, forgotten stone foundations, a pool house and a much-patched tennis court for establishing distance. On a warm afternoon Pat would find me reading science fiction in a lawn chair near the tennis net. Picking up a paperback, he would skim pages wearing a troubled expression, make a derisory comment about my lack of maturity, and then, if I asked neutrally what was up, describe the paternal tantrum that had finally driven him from the house. Rejection hurt him, hurt both of us. Pat kept trying to cure the defects in him that had angered our father, while I pretended stubborn indifference and even cultivated a few habits and interests that I knew would earn me the scorn that came anyway. Scorn sought was a matter of choice, a source of pride rather than humiliation.

On Sundays dinner was at four. Ten minutes before the hour, I parked beside a Cadillac I didn't recognize and a dozen feet from my brother's dented Jaguar and walked into the center hall. It was so quiet that the main house might have been empty. A carpet that was older than either of my parents muffled footsteps. I passed the twin staircases and headed for the back rooms. A few feet from the door to a game room, I heard a half-familiar voice before seeing its owner.

The voice said, "Splendid kill, Patrick."

My father chuckled with pleasure. "One of my damned fool sons was making such a racket that I almost missed the shot."

"Where did you take it?"

"Ah—I own a small farm over on the Eastern Shore. One of the privileges is hunting the land myself."

By now I recognized the voice. It said, "Do you cultivate the land?"

"I lease part of the acreage to a neighbor. For me, the property is a weekend retreat."

"Ideal for a sportsman," the voice said.

My father warmed to the description of himself as a sportsman. "Yes, yes—it takes the city cares away."

A visitor's admiration of only one object in the game room could have set my father purring, and that was the head of a young buck he had shot fifteen years earlier. The damned fool son at the scene had been Pat, sitting on the back porch with a radio when the deer wandered across a field and came up to investigate and according to Pat, was sportingly blown off its feet from a bedroom window at a range of four yards. I wondered if my father felt a glimmer of shame as he threw back his shoulders and accepted the mantle of sportsman or whether he remembered tramping across a frozen field at dawn, gun in the crook of his elbow, spotting a flicker of movement in the distant trees before the sky had lightened. One version could have become as real as the other.

"Getting away from the city is a necessity," the voice said.

I stepped into the doorway and said hello to Simon Povane. His large face registered no surprise, only pleasure. "So nice to see you again, Richard." He held out a hand.

"You've met?" my father said.

"Bumped into each other at the symphony," Povane said.

"No doubt he harangued you about how awful everything was?"

"Not at all. Richard was quite complimentary of minimalism."

"He loathes the stuff," my father said flatly.

Povane gave me an appraising look. "Well then, perhaps he was being tactful."

"Not his strong suit either," my father said. "He was deceiving you. Richard likes to play games with people. It gives him a sense of superiority."

Povane searched my face for a reaction I made certain wasn't there. "I may have misunderstood," he said. "We shall settle this. Richard, how *do* you feel about new music?"

"It's good to challenge the audience," I said and saw my father's face darken.

"The little hypocrite doesn't mean it," he said.

My mother appeared at the doorway, tall and elegant and suspiciously auburn-haired. Her smile always took in the room and anyone who might be present, but her pale and pretty gaze lighted nowhere in particular. "I hope Mr. Povane doesn't take you two seriously," she said. "Laurel and I have been inspecting the garden. The azaleas *are* a little spotted, dear."

"Tell the gardener," her husband said.

"It's a lovely garden, Mr. Welles," said a young woman who had come up behind my mother. I got a quick impression of a flowered sundress with a matching jacket, suitably informal for Sunday afternoon dinner, and a pink brocaded band holding back blond hair that reached almost to her shoulders. She was as tall as my mother, which meant five-ten in low heels.

"Laurel, this is Richard Welles," said Simon Povane. "My daughter works at our downtown office."

"It's a pleasure, Richard." She stretched a hand forward. Good fortune had saved her from inheriting her father's build or features. Coming to stand beside him, she was half a head taller, and three of her could have hidden behind his width. She didn't bear much resemblance, either, to the pale, withdrawn woman who had been with Povane at the symphony. Laurel Povane's bearing spoke of expensive schools and enough money not to have to make too much of their names. She had amber eyes, a tall forehead, wide lips and crisp features. Not the kind of girl you would overlook in a crowd or would forget once having seen, and I remembered her very well and on close inspection now found nothing wrong with my first appraisal. It had been just over a week since I had seen Laurel having dinner at the Ruxton Club with my brother.

"I have the odd feeling we've met before," she said.

I left the gallant response (*I would remember*) unspoken

and said, "That happens a lot; Baltimore is a small town. You've been over here longer than your father, haven't you?"

She laughed. "Five years longer. Four at Harvard, one at Merrill Lynch. People tell me my accent's almost gone, but it comes back when we go home for a visit."

Pat came downstairs twenty minutes later, looking scrubbed and alert but nonetheless hungover. He permitted himself to be introduced to Simon Povane and then to his daughter without letting a word or gesture suggest they had met before. Through dinner his long face wore a small version of the smile that took over when he was getting away with something.

Povane understood that the essence of good business talk lay in knowing when to let matters drift. He got into a spirited discussion with my mother of English hybrid roses, about which he sounded knowledgeable, and teased Laurel gently for having a tin ear like Richard's that couldn't appreciate anything since Bartók.

I watched his smiles and blunt gestures, listened to his banter, and concluded that Mr. Simon Povane was an essentially dishonest man. He spoke to cajole, win over, entertain, influence, distract and charm all at once. Aiming to enlist my father's support for his investment, he sold himself naturally and comfortably, as only an experienced pro could advertise a product both familiar and reliable. If there was any negative information about the Povane model, bad experience braking on hills or with the rear window defroster, the data were hidden in a safe in a back office the customer would never visit.

All right, I asked myself, *what did it matter?* Every social animal learned how to present itself. Even being truthful was a kind of sales pitch. My favorite disarming tactic with clients was to admit to some minor lapse, and unconsciously I picked them with care. Amusing was desirable, embarrassing was marginal, nauseating was to be avoided. A customer enjoyed hearing that you had lost money in such and such a stock. But as the bloody-nosed nightclub comic said, the success of jokes about impotence depended upon the experience of the listener. I realized how deliberate my stories had become only when I found I was inventing stock market losses after a particularly good year.

Fallibility was a marketable product, as were quiet intelligence, not-too-sharp humor and assorted social graces. Normally you accepted the presentation while knowing that the smiling person wasn't always so self-effacing, intelligent or good humored—that he or she inevitably was pig-headed on occasion, obtuse, foul-tempered—but a best face could be offered and accepted provisionally, because the pretender's effort to make himself attractive said the observer was worth the effort.

What mattered was motive. Winning over the acquaintance was an acceptable end in itself. The effort became repellent if the purpose was to grab the old lady's bank book, or lure the gullible young man into a mousetrap, or undermine the office rival.

Listening to Simon Povane, I felt the conviviality had no life apart from his business or social interests. It was a learned grace that had no personal importance for the ambitious man sitting across from me.

The tiny brokerage house he had acquired, Wood Chatwick, fitted him as badly as a schoolboy's suit. I wondered again what use he had found for a faltering retail stock firm with only one office, and that one sited not downtown but in a northern suburb. When there was a lull in conversation, I said, "Are you finding the retail business difficult?"

"More nonexistent than difficult," Simon Povane said. "It was bad a year ago when we purchased Wood Chatwick. Things have gotten worse I dare say. The individual investor no longer trusts the financial markets—perhaps with some reason. Fortunately the price we paid for that firm was commensurate with its prospects." He waved his wine glass in a small circle before setting it down. "The question now is whether we have enough at the firm to build on. There are directions we could go, of course, besides courting the small investor. If I could recruit several stock analysts, we might create research services that would attract the business of banks and pension managers."

My father never missed an opportunity to fault operations

on Harvey's watch. He smiled wryly and said, "Ambrose & Welles has at least several analysts on the payroll who could be dispensed with. You won't get a warranty from me on how much institutional business they'll drum up."

Povane chuckled. "I would rather steal your good people than receive a gift of castoffs."

"Now," my father said in a cautioning tone, "you're not thinking like a partner at Ambrose & Welles. These days we treasure what should be cast off. Cutting out the deadwood is well nigh impossible." His glance barely flickered to my side of the table. "Our managing partner, a very likable chap, finds terminating people anathema. He's a bit out of his depth, to tell the truth."

"You believe Ambrose & Welles needs reform, I take it."

"May not survive without it," my father said briskly. "Everyone at the firm knows the realities of today's marketplace. There is no room for coddling mediocrity, no profit in rewarding failure. It's not merely my judgment—*our* judgment, as I speak for other senior partners—but the judgment of the market. No firm dares drift on a rudderless course if it hopes to be around next year."

Watching Simon Povane, I tried to read his reaction to my father's bald invitation to join him in a purge. It was too crude, I thought, and Povane would suspect a trap. The broad face gave up nothing, but the pale gray eyes glittered in merriment—because, it struck me, he had gotten an absolutely reliable reading on Patrick Welles, Sr. through his daughter Laurel, who had bent her elegant head close to my brother's. So he could guess my father's capacity for subtlety. His response was to the point. "If one has to chop, I've always been in favor of doing it quickly. It's best to catch them when they're not looking."

"That's *awful*," Laurel protested. "And you're not that kind of businessman, no matter how hard you pretend."

He looked at her fondly. "My daughter believes that every error can be mended; in her world there are no lost causes. That optimism can be expensive, my dear, if you're running a business that faces harder-headed competitors."

"It's better than just cutting people *off*," she said. "He

doesn't, you know. We still have people in England who worked for Daddy when he started. A couple of them would have been forced into retirement anywhere else."

"They still perform their jobs," Povane said. He looked at my father. "Do you confide to your offspring every time you give somebody the sack?"

"Not likely!"

My mother leaned toward the girl in mock confidence. "Patrick isn't the bear he pretends, either."

Her sweet words, born more of hope than experience, elicited no flicker of a smile from the head of the table. Patrick Welles looked through her and said, "Simon, why don't we talk privately in the library?"

Neither Pat nor I was invited. Laurel attached herself to my mother and gamely pretended interest in an expedition to the herb garden that the cook maintained behind the kitchen. Pat followed me down to my car. "Let's talk," he said with a flick of a thumb. He headed off the gravel between boxwoods that funnelled us down to the pool house Grandpa Welles and a brother built after the First World War. "Povane seems a pretty solid fellow, don't you think?"

"A veritable rock," I said. "I saw you and Miss Povane at the club the other night. It's not a very discreet rendezvous."

His look of sunny self-satisfaction vanished under a brooding cloud. "Why do I care about discretion, little brother?"

His tone resolved the question. I said, "Why did you pretend you hadn't met her before?"

He laughed. "Would you want a bull like Povane thinking you're screwing his daughter?"

"I would be surprised if you were."

"Don't be." He folded his long arms and grinned, happy again. "A few months ago, I ran into Laurel at the Rusty Scupper; the same night we tore up the sheets at her place for four hours."

"Congratulations then. What do you suppose Mr. Povane is promising our chairman right now?"

"That two wise men will act together for change," Pat said, making it sound like a rehearsed campaign promise. "And when it's done, one of the wise men will regain his rightful place as managing partner. The old man thinks he'll be the one."

All his talk about not betraying the old bastard, I thought, had been to convince himself. Suddenly I was sick of his denials, his pretenses, his lies. The excuse I summoned so often, the specter of Patrick senior, no longer seemed adequate. Pat *could* have broken away, *could* have taken on the burden of himself, I thought—knowing he couldn't have. Bitterness welled up and found expression in my words: "And what is Povane promising you?"

"What do you mean?"

"You wouldn't pass along information for the fun of it, or just because Laurel is a good sport in bed. You're not that dumb. You must expect something. What is it?"

"Nothing—" His anger deepened. "I haven't passed—"

I stared at him.

"You're such a smug, sanctimonious shit!" he said between his teeth. "I'm fed up talking to you."

You'll manage when it suits you, I thought, turning away.

He caught my shoulder and spun me around as his unoccupied hand came up, clenched and unexpected, and connected under my nose. I fell back into the boxwood and was caught like a drunk sprawling into the arms of friends. The branches didn't fling me upright. Only one foot was in contact with the earth, and I subsided gently. My eyes stung. The last time my elder brother had hit me, twelve years ago, it had also been a sucker punch. Pat believed in one-punch disputes.

He had gone when I got onto the path. My nose was spattering a good striped shirt. I stuffed a handkerchief under it and went up to my car. Pat was nowhere to be seen, though the Jaguar was still skewed against a lavender-flowered hibiscus. The Cadillac that must have been Povane's sat between Pat's car and mine. I leaned against a fender and stared at the path down to the pool house. My brother had learned at least how to pick his moments.

Behind me the front door to the house opened and jolly voices rolled across the porch. Presenting my bloodied nose to strangers didn't appeal to me, even less letting my father get a look at the damage. The top was down on the car, offering no refuge there, and turning my back and walking away couldn't be counted on—somebody might call out. So I elected the only other undignified option and slid down beside the door—out of sight unless they went ten paces out of their way. My father came part way down the path with Povane and his daughter, delivering his set piece on local politics, which he felt suffered from a lack of participation by the "better-quality" people. "I'm guilty of the same neglect as the other old families," he said, "but one never seems to have enough time."

"Politics usually isn't the best use of an intelligent man's resources," Povane said, still accommodating.

My mother called that Patrick was wanted on the telephone, and they said good-byes. Povane and his daughter went to the Cadillac and spoke across the roof. The last words caught my attention, as Povane's voice lost its agreeable purr: ". . . wouldn't worry if it were just the two of them. The young bastard is sneaky. He caught me out on music, which doesn't matter. But he notices everything."

The sound of his annoyance redeemed the afternoon. Assuming myself to be the young bastard in question, I suppressed a smile that would have hurt.

"Your vanity's wounded," Laurel said.

"No. Take my word for it. Richard is trouble."

There was a light laugh. "Shall I transfer my affection to Richard?"

"No! Enough is enough." He sounded as if he were pleading instead of ordering.

Her laugh was stronger, mocking him. "Yes, Daddy."

Even after they had driven away, I sat against the car door for a few minutes, wondering what Simon Povane and his daughter might look like with the genteel masks fully removed.

14

I called Anne Hargrave and asked how much she knew about Simon Povane. It was almost seven-thirty and the sky's reflection was fading in the glass-walled office building two blocks north. The streets were empty unless I looked toward the steel-framed green pavilions hugging the waterfront, where shoppers and diners strolled even on a Sunday evening. I had changed my shirt, put on canvas shoes, and opened the window behind the sofa, enjoying the silence and the absence of treacherous company.

"I thought I told you what I knew," Anne said.

"You told me he's on the symphony board and has been generous with his money."

"Well. . . . That's about it. I guess he's well-liked, or at least hasn't made enemies. You learn the most about someone from people putting him down. Nobody's commented on poor Simon's business flops or on an unfortunate habit of stiffing waiters. That may not be true, come to think of it. I haven't *heard* anything like that, but maybe I wouldn't. I'm just a junior investment banker, and we don't travel in the most august circles. Let's say the other members of the symphony board like him. I'm pretty sure of that."

"Who knows him well?"

She thought for a moment. "Mr. Eckland seems to have a lot to talk about with him."

"Peter Eckland?" I said. He was a senior partner at a law firm that prized its access to prominent politicians. When a commission had to be mustered to review a matter of public policy, either Eckland or his nominee presided, as often as not, and kept a professional eye out for an array of commercial interests. The affinity between Eckland and Povane was easily imagined: The Ecklands were devout Anglophiles who kept a house in London, and Povane was an authentic article with the tact not to curl his lip at American lawyers who longed to call themselves solicitors. If Povane worked them as skillfully as he did my father, he would have assured Peter Eckland at least once that but for an accident of geography the American would have been born English, almost certainly titled. To which I could imagine Peter chuckling and confiding that yes, he had always had an affinity for the other side of the pond.

For all his vanity, Peter Eckland wasn't a total fool. If I sought information on Povane from him directly, the effort could backfire. I put his name back on a corner shelf and after saying goodnight to Anne sat back and made notes about every fact I knew of our firm's prospective investor. They were startlingly few. The list expanded if I went afield from scarce specifics—English businessman controls money manager, broker—and let in opinion and conjecture. Then I could include the judgment that Povane was shrewd and tougher than I thought. And perhaps more oddly wired. Laurel's delicate taunting laugh kept singing in my memory. *"Shall I transfer my affection to Richard?"*

The mocking note in her *"Yes, Daddy"* was more like a lover teasing an abandoned partner than a daughter replying to a father. What kind of man sent a daughter out to collect business intelligence in bed? Or at least nodded to the procedure? One who would permit little to stand in the way of an objective. That seemed safe to say.

Assuming Laurel *was* his daughter. . . .

But probably even if not. I didn't need to consider Laurel to know that Simon Povane was a pusher. But so what? I wondered if I wasn't reacting like a typical threatened executive, who saw his comfortable job at risk and decried any interloper as a predator.

I couldn't deny I was comfortable—too comfortable—at Ambrose & Welles.

I went into the large gourmet kitchen that never got much of a workout and heated a small pot of water, tossed in a bag of Earl Grey, and noticed the glossy program from the symphony lying on the breakfast counter beside a stack of mail. Exactly where I had dropped it Wednesday night, congratulating myself on a successful social outing without the slightest hope of repeating it.

I flipped open the program to the pages listing prominent supporters of the orchestra, who were tiered according to the size of their contributions. I found Mr. and Mrs. E. Peter Eckland in the Maestro's Circle, which meant they chipped in at least $10,000 but less than the $25,000 that would have admitted them to the Silver Baton club. Most of the names at the loftier levels were corporate sponsors and charitable foundations. Up in the Gold Baton class, where the dues started at $50,000, my eye stopped at the name Consolidated Illuminating Corporation. Our erstwhile client spread contributions over an array of worthy causes, trying to buy the goodwill that its rate payers refused to exchange for light and power. The effort was most likely futile; no management consultant had concocted a formula for making a public utility attractive to its customers, many of whom would grind their teeth upon finding that their monthly payments were financing orchestras, AIDS hospices, and animal shelters. It wasn't Con-Ill management's fault that some businesses aroused the latent Jacobin in everyone.

I turned a page backward and glanced over the board of directors. E. Peter Eckland was there, along with his countryman Simon Povane. If Consolidated Illuminating hadn't been on my mind for more than one reason, I wouldn't have looked twice at the name of the power company's vice chairman, Jack Rosenberg, who was listed a few steps after Simon Povane. As it was, the name had an effect on me somewhere between electric shock and light flooding an unexpected room. Once you realized there was a room, the response became *Of course*. It made such sense. Most of the dealings between Ambrose & Welles and Con-Ill occurred at a lower level than vice chairman, but both Rosenberg and his boss had the final word on how stock sales by the utility were handled—and by whom. Either directly from Povane, or a bit more circuitously from Eckland via Povane, Jack Rosenberg could have gotten the story of my ignominy in Louisiana. It was the kind of dirt Pat would pass along joyously to Laurel, and that Povane would recognize as a promising tool for opening fissures at Ambrose & Welles. Partners seeing a big account vanish wouldn't be especially loyal to the firm's management.

There were other ways Con-Ill could have heard the story, but probably not many where I could find the talebearers all named on one page.

I had to wait until Monday to talk to Ulrich Lenz. He rarely went to lunch, gobbling cheese sandwiches at his cramped desk if the trading slowed for a few minutes. I walked over to the Kennelworth Mercantile Center and slipped into a chair next to Ulrich's. He had his feet up and was using his chest as either a table or a plate. He smiled across an expanse of crumbs. "Have you been watching Winners Electronics? Look at the screen." He hooked a thumb toward the amber monitor with stock symbols and prices marching across it. "It's every fifth trade, five thousand shares at a time."

I leaned forward, staring past his head. The symbol WELE, which I assumed belonged to Winners Electronics, flashed across twice in quick order, each appearance announcing the purchase of a large number of shares at a price twelve cents a share higher than the previous trade. Somebody wanted to own the stock badly enough to push the price up for it.

"Is there a takeover?" I asked.

"Don't make me laugh. Do you know what this company

does? No? They sell televisions and stereos to people with lousy credit. It is a concept that is sweeping the South and creeping north, and WELE's stock price has doubled since May. Our firm brought them public last year."

"Congratulations," I said.

"No, we should be ashamed. The company is doomed. One, two, three months after these people buy the expensive components or humongous-screen TV, Mama loses her job and Papa lands in jail. Or perhaps Mama sends Papa to the hoosegow. They stop making payments on the TV, which the kids have wrecked anyway. Do you think they care if Winners Electronics gains a judgment against them? No! Their *landlord* has judgments against them. Their used-car dealer has judgments. So what? So three or four months have gone by and Winners must repossess a toy that doesn't work anymore, assuming their wonderful customers haven't loaded up the car by night and taken the TV back to Arkansas with them. By then Winners has taken in maybe a hundred dollars in installment payments. Say it got fifty as a down payment. That's one-fifty recovered on a piece of equipment that may have cost it one-forty before corporate overhead. But actually, when you add in all the costs of running the business, the price is higher. So you've got a real, cash loss. But when they sold the equipment to Mama and Papa, they took the entire sales price into revenues and profits, just as if they had been paid in cash rather than in a deadbeat's IOU. So it looks like WELE is going great guns, selling to the trailer parks and shantytowns, when in reality they are losing money. It is fine until their auditors complain about six months from now that WELE has not set aside enough cash to cover its losses."

If that happened, the company's profit reports for the last several years would go back to the accountants' desk and be rebuilt as losses. A bank that had been a friend would cut off credit, and suggest quick repayment of its balances. The stock price would crumple. Both Ulrich and I had seen how quickly disintegration could sweep away all the hope, greed and daydreams that had carried investors for years. Rather like a roller coaster derailing at the top.

"You used to work in London," I said.

"For three years," he said. "The rainy people's revenge on a superior race."

"Was Simon Povane much of a presence?"

"Circling the wagons, Richard?" He smiled when he got the idiom right, which was often. "Never heard of him. If he wasn't a trader, I might not have."

"Do you still have friends you could ask?"

"What shall I ask?"

"His reputation. Does he build or wreck. That sort of thing."

Ulrich's attention wavered between me and the insistent yammering demands of the market. The phone burred and he sold ten thousand shares of Winners Electronics at an eighth of a dollar more per share than the last price. He swept bread crumbs from his chest, sat slightly more upright. "Now, Richard, I am short fifty thousand shares of Winners. Most of the shares have gone into the accounts of our own customers, upon whom our most retarded securities analyst has been inflicting luminous reports extolling the company's exponential growth. This same imbecile has adored two other wonderful growth companies that have gone bankrupt in the last eighteen months. I had sold short a few hundred thousand shares of each to our customers by the time the bottom fell out."

"I hope they thanked you," I said, wondering if Lickety Lube would end up being marketed to the public by Ulrich's firm so the retarded analyst could nudge the shares and Ulrich could sell them short to customers who, despite all the reasons not to, kept coming back for more.

"You should have come along on Saturday," Ulrich said. "I rented the *Dunuthin'*, met two lovely girls we've met before—mind you, at the same bar—and fornicated each while the other took the helm." He saw my grin and said, "What is wrong?"

"Nothing. Go on."

Frowning suspiciously, he said, "It was an ideal weekend. We spent the night at Smith Island, investigating the deformities of the inbred natives, and picnicked Sunday morning in a cemetery. It was decadent. Sue-Sue said she missed you, at least until I showed her how a hero fornicates her. Are you sorry now that you accepted family obligations?"

I balanced a punch in the mouth against listening to Ulrich hammer Sue-Sue or her friend and decided the lip didn't hurt.

Ulrich's manager came back and the couple of traders who slouched at the desk straightened and exchanged businesslike chatter and the phones started ringing. I got out of the way of commerce.

Pat avoided me for the rest of the afternoon. One of Wister Burns's troops sidled by trying to recruit co-conspirators and left disappointed. At five-thirty I was immersed in another prospective client's financial statements—this one a publisher of magazines on gourmet cooking and other special interests who wanted to buy out a handful of other investors. He couldn't get a bank loan. Did we have any ideas to help him? His real problem was that he had a profitable business and his investors knew it. Their spokesman had demanded top dollar.

On those terms the banks wouldn't play. If he paid top dollar, there wouldn't be a cushion in case the nice business ran slack for a while; no cushion for him, none for the bank. I was torn between advising him to tell his investors to forget the whole thing—the thought of sitting with their shares for ten years might soften them up for a lower price—and suggesting he try to pay them off with bonds or preferred shares issued by his own company. He would still face hefty interest charges every month, but the risk would be borne by the people getting the benefit instead of by disinterested bank patrons. I was on the verge of flipping a coin when the phone rang and Laurel Povane said cheerfully, "I hope you don't think my father was too pushy."

"Not at all," I said.

"He has a one-track mind, which I guess has made him successful. But sometimes he seems overbearing. He's too used to being in control of every situation. After meeting Patrick senior I got a feeling you may know what that's like."

"It sounds familiar," I said.

"Daddy was furious with himself last night that you caught on to his pedestrian musical tastes. He really doesn't like anything that much. But he endures concerts because somebody—I think it was his old friend Theo Willard—told him businessmen have to appear to be multidimensional, even if their hearts are made of tin." She gave the high, feather-light laugh that I had heard above their car. It had been brutal then. Now it was a chime singing warmly on a summer day. It could be whatever she wanted, I thought. "Anyway, Richard, that's not the reason I called. I'm inviting some friends out on Friday evening, people more our age, strictly for nonbusiness cooking-out purposes. Could we see you?"

"I'd like to bring a friend," I said.

"That's wonderful," she said without missing a beat—although "a friend" couldn't have fit with the intelligence she had collected. Laurel gave me the address and the time—anything after seven—and hung up with the cheery certainty she had made a new friend.

I called Ulrich and added Theo Willard to his research list.

When Anne Hargrave raced back from an appointment, jammed two panicked phone calls into three minutes, and then kicked off her shoes with a sigh, I said, "What do you make of Povane's daughter?"

"Povane? Is it always Povane with you? I'm close to bringing in my first solo client, one with a decent business to sell, and you ask about Simon Povane."

"About his daughter. They could be running this department in a month—Simon and his daughter. Congratulations on your client, if you get him."

"If I get *her,*" she said with a smug girls-in-solidarity smile. "I didn't know Mr. Povane had a daughter."

"Blond, silky, smart, amber-eyed."

"Shit. I was feeling so good a moment ago." She put her chin on her hands and stared from her green eyes under mousy hair that looked all right, soft enough for most purposes. I decided to leave off the bits about tall, full-busted, wide-mouthed and regal.

I said: "I've got an invitation to bring along a friend to meet Miss Laurel on Friday evening. Do you want to size up our new boss?"

"I've got a date Friday," she said from atop her hands.

* * *

On Wednesday Ulrich swaggered in at four-thirty, leered at Anne and a couple of passing secretaries and declared he was buying if I was drinking. We went over to Poppy's. "The first thing you should know about Simon Povane is he isn't English," Ulrich said. "New Zealander, migrated to the U.K. twenty years ago, started a general import business—powdered casein from the homeland—and went bust. Subsequently Simon hired on at a stockbroking firm in the Midlands and a couple of years later bought control from the boss's widow. The only reason one of my old chums knows anything about him is that Povane got into a jam six or eight years ago using rough tactics in a takeover."

He paused to finish a Samuel Adams and wave for two more. When he told me about his days in England, he sounded like a downed Luftwaffe pilot trying to pass for a Bristol pipe fitter.

"There was a trucking company, family controlled, regionally traded stock—a hundred shares twice a week by appointment. Povane and some backers had a go at them, according to my friend. They bought shares quietly for about a year, got ten percent, found a little block held by a disaffected cousin and took an option on that, and asked for seats on the board of directors. The people in charge told Povane to piss off. That was when they started getting their tires cut and having roadway accidents, couple of drivers beaten up."

"Was Povane charged?"

"No. One of the hirelings testified a guy named Finley—my friend thinks it was Finley—put him up to it. Finley denied being associated in any way with Povane's group. Povane agreed one hundred percent and made suitable noises of horror at the strong-arming. Nobody believed him completely, so a bad odor attached even though he couldn't be prosecuted. His group sold its stock to a conglomerate that engineered a friendly takeover of the trucking firm. Finley, maybe it was Findlay, served nine months in prison, came back to Manchester and got stabbed in a men's room."

Ulrich watched my reaction, which must have been interesting. He said: "A couple of years later, Povane was finding it hard to do business with reputable people and chose to migrate to the Colonies—my chum thought he had gone to Canada rather than to the States. You've probably got enough there to block him, don't you think?"

I nodded dumbly.

"That's good. Now, you called me asking about Theo Willard. Jerome Theobald Willard is an old-school gentleman in London who manages other people's funds and has a seat on the exchange. I talked to him this afternoon. He knows and admires Simon Povane. Simon is a cultivated chap like Theo, a businessman of exceptional integrity, a strategic thinker par excellence, and—listening between the lines—a good sport you can invite home knowing he won't ravish the scullery maids or bugger the butler. How did you know he would vouch for Povane?"

"The name was dropped in passing by his daughter . . . too conveniently."

"Theo sounds about eighty years old," Ulrich added. "Perhaps Simon helped him across Piccadilly Circus one morning."

"Or told Laurel to sit on his lap," I said.

He scowled at me, said with deliberate pomposity: "You are a case study in sexual frustration. It leads to disgusting images."

"I know," I said.

He pounded the bar. "This weekend, you *must* come sailing! We will pick up four girls. I will tell one she must settle for the pale withdrawn boy, and I will quench her unsatisfied yearnings the following weekend."

"You're too kind."

"You do not have to mention it," Ulrich said.

15

Daddy bought this place before he found out how hard it is to get into the island's only club," Laurel said. She had shown us a garden that had wilted in Gibson Island's humidity and taken us up a back stairway to a wraparound second-story porch, which gave a shimmering evening view of the Chesapeake Bay. The island's marina was just around a bend, and a half-dozen sailboats were bending into a breeze that promised deliverance to a safe harbor, Bloody Marys, and the practical conversation of other sailors. It was a bonus that the harbor was on a privately owned island where a gatehouse blocked the urban problems that might drive down the highway.

My brother was in a cheerful mood. He waved his whiskey and water in the general direction of the club. "Did Simon finally get accepted?"

"Finally. Judge Porter, who put him up, gave good advice: be as inconspicuous as possible. That's a test of will for my father, but he managed. So now we get the best of life here, boating and entertaining at the club. Did you have any trouble getting onto the island?"

The guards had held me up for less than a minute as they checked the evening's guest list, then offered directions to Bridge Street. Pat, lounging in the passenger seat—he had asked for a lift that morning after parking his Jaguar in a ditch the night before—had jeered at them for taking the precautions they were paid to take. "Little men, big authority," he said as the slipstream pouring over the windshield lifted his hair. "You ever notice how they go together?"

"Yes," I said.

"I hate petty authority," he said.

"They didn't frisk you."

He leaned his head back staring at a canopy of elms that gave him no more pleasure, from his expression, than the island's guards had done. He muttered, "Jesus, the wisdom of Mister Diplomacy."

I thought about getting him more riled by saying, *They save frisking for the way out.* Didn't, because it could be a long evening with or without a fat lip.

"A lot of people get blackballed by the Gibson Island Club," Laurel said, pressing a leg against the wooden railing. "They don't like politicians, especially celebrities from Washington, and Judge Porter said the membership committee would sooner burn the place down than accept anyone from show business. No vulgar power or money is welcome, but if one has a delicate touch, power and money become influence and breeding. Those fit in nicely with the gentle image. Even Father, a snobbish Englishman to the bottom of his soul, thinks it's all a little constipated."

Pat drew back, pretending horror. "How does he feel about those of us who live in Ruxton?"

He was acting, but only partly. In his own estimate he was a gentleman, a believer in noblesse oblige as long as he wasn't provoked, and although he hadn't much money he regarded the family assets as jointly owned and therefore conferring on him some of the status of a slightly rascally fellow who didn't have to work for a living but chose to as a mark of character. It was a popular image in either enclave.

She folded her bare arms and looked him over in a considering way. "People in Ruxton, I think, have more fun."

"We always try," Pat said.

She gave him a low-intensity grin. Whatever schools she had attended before Harvard had taught her about handling men. I had seen Pat stroking a conquest in public like a trainer patting a mare who had been good over the jumps. With Laurel Povane, his public manner was friendly and flirtatious but not possessive. If it hadn't been for her high, brutal laugh outside our house, I would have doubted his claim to have torn up a bed with her. If it hadn't been for that laugh, I thought, I would believe her as she presented herself right now on the porch—cultivated but not constipated, mischievous but proper, all silk and grace and strong girl lines, at ease with the welcome company of prospective friends close to her own age.

She turned the smile on me, intercepting whatever thoughts I was letting loose, and said, "You said you were bringing a friend."

"She stood him up," Pat said.

"I'm surprised." She seemed aware that the remark won no points with my brother. "Is it true?"

"Another engagement," I said. Then added, for no reason, one of those amplifications you would later retract a million times if events could be undone, "Miss Hargrave sends regrets."

Her blond head tilted. "Is she as pretty as the name?"

I mumbled something that caused both her and Pat to laugh, and we went down the side steps to a brick patio set with tables and chairs. My brother lighted torches above the line of peony bushes at the periphery while I made drinks. Two couples in their twenties arrived together, the men with hair cut short on the sides and long over the back collar, faces sunburned and glowing from having gotten an earlier start on the evening. The girls were unnaturally blond and improbably pneumatic in short Day-Glo-lime-and-pink jumpers. Laurel introduced them as Jan, Jackie, Bob and Pete, friends from a downtown health club.

Bob and Pete set a plastic cooler between chairs, where

the four gathered and filled a table with cans of beer. They were trading stories about the bouncer at a bar they had left, whose shoulder Pete or Bob had dislocated, possibly with Jan's help. If biceps counted, she could have done it herself.

Several people arrived from Laurel's office. We started steaks and salmon on a long grill as the party broke down into two mismatched groups. Laurel hovered between camps, chatting as comfortably with the jocks as with the financial drudges. Her tone and manner changed only slightly as she went back and forth, but to each group she somehow conveyed the sense she was one of them.

I zeroed in on a young man from Laurel's office who looked a year or two out of college, wore short-trimmed hair and wire glasses, and tried to hide the fact he was impressed by the presence of two brothers from Ambrose & Welles. His name was Tim Smith. He was ambitious enough to have his sights set on a firm larger than Povane's Overseas Asset Managers, and he was eager to display his knowledge. It made finding out things about the firm easy, and restraining him became the problem. We went through the size of the assets Povane had attracted, the latest year's return on the firm's investments, and the apparent strengths and failures of running portfolios containing a lot of foreign securities—all that in the first couple of minutes over gin and tonics before Laurel noticed we were talking. When I tried to break it off with a cheerful nod, he followed me toward the food table chatting about one of Povane's less satisfied accounts, as though he had been interviewed, hired on the spot and felt free to spill all his former employer's secrets.

Laurel was coming within earshot, drawn by his earnestness. I headed straight for her, waving my second drink in too wide a circle. "Tim says you're the world's best office manager," I said loudly.

He hadn't. To the extent that Tim had implied anything, it was that Laurel Povane was Daddy's gale-force bitch.

She glanced at his surprised look, knew that wasn't it, and played along. "Tim is our best junior portfolio manager. But Timmy, the affairs of Overseas Asset Managers can't be very interesting to Richard Welles."

"Oh, I'm impressed by the way you and your father have made it grow," I said, giving up the doubtful secret that Timmy had been indiscreet and I had listened.

"We've worked very hard," she said.

Pat came over, handed her a drink, and hovered. He grinned amiably in my direction and told Laurel, "Be careful or Richard will end up knowing everything there is to know about your business—and your private life."

"Someone else gave me the same warning," she said. "Is your brother really so nosy?"

"It's his job and he does it obsessively. Knowing things about people gets to be an end in itself, doesn't it, little brother? Then he begins to think he *understands* you! That's really hard to take."

Watching me, Laurel put a hand on his shoulder. "You're not being fair to Richard."

Pat answered. "You don't know him."

Laurel sipped her drink. "Do you study yourself, Richard, or just other people?"

"Neither, really, beyond the call of duty."

"If you understand other people," Pat said, "you control them a little. You push their buttons and guess which way they'll jump." He was still grinning, still pretending this was light ribbing.

"And do you know how your brother will jump?" she asked me.

"Seldom." I had a sore lip to prove that he could still surprise me.

"It would be a help in the stock market, wouldn't it? Knowing what people will respond to, what they might accept and believe or turn skeptical of."

It was an oddly naive remark, and even Pat noticed. "Ambrose & Welles is always trying to guess what turns the masses on. If retail boutiques have been hot, you'll see us underwriting more retail boutiques. We'll find a nicer way to describe it," he added, "but basically we sell whatever has been successful."

"It's a pity we can't use Richard's cleverness to know what will be successful *next* year."

It was what she had meant all along—too bad you couldn't make a guess about human behavior and get a jump on the markets. People looking at markets from outside imagined it was possible. A few obsessed professionals agreed. They saw the psychology of crowds in motion, pushing prices higher for no good reason except that prices had gone up yesterday, and they constructed charts and graphs documenting the movements and hoped they had a reference point for predicting what the vast, amorphous crowd-mind would do tomorrow. The predictions worked about half the time—and failed about half the time. The crowd had too many variables, too many cranky, contrary, smart, stupid, informed, ignorant participants, for its behavior to be reliable.

"If you find a system that works, please share it with me," I said.

Timmy Smith, who had been left out of the conversation, stood close, hoping for a chance to repair himself with Laurel. "What Richard and Patrick are saying is that predicting markets is statistically impossible," he said with a smug, scholarly smile. "Everything regresses to the mean—you can't escape that, can't do a lot better than the average. Isn't that right, Mr. Welles?"

I nodded.

He went on: "You can't because the mean represents the random distribution of results in every pursuit—gambling, investing, marriage. Most of the results fall toward the center, trailing off toward either side. If you try to influence the outcome to put yourself on the side of superior results by adding or removing some factor, you're just as likely to end up doing worse than average."

Laurel stared at him as though a fish had begun reciting Shakespeare. Her smile was brittle. "I didn't know you were so erudite, Tim."

His face turned pink, but he had drunk a bit and with a twenty-five-year-old's recklessness couldn't resist going on: "Mr. Povane wants to get better investment results by focusing on foreign stock markets. But every time we jiggle the portfolio mix, adding a little London at the expense of Singapore, we run the risk of making things worse than if we had stayed put with equal parts of all the markets."

Laurel said sweetly, "Our clients hope our judgment on where to invest is worth the fees they pay us. I like to think our portfolio managers agree."

His eyes were miserable as he watched something he had gotten used to seeing beneath her smile. "It's just the academic view," he said.

"Of course." She added, "Perhaps we can discuss this further Monday morning."

I watched him walk off, shoulders slumping, into the sultry August evening. His hopes of a vaulting career advance had crashed. His springboard from Overseas Asset Managers into Ambrose & Welles looked like a trapdoor with no job underneath.

"C'mon," Pat said to Laurel, "I'll buy you another drink."

Simon Povane and his faded wife arrived just before eleven, and after looking out onto the patio from a screened porch the woman disappeared and lights popped on elsewhere in the house. Simon came outside, arms bulging in a plaid short-sleeved shirt, shook hands with Pat and me, practiced small talk without engaging more than a fraction of his attention. He made himself a gin and tonic, sampled a pasta salad, and walked the perimeter created by the chemical torches, glancing back at the lighted house.

After Povane went indoors and I made noises about driving back, Pat announced he was staying. So I set out along the empty Mountain Road by myself, which made it easier to turn south toward Annapolis.

Ulrich was aboard the *Dunuthin'*, the taut lines of which reached down from the pier as the tide rushed out of the Severn River basin. He was alone—for which I thanked the occasional failure of neolithic charm—but undiscouraged about the weekend's prospects. He was also seven-eighths drunk, which was about right for one A.M. on a Saturday.

"Free the lines," I told him. "We can still make it into the bay." With the *Dunuthin*'s light displacement, we had made it across everything except mud flats.

"Are we going after girls, Richard?"

"Yes, yes. Can you stand?" I dropped a bag of groceries from an all-night market into the cockpit.

"If the rocking stops, I will try."

I cast off the bowline, rolled and stashed it, went aft and helped Ulrich with a tangle of rope that seemed to have snaked around his bare feet. "Are we gassed up?" I asked.

"I do not forget these things, Richard."

I checked, and the small inboard's tank was close to full. Birney Weyer, who ran the Bay Brokers marina, usually made sure that water and gas tanks were topped. I turned on the running lights, started the engine and left Ulrich at the helm while I ran along the rail and fended off a concrete piling. The marina was brightly lighted, and a couple of rows over from us there was a quiet party under way on somebody's old Trumpy. As soon as we hit the channel the lights were behind us and it became a job of spotting markers by reflected light and watery phosphorescence.

The cooler air brought Ulrich awake enough to ask where we were going. When I told him, he shrugged. "This woman must be hot."

Ask my brother, I thought, and said, "She's interesting."

At five-forty A.M., we came around a channel marker in a spray of rain and spotted a cluster of houses hugging the shoreline. Ulrich tacked west until we approached the sandy band of causeway that connected the island to the mainland, where the flag of the Yacht Squadron flew above a modest frame building. I had made the approach a dozen times in the last couple of years while dating the Donners's lawyer daughter. The romance had worn off but I had remained friends with her parents, distantly civil with Mary-Alice, who was a fierce litigator of her boyfriends' torts. Any weekend that Mary-Alice and her fiancé weren't visiting, I could count on a ready welcome at the summer house.

At six, the harbor boy showed up, assigned us a mooring and allowed Ulrich to replenish our supply of ice. I used the *Dunuthin*'s galley to scramble the eggs I had bought, threw in some bacon, and ate sitting atop the cabin while Ulrich used the bathhouse on shore. He came back before I had finished, blond hair wet and standing straight, and averted his glance from the food. "This isn't the weekend I had in mind," he complained.

"It may be more interesting," I said. Whether I could deliver on that promise wasn't certain. The problem on a privately owned island was getting around without arousing interest. Coming in by boat was a tolerable start, because the nautical souls treated other boaters as equals, give or take a bit of manners and money. An off-islander coming in over the narrow highway confronted guards who were paid to be less democratic. Deck shoes and yachting caps be damned. They knew: *You didn't belong.*

My face was vaguely familiar to probably a third of the island's residents, the ones I had passed a few times in Mary-Alice's company, the ones who might remember someone they had seen at dinner with the Donners, a fair number of regulars at the Yacht Squadron. None of them would raise an alarm if I took a stroll. If anyone asked, I could be visiting friends. The problem lay in doing what I wanted to do without running into Simon Povane, his daughter or my brother Pat.

16

The chance didn't come until Sunday morning. For part of Saturday Ulrich and I sat under the aft deck tarpaulin, rolled the radio up and down the dial and played cards. His griping about the chaste weekend I had forced on him was an intermittent rumble beneath the strains of a university station's light opera. At a decent hour I used a phone ashore and got Raye Donner. She hadn't been planning anything that morning. Jack was in Washington, and Mary-Alice and Spencer weren't expected until evening. We were welcome to come up to lunch. And yes, she would see if she could arrange what I wanted.

I came back to the boat. Ulrich was wiggling his chest muscles at two girls on the bow of a Gulfstar moored about twenty feet away. When I told him we had a lunch date with Raye Donner, he gave up on the girls and said, "She hopes to win you back for the daughter, yes?"

"No, she likes Spencer."

"*She* wants you then."

"She's happily married."

"Then she wants *me* and uses *you* as an intermediary."

I said, "Don't let on you know." I went below and dug through my duffle, came up with a razor and shampoo, and went ashore to prepare in case forty-six-year-old Raye Donner really couldn't resist her daughter's ex.

She delivered a loud but passionless kiss and drew us past the front studio cluttered with her canvases and drawings and into the air-conditioned living room. "What are you boys up to?"

"Espionage," Ulrich said.

"I always wondered about you," Raye told him. "And you, Richard?"

"Espionage, too. We sailed up from Annapolis to spy on your neighbor Simon Povane."

"They're not neighbors, my dear. They just bought the Henreder place over on the other side of the island. But I did what you asked. I called and invited her without mentioning you. It's supposed to be just us girls, tomorrow at one P.M. I don't know how I'll get rid of my daughter by then. And I'd *better.* Your name is still mud in some parts of this family, probably with good reason though I've never asked for details."

"Thank you for setting it up," I said.

"It had better be justified. I trust you a long way, for some reason, but helping you deceive someone doesn't feel good."

We had lunch on her back deck, which overlooked a stretch of shaded ground where not much but pachysandra grew and a dozen jays, robins and finches jumped in and out of two widely spaced stone baths. Ulrich tried to entertain her with his recollection of having had to kedge off a sand flat in the Grenadines by wading out to deeper water carrying the anchor through a school of glittering coppery barracuda. His delivery was as ebullient as ever, and Raye laughed and oh-my-godded at the right places while her eyes remained wary and her shoulders stayed straight, never leaning into the joke. She found Ulrich civilized and charming and expected him to metamorphose at any moment into one of the ebullient executioners of her mother's parents.

Ulrich's story ended with the appearance of a hammer-head just after he freed his boat and retrieved the anchor. "If all those teeth had arrived five minutes earlier, I'd have cut the anchor loose rather than go back into the water," Ulrich said.

"Well, *I* wouldn't have gone through the barracuda," Raye said. "So I would still be sitting aground."

"In truth I only saw them when I was halfway through the school. Going ahead made as much sense as turning back."

Raye's smile softened. "That's what I tell myself halfway through a painting. No point in turning back, my dear."

Ulrich and I walked back to the anchorage, and midway through the afternoon, when he had exhausted the question of whether Raye Donner's passion was greater for me or for him, he asked, "What is it which you expect to find out tomorrow?"

I couldn't answer. For the life of me, I didn't know. After Sunday was over, maybe. . . .

"Why, Richard! What a pleasant surprise!" Raye flung the door wide and spread her arms, voice rising with disbelief—a little heavy on the irony, I thought. "And Ulrich! You brought Ulrich!"

As I rolled my eyes, she laughed silently. When I stepped into the hall, she leaned close and whispered, "I'm not the only one who's in for a surprise. Come into my parlor."

We went into the parlor. It wasn't much of a surprise to see a compact young brunette with hazel eyes sitting on a sofa arm, fingers of one hand hooked into a tennis racket, the other walking delicately along Spencer Coughlin's polo-clad shoulder. He made as if to get up and the fingers pressed down. He subsided but sketched a friendly wave. "Surprise, surprise."

The solid, practical white Saab in the side driveway had warned me. I waved to Spencer and said hello to my ex-girlfriend. Before answering, Mary-Alice threw a glance at her mother, more suspicious than annoyed. "You're the last person I expected to see today," she told me.

"We docked an hour ago."

Raye skirted past Ulrich and said, "We were just about to sit down to lunch with our new neighbor. Let me introduce you."

The new neighbor sat quietly in an overstuffed chintz chair, gray-streaked hair tied back, hands folded decorously in the lap of a denim skirt. On top she wore a red T-shirt. There were no earrings, no lipstick, no other visible jewelry or adornment. Her eyes were dark and placid.

"We met at the symphony," I said to Simon Povane's wife. "My name is Richard Welles. This is a friend of mine, Ulrich Lenz."

"You know each other!" Raye said, irony untamed. "Baltimore *is* such a small town! Carlotta, they would bore you to death with their sailing adventures if I let them. Ulrich is the bigger bullshitter."

Her expression hardly changed. "Richard is a friend of Laurel. My daughter Laurel," she said. She could have been describing her relationship to a fence post.

"Perhaps she can join us next time," Raye said.

Mary-Alice shook her head, laughing openly at her mother, and tugged at Spencer's collar. "C'mon, Snooky. The dining room can't hold us all. We're going to do an hour of tennis, if Spencer can last that long. It was nice meeting you, Mrs. Povane."

As she and her fiancé passed us, Mary-Alice said, "I need some investment advice, Richard. Can you spare a half minute?"

I followed her to the front door.

She spun on me, her small tanned face barely containing her grin. "Is her daughter a zombie, too, Rich?"

"No, but maybe overrefined."

"I'm sure you're a proper couple."

She patted my chest. She knew she was the cutest when she was being wicked.

Raye did her best during lunch to help wring information out of Carlotta Povane. She asked leading questions that I couldn't have. Did Simon have interests outside the investment field?

Had she and her husband met so-and-so? How long had they known Judge Porter? Wasn't it muggy on the island during the summer?

"English summers are milder," Carlotta Povane said without inflection.

Raye Donner looked at the woman with annoyance giving way to concern. Carlotta wasn't detached so much as nonreactive. She sat, she ate, she heard—and none of it touched her, none went beneath the placid surface and nothing came back from there. Perhaps, I thought with a deep chill, there was no *there*.

"So Richard and your daughter are friends?" Raye asked.

"My daughter Laurel," the woman said.

"Did you go to school together, Richard?"

"No, I went west. I've forgotten where Laurel went." I looked expectantly at the tranquil face across from me, into deep brown eyes that only slowly understood that something was expected and then searched in vain for an equivalent of "English summers are milder."

After a moment, she said, "I'm certain I'll remember."

"Help me with the coffee, Richard?" Raye's smile disappeared in the kitchen. "If I could see one bruise, I would say she has been beaten into submission. It was like this for the twenty minutes before you arrived."

"She could be on medication," I said. *Or lobotomized,* I thought unkindly, *or undergoing shock therapy.* Anything that disintegrated the personality or made it run off and hide deep, where it could be safe.

"Do you think so?" Raye said, face hurt for an injury we might have invented. "At first I thought she was just cold, an oh-so-reserved English bitch. Do you think she knows we're prying about her husband and just doesn't want to let anything slip?"

"I don't think she's sure what day it is," I said.

We went out and found Carlotta Povane showing no discomfort under Ulrich's frankly clinical stare. I had an impression that Raye and I could have held our kitchen conversation in her presence without effect.

"Would anyone prefer iced coffee?" Raye asked. There

were two yesses before her gaze stopped at Carlotta Povane.

"That would be fine," the woman said.

Ulrich and I walked her back to Bridge Road. I let the journey pass without trying more small talk. I wondered that Povane let her go out. He must have concluded it didn't matter. We reached the Povane's house. A trellis with parched roses arched over the driveway, which was empty.

We stopped, and I said formally, "It was nice meeting you. Give my regards to Laurel."

"Of course." Her eyes searched my face. A small part of her struggled to come out of hiding. She said, "You seem nice. But you're part of all this, aren't you?"

Whatever "all this" encompassed, I knew the right answer. "No, I'm not."

"You're lying. You must be. Well, I'm being good, *aren't I?*" For the first time her voice carried an edge. She said, "I'm being very good!"

She spun and hurried up the driveway, not looking back. I took a step after her, heard the whine of a car engine and leaped aside as a convertible turned into the driveway, lacquered red finish reflecting the sky and trees. The car stopped beside me. The driver didn't recognize me, nor I him. Laurel Povane, her blond hair loose and wind-tangled, her upper torso bare except for a pink flowered halter, placed a hand on the driver's shoulder.

"Hi! What a surprise!" she said, with better cause than Raye had.

While she spoke I felt the driver's silent inspection. It was a close, inch-by-inch reading that occupied his full attention. His lack of subtlety was meant to be disarming. I could see his eyes moving behind wire-rimmed sunglasses but not their color or expression. He was grinning through a forty-eight-hour beard. His hair was black and curled tightly against a skull that seemed to narrow as it rose from the shadowed jaw, which sloped outward like a brick ledge. His hands on the steering wheel were large but graceful. It was hard to guess, but he probably stood at least six feet. He held out a hand. "Hi—I'm Paul Cook."

I introduced myself, neglected Ulrich. "We just docked this morning," I said, more to Laurel than to the man.

"You got a boat here?" Paul Cook said.

"A twenty-six-foot Johnstone."

"Nice for racing."

"I'm too lazy to race."

Laurel gave a darting glance up the driveway. "You were talking to my mother."

"Walked her back from lunch, actually," I said. "This is a small place. Ulrich and I were visiting a friend, and who should be there but your mum. I don't think she's feeling very well. She was pretty quiet."

The girl climbed out of the car. "She's like that."

She stood with her hands on her hips, face as set as when she had been measuring her junior portfolio manager for walking clothes on Friday night. Some little switch in her head sent a message, and she remembered to smile. "You didn't tell me you were coming back this weekend."

"I didn't want to intrude."

"It wouldn't have been an intrusion. Well—I would invite you in but I'm a mess. And unfortunately, I've got a dinner appointment in town. . . ."

"We're taking the boat back this evening," I said.

"Then another time."

"Another time."

Paul Cook lifted the glasses and I got a glimpse of the eyes. They were amused but not friendly, holding something like an unpleasant adult's contempt for children. "I've got to shove off, fellows. Happy sailing." He waved over the top of the windshield at the girl. "See you, Missy!"

Ulrich waited until we were around a bend in the road. "She is a nervous woman," he said vaguely.

"Mrs. Povane or Laurel?"

"Oh—they are odd geese, too. I mean your ex-sweetheart, Mary-Alice, who gets hysterical and vindictive at the sight of you. Her Chester must be short-changing the lady." He smiled smugly, having gotten around to the Ulrich Lenz explanation for all life's hysteria, vindictiveness and melancholia.

"Spencer," I said. "Spencer, not Chester."

"He looks like a Chester."

"He looks like a Spencer."

"My point exactly. Who can tell the difference?"

"Mary-Alice, according to you."

"If she had had *me,* she would find you both wanting, not just Spencer."

I didn't remind him that Mary-Alice had given up on me and showed no sign of throwing in the towel on Spencer. She wasn't on my mind. Mrs. Povane was, and Laurel—Laurel, her daughter Laurel. "Missy" to her friends—at least to today's friend, another pickup from the athletic club, I supposed.

If I believed that, why had I lied about the make of our boat and when we planned to depart?

"I'll check tomorrow morning's weather," I told Ulrich.

"Whatever you like, Richard." He had been prowling the docking area, hadn't been invited aboard anywhere, and was acting aloof. Asking with no trace of tact, he had identified a fat Bayliner at a farther-out mooring as Simon Povane's. "It is a classical name, the *Alcyone,*" he said. "You do not recognize it, of course."

"No."

"Alcyone drowned swimming out to meet her lover," he said. He pulled his feet down from the railing without unbalancing the beer can on his belly. "I have been making calculations based on recent observation. The average age of the women on this island is between sixty-three and eighty-eight. It is not a very interesting place to visit. I am sorry that you employed pressuring-gang tactics to bring me along."

"Quit your bellyaching," I said.

He finished his beer and went below. I sat and tried to remember Paul Cook's sunburned face—and fasten on what bothered me about it.

* * *

The *Dunuthin'* rocked suddenly after one A.M. and I came awake. A compact brunette switched on the cabin light to check who was on the berth, then turned it off. Her slacks and shirt came off in the dim light from above decks. All economy of motion. One hard slap of a bare foot on the floor. Then she straddled me on her knees, groped and joined us with the delicacy of rushed hands stuffing a brief bag.

I was mean enough to ask after Spencer.

She bent forward and grasped my shoulders, choked down a sigh. "Sent . . . Snooky . . . home. Okay w'you?"

Forty minutes later Mary-Alice came out of a light doze to tell me it was a shame I wasn't more ambitious, or stronger-willed, or easier to get along with. This, that and the other thing. Her complaints turned to a muddy whisper as sleep switched off the busy mind and silenced the sharp tongue.

17

We left at first light and made it back to our respective desks before noon. Laurel's junior portfolio manager Timmy was still on the payroll. I caught him late in the afternoon, when the top executives at Overseas Asset Managers had gone home. He sounded bored and dejected.

"I hope I didn't cause you any trouble," I said.

"Why should you have?" His tone was gruff before he remembered a faded hope of landing a better job. "I mean, there was nothing out of line in our conversation. We just talked business. I enjoyed it, you being so knowledgeable."

"That's what I intended. You never know how someone you work with will take an innocent remark."

"Tell me," he muttered.

"Actually, I had hoped to catch Laurel just now," I said. "When we were talking Friday evening, she mentioned the name of a hotel company in Europe that I should look at. You wouldn't know its name?"

"No." He wasn't going to say anything more but then

couldn't resist. "She must know the hotels. She's away a lot."

"Do you get to use more of your own investment ideas when she's traveling?"

"Not really. When she was away in June, I figured here was my chance to show what I could do. Some chance! Mr. Povane came in every day to run things."

"Tough break."

"She went to London, she said, but didn't bring back anything for anybody, not even a scarf for the secretary."

My mind wandered away from his complaints. "Did she call in to see that her father was running things right?"

He chuckled. "She's the type, isn't she? I don't like to bad-mouth people I work for, but they're both pretty intense. Not that you shouldn't be in our business, I mean, it's other people's money and you've got to treat it professionally. But they get excited about little things."

"Like what?"

"Paper clips," he said, "and security. You'd think someone was going to run off with the client list the way they guard it."

"Well, they probably don't want Ambrose & Welles raiding the list. You can't blame them."

"Fat chance you'd have. The few names I've seen are all from the U.K. and I guess one from New Zealand."

I said casually, "Is Theo Willard still aboard? Jerome Theobald Willard?"

"How did you know?"

"There are no secrets in our business, Tim. You know that."

"There are secrets around here," he said.

I stared at the ceiling, wondered whether I was enough of a shit to tempt him again, and said, "What are your plans for the next few years?"

He swallowed audibly. "I like managing money, but it would be nice to work with a larger client base. I'm good with clients. That's sort of wasted here, since I don't get to talk to them."

"It sounds frustrating," I said. "I can't promise anything. But the fellow who runs our money managing department always needs good people, and it couldn't hurt to talk."

"Well . . . I *can't* today," he said, regret plain that his chance to be seduced might slip away.

"I'm free tomorrow," I said.

Peter Eckland was more sophisticated. Baltimore is a small enough town that its legal eminences take phone calls from the Welles boys; small enough that if it was Pat on the line Peter Eckland would have the name of his firm's best tort lawyer on his lips before lifting the receiver. If Richard was calling, it was probably business, some dreary detail in a prospectus that he wanted to quibble over—except that Eckland's firm didn't do our securities work. He came on the line courteous and formal. "Yes, Mr. Welles. How are you?"

I hadn't quite decided on my pitch until that moment. I couldn't expect much if I just asked him to spill everything he knew about his fellow symphony benefactor Simon Povane. I wouldn't get far pretending I wanted to sell him a piece of one of our deals. We traded courtesies and I said, "We have a client, an older woman, who is thinking of making a bequest to the symphony through her estate. She asked me to look into the idea and I thought of you."

"Oh, yes." His tone went from neutral to condescending. "I'm quite active on the board. We're always delighted to see bequests."

"Would you have time to go over a few possibilities?"

"Certainly. Do I know the lady?"

"Yes, but I've promised to keep her name quiet for a while. We're talking about a fair amount of money, and she's worried that if the gift ultimately goes somewhere else, there might be bad feelings."

Someone else might have quipped, *Only in proportion to the gift's amount,* but Peter Eckland said, "I assure you the symphony *never* harbors ill feeling toward donors who find other worthy causes. What exactly did you wish to discuss?"

"We need guidance on what it might take to endow a chair."

Half a million bucks was the short answer. Peter Eckland decided he had time for me to drop by his office. It wouldn't take him more than ten minutes to worm the old lady's name out of me.

He was gangly and somber, a farmer's scarecrow from the Delmarva shore in a two-thousand-dollar double-breasted suit. He was about forty but looked older, with thinning black hair combed straight back from a low forehead, a long knobby nose, a chin made of two crab apples. For all his useful connections, his family wealth, his Yale-Princeton-or-wherever education, I'd heard that he felt bad about not having gone to Eton and eaten bangers, about having missed out on what he might have been if he'd been born an Englishman. Across the pond was where men were gentlemen, where they carried brollies and gathered in warm evening clubs without raucous swimming pools out back. I thought of Harvey's bouillotte lamps and duck engravings and supposed my own affectation, my own reaching, lay in rejecting as much tradition as I could. And I was just as determined about it as Peter Eckland was about owning bespoke suits.

Nothing could be done to make his office look quaint. The Midlantic Life Building, where Peter's firm had three floors, was hopelessly modern, with sliding glass doors and pipe-railed balconies on four sides. He had adjusted by deciding that he was in modern London, where during working hours a tradition-conscious solicitor was tuned into the share price of the Chunnel consortium. The photos on the ledge behind his desk included Peter and Prince Charles in polo garb, Peter and an overweight man in dinner jackets on a balcony overlooking a trading floor, Peter standing alone on a mossy hillside in a green-plaid kilt.

He sat me down and asked, "Does your client have a particular kind of chair in mind? A particular instrument, I mean?"

"Bassoon," I said. "She's very fond of the bassoon."

He looked at me steadily. "Well, that would be a *most* welcome bequest. Has she thought of a living gift? She would get the enjoyment of seeing her name on the chair—the Etta Kay Smythe Chair for the Bassoon." He grinned, waiting for me to come up with a more felicitous name for a bassoon endower than Etta Kay Smythe.

"Etta Kay would be pleased," I said.

It wasn't hard to set the conversation drifting toward his second homeland (if we ignored the rowdy gangs of drunks abroad after the pubs closed, life was so much gentler in London) and from there to mention that I'd met Simon Povane at the symphony.

"Oh, a wonderful chap!" Peter's long face brightened. "Simon's quite an asset on the board. He could be an asset elsewhere in town as well, if more people appreciated him."

"It's an insular town," I said.

"Quite. Quite."

For half a second I heard Ulrich doing his kraut-in-London routine *"Quite, quite, old swine!"* and could barely force down a smile. I said, "He seemed knowledgeable about music."

"Oh, yes, of course he's that—or at least familiar with a lot of the works a major orchestra must perform. That's as much as you can say for many of the board members. They know Beethoven from Brahms, unless you give them a snippet of Brahms that sounds like Beethoven. Then they're lost. It's just as well. We're not there to create the programs."

"What other of Simon's talents is the city missing out on?"

"He's a bulldog at getting things done. The rest of the board could let the best ideas die of old age. Not Simon. He jumps up and down—in a manner of speaking. He cajoles. He shouts. Gets red in the face. Pretends most convincingly to lose his temper. Altogether effective. Can't you think of a few things in town that could use a touch of Simon?"

Ambrose & Welles, I thought.

"What do you think Simon's business plans are?" I asked.

"Big, I'm certain. Baltimore can't contain him. He's got his sights set on building a string of small brokers and investment banking houses." Peter Eckland leaned back and chuckled. "You chaps had better watch out. Your father's tough, but he's no match if Simon takes a shine to your firm."

He locked his fingers across a knee and brayed at the idea.

I walked back to the office in the sweltering afternoon glare imagining a bear named Simon tearing up the Ambrose & Welles campsite and then romping off to New York or L.A. to knock over trash cans at another family-owned, dissension-ridden firm.

Looked at that way he was part of the natural order. Inconvenient if one lived in a camp where the garbage cans were left uncovered. But no more or less moral than other natural predators.

Except that I knew there was more to Simon Povane than he let Peter Eckland or my father see.

At the office, I tried phoning Ulrich, but the market had closed and he was gone.

As I hung up the phone, Anne Hargrave appeared at the front of the room, briefcase and businesslike black jacket in hand. It was nearly six-thirty. I hadn't run into her since Friday.

"How was your blonde?" she demanded.

"A piece of work. You'll like reporting to her."

"It was noticed by certain people here that as of eleven A.M., you hadn't returned from the weekend. It must have been a great party."

"Is two days on a small boat with Ulrich Lenz your idea of a great party?" There had been a few hours of Mary-Alice that I didn't mention.

"If Ulrich could put up with me for two days, I could put up with him. That's one macho loudmouth who would come back a whipped puppy." She leaned back in her chair, savoring the prospect.

It was a fantasy blow for womankind, I thought. If I understood her at all—a dangerous assumption—she would swim ashore from two miles out rather than spend a weekend with Ulrich. Even Mary-Alice Donner, who was as pragmatic about sex as an electrician testing plugs, had never warmed to Ulrich's hungry grin.

"You would give him hell," I said.

The phone rang, my direct line, and I answered.

"My, aren't you the diligent little soul!" said Mary-Alice. "I didn't expect to find Richie Welles, gentleman investment banker, at the office so late."

"I got a late start," I said.

"I just wanted to let you know that I've been kicking myself all day for coming to see you. Spencer has too much on the ball for me to treat him that way. So we'll call last night an aberration, all right? I mean, you and I aren't back together just because we had a good time. Do you understand?"

"Yes," I said.

"I hope you can deal with this."

"I'll try."

"You're a sweet person, Richard, but you could stand to be more assertive, do you know that?"

"Yes."

She hung up, I hung up, and Anne Hargrave looked across her desk. "What's so funny?"

"Nothing. Would you like to have dinner?" There—I was being assertive.

She said, "Sure."

We argued about where, agreed the harborfront places were boring, and drove the clotted artery to Annapolis in thirty-five minutes, a record. At eleven-thirty, when they threw us out of Middleton's, it was almost too late to bother driving back. Almost. Neither of us was assertive enough, adventurous enough, reckless enough, or passionate enough to seize the moment. So it slipped away. We drove back with the long silences of gentle disdain that cowards save for one another.

I came awake later, in my solitary bed, mind running at high speed. It told me, over and over in detail too vivid to deny, what had bothered me about Laurel Povane and her heavy-jawed friend Paul Cook.

I could see them in the red convertible, sun-dazed and languorous until they saw me with Carlotta Povane. I could see them in their shorts, smell the tanning oil, hear our conversations. After which he had bid her farewell.

He had called her "Missy". . . .

The last place I had heard that name was New Orleans.

18

Timmy showed up at an upstairs harborfront restaurant looking every bit the straight arrow. In twenty minutes, I had wheedled out of him the names of several British clients and more or less guaranteed that a bright opportunist could be heading our money management division two years after walking in the door.

I ordered two more John Bulls. "Do the U.K. clients know one another?"

"I'm pretty sure they do. Mr. Pixter came in at the same time as Mr. Willard, six months ago. They and Mr. Kerwin-Jones and Mr. Philiponis are all in pretty much the same things, gilts and U.S. Treasuries."

"Not very aggressive."

"I know. Mr. Povane says he's waiting for the right opportunity for them. He usually moves faster. With the regular pension plans we've got from American customers, the portfolios are all over the place—Spanish banks, Italian steel, South African breweries—I'm not sure all the clients know about that last one; the public employee funds we've got aren't allowed to invest in South Africa."

"Do you buy the ADRs?" I said. The American Depository Receipts, ADRs for short, were issued by U.S. banks to cover foreign securities held abroad. They provided a convenient way for international shares to be traded on American exchanges.

"No, we buy the shares directly," he said. "Mr. Povane still has connections with brokers in London, and they hold the actual stock certificates for our accounts. That makes it a lot easier to buy and sell."

"Wouldn't it be still easier to hold ADRs over here?"

"I suppose. But lots of the companies we buy are too small to have ADRs. You know, not many Americans know their names, so there's not much interest in buying them, so no bank puts out the ADRs. But Mr. Povane thinks the little companies are the best investments."

"Does he make most of the investment decisions?"

"He pretends to," he said, resentment surfacing. "So does Laurel. They're both great at snowing clients with names and numbers on companies no one else knows anything about. But Mr. Povane relies a lot on ideas from his brokers in London."

There was nothing unusual in that. A lot of money managers depended on brokers. And the people in London would be closer to what was going on in companies there. I asked Timmy, "Which brokers do you use overseas?"

"Just the one outfit, Mr. Willard's."

"Theo Willard's?"

"Right. It's in the financial district—the City—Jerome T. Willard Company."

I looked away, out over the clutter of masts rimming the waterfront. I had guessed wrong. Theo Willard's relationship to Povane was far more important than having bounced the easy blond daughter on his lap.

Far more intimate.

Ulrich had left his office for the evening, and his number at home didn't answer. I set down the phone, stared vacantly across the empty desks of Ambrose & Welles's investment banking department, and mentally compiled a list of what I'd learned over the last few days from Timmy. When I scratched it down on paper, it didn't seem to amount to much:

1. Laurel went away in June. Said England. (Didn't bring back gifts.)
2. U.K. investors Willard, Pixter, Kerwin-Jones, Philiponis are mainly in bonds easily converted to cash. Waiting for the right investment.
3. U.S. clients' securities are held abroad at Theo Willard's firm.

The first item I set aside until I could talk to Stu Harris.

The last item wouldn't matter if Overseas Asset Managers and London's Jerome T. Willard Company were both on the up-and-up. On the other hand, if Overseas Asset Managers failed to open for business one morning and the Povanes had left town, how much of the American clients' assets would be found? The answer might be: Not much. The securities were held by the London broker. If Jerome Willard Company closed the same day, the clients' money would be out of reach and—if Willard had done his job right—all but impossible to trace.

For looting careless pension funds with tens of millions to spare, the arrangement looked ideal.

If Willard and Povane were a team, where did those other three cash-heavy U.K. investors fit in?

I tried Ulrich again, itchy to have his London contacts check out Pixter, Kerwin-Jones and Philiponis. He answered, listened and said he would give it his best.

I phoned Louisiana and got somebody to track down Stu Harris in the shop. A few minutes later he came on strong and buoyant. "How ya doin', buddy?"

"Just fine. How are things down there?"

"We're gettin' busy. I told you the Gulf wouldn't stay down forever. Two more drilling rigs started jobs last week, and that means our supply boats will get work. Your money's safe."

There had been no more sign of trouble. No success, as far as he'd heard, in finding Loren Menard's boss. When I asked, Stu described his meeting at the hotel with Charlie Fentress and an assistant. It was pretty much as I had remembered.

"What was the assistant's name?" I asked.

He thought and the line was silent. "He called her Missy or somethin'."

"You feel like coming up to Baltimore?"

"Now why would I do that? I tol' you, we're busier'n a rooster with two peckers."

I told him why.

"Yeah. . . ." his voice trailed off. *"Is that all?"*

My bloody-nosed eavesdropping on Laurel and her father wouldn't mean much to him. I said, "Nothing else specific."

"Cripes, you call *that* specific? Richard, have you gone off the deep end?"

I described Paul Cook. "Big jaw, whiskery, little head, a grinner, suntanned, about thirty, strong-looking."

"That *could* be Charlie Fentress," Stu admitted. "Except his hair wasn't black; it was brown and curly. The rest fits."

"It would explain why Fentress hasn't shown up in Texas."

"Why would he be up your way?"

"That takes some explaining. Will you come up?"

"If you're right, the son of a bitch cost me money, blew up my boats, and I guess he killed Ellis and Marsha. I'd like to get my hands on him. Have you told the Feds?"

"Not yet. They don't bet on my hunches."

"They don't know you," he said.

We hung up and I sat wondering if maybe I *had* gone off the deep end. Did I really believe that Laurel Povane was the young woman who had helped Charlie Fentress loot Harris Marine? How would either of them have known there was a Harris Marine to loot?

"Missy" was an awfully thin thread.

19

Harvey Breton was quiet and unthreatening, reliably gray except for the sporty motif of ducks in flight that recurred in gold bands across his navy necktie. Not at all the image of a bushwhacker. He came around to my office and in a deferential manner invited me down to his. He closed the door. "Yesterday Leviticus and Mortimer transferred their partnership interests to Simon Povane. Mr. Povane and I had a pleasant lunch today. He would like to be considered a member of our family."

He waited for me to say something.

I obliged. "That was fast."

Harvey shrugged. "Perhaps he sensed opposition building. Would you know anything about that?"

"There were a few rumbles." I thought of Wister Burns, laying in stores and counting friends.

"Come come." He was as close to scowling as I had ever seen him. And he had spoken as harshly as I had ever heard him. *Come come.* "Mr. Povane tells me, in fairly convincing detail, that you seem to bear him an irrational personal animus. That happens to coincide with your father's comments, which because of my generally high regard for you I had ignored. Simon says he doesn't know what it's about. Your father says you harbor some resentment over Simon's daughter—I gather she's been seeing your brother?"

"She has."

Harvey leaned back, regarded me with an expression I couldn't read. "I haven't let it affect my opinion of you that you appear to be a very lonely young man who to a certain extent has isolated himself. There's, ah, your family situation, which I sympathize with. The problem is that Simon Povane alleges you've gone to some lengths to upset this transaction, including dangling a promise of employment before one of his staff people in return for confidential information. Further, he says that you contrived to interrogate his wife, who apparently is in fragile health. Simon is willing to overlook this behavior in the interest of having a harmonious relationship at the firm. But tell me: *Who in hell* authorized you to take such steps?"

The door opened, and Patrick Welles, Sr. leaned in. His large head inclined toward Harvey like a granite monument nodding to a street sweeper: giving acknowledgment, not approval. One hand was tucked into a trouser pocket. He stepped inside. "I didn't realize you'd have him in here, Harv. I heard your last question but no answer. Who the hell indeed told you to put your nose into Simon Povane's affairs?"

His glower couldn't quite conceal pleasure.

"Who the hell?" he repeated.

"Would you like to know what I've found out?" I said.

"Good God, I'd like to know why you don't expect us to be sued! If you'd spoiled the agreement, both Leviticus and Mortimer *and* Povane would have had causes of action. Povane does anyway. His wife could have a relapse, and the firm would be morally bound to pick up the bill. You're more stupid and irresponsible than I imagined." His eyes glittered, anger feeding anger.

"What kind of relapse?" I said.

"What kind? Are you a medical doctor now?"

I had dealt with him for too many years to let the inner trembling reach my voice. I said, "I thought you might have wondered."

"This time you've gone too far. A father cannot cover up for a son's failings forever. Not to the point of betraying other responsibilities."

He believed in himself, in his permanent righteousness, in his conviction that one son was well-molded, the other a miserable failure, that one was reliable, one treacherous. If he knew all of the fragments of fact and gossip and clever insight that Pat had fed to Simon Povane, the knowledge wouldn't change his mind. At worst, the older son's indiscretion would be put down as a misdemeanor borne of healthy lust. More likely the information would travel from ear to brain and make no indelible mark. So I sat and couldn't help yearning for his approval, as I had for nearly thirty years, and couldn't help recognizing that it was the ability to live without Patrick senior's approval that had left somewhere within me a reasonably firm core of personality. The core was slightly prickly and wary of entanglements—as evidence, my readiness to drive home last night—but not hostile to the world. Even hedgehogs shared their burrows sometimes.

My father looked away from me, directed a beam of ill will at Harvey. "Whatever you do about him is up to you. The partners will support you."

He left.

Harvey stared across the desk, reached out and switched off the little antique lamp. "It appears I've been invited again to fire you," he said without inflection. "With the support of the partners. I wonder which ones."

It was a rhetorical question. I didn't answer.

He leaned back and sighed with the indifference of a gray, safe man who knows he has been designated as a short-timer. He said softly, "Perhaps you could tell me what you've learned about Mr. Povane?" As I stuck to the facts I had learned from Ulrich and Timmy, he said little. Then he sat straighter. "Does your father know any of this?"

"No."

"The deal is done. If there was fraud or misrepresentation,

we might be able to get Povane's partnership frozen. But it would be rough going."

He didn't dismiss me with the usual "We'll talk later." He didn't tell me to clean out my desk. He stared at his own desk as though he saw an outsider's fingerprints on it and said, "If you learn more about my new friend Simon's investors, will you let me know?"

He didn't have much hair to let down, and he was out of practice, but he had done his best.

20

Laurel and I had lunch at Dominique's, where there was a reasonable chance of being seen while pretending to be discreet. It was a perfect place for a capitulation meal: her choice on my invitation. Richard Welles the coward thought it best to make amends with the Povane family and hoped she would present his case to her father, who might be generous enough to present it in turn to Patrick Welles, Sr. Young Richard was shaken by the prospect of unemployment.

She had nothing to fear from me and was relaxed. Her smile was blond sunshine and summer air. "I'd gotten the impression you weren't all that serious about your career. Was that a pose?"

"It's easier to be cynical when the rent is going to keep getting paid," I said. "The way things stand, that might not be for much longer." I finished off a half-glass of wine in a gulp, twisted around to look for a waiter. There was a bottle of Brouilly on the table, empty; it had been three-quarters gone when she arrived, given with my compliments to the sous-chef, though she didn't need to know that. Now I was desperate for a refill.

The waiter came, and I raised a silencing finger. "Make it our secret—we'll take another bottle."

He probably assumed I had the sheets already greased for her over at the Brookshire. He lifted the dead one away, and Laurel gamely took a second sip from her glass.

Her glance wandered around the dining room, which was too brocaded and nineteenth century to be believable. It was a place for keeping up pretenses—and for keeping on nice-people masks. She had dropped hers just once in my presence, and I had only heard its absence in the taunting voice, hadn't chosen to look over the cars to see what face was teasing Simon Povane. *"Shall I transfer my affections to Richard?"* The sweetness had vanished when she sent Timmy on his way, but its absence revealed only empty, professional coolness. Not the stripped-away truth that must have accompanied *"Yes, Daddy."*

She set down her glass. "Frankly, I'm puzzled. Why are you so set against Father buying in?"

"I wasn't dead set against," I said. There was a whine in my voice.

She gave me a later-afternoon version of the smile, when the air was full and still. "Well, Richard?"

"I just like to know what's going on—who's coming in. Nobody at our office knows much about Overseas Asset Managers, so I asked around and got a clean bill of health on you."

If Ulrich's telephoning all over London hadn't gotten back, she might also believe that.

I added quickly, "I didn't realize your mother was ill, or I wouldn't have bothered her."

"That's what upset Father most," she said. "They've been together forever and she means the world to him."

I said, "And she means the world to you, of course."

"Of course." Nothing in her face changed, but she threw her dart with unerring accuracy. "You're from a close-knit family—it's an unparalleled source of strength, don't you agree?"

"Unparalleled," I said. "About talking to your father . . ."

"Oh," she said, "I'm afraid that won't help you much, Richard. My father's a pussycat. A patron of the arts, fine English gentleman. But he's also unforgiving. He finally realized that you have been bullshitting him every time you met. It's a weakness you have, thinking you can make people play your games. I'm afraid my father and I agree that you wouldn't fit in at the new Ambrose & Welles. We're *very* sorry."

"I thought maybe. . . ." The whine was on both knees pleading.

"You thought you could try to undermine us and then say 'Oh, I didn't really mean it.' That was a bad wager, Richard. But look at the bright side. You and Timmy will have hundreds of free hours to carry on your discussions."

I looked down in guilty silence.

"Perhaps you could beg your father to withdraw his support for the transaction," she said. "Do you think that would have much effect?"

I didn't answer. To answer with the truth was to be humiliated again.

I filled my glass and stared into it.

And very pleased with herself, because she just couldn't help it, she got up and said sweetly, "We just don't care about you."

Two minutes after she left, Stu Harris lumbered to the table, face dark. "It's her."

"Are you sure? You couldn't hear her voice."

"Don't need to. Blondes all look sort of the same, I know. And her hair was put up different before. More fluffy 'stead of sleek, and she was dressin' like Texas girls do when they're making their first good money. But the face is the same, always smiling. You think she smiles when she shits?"

"She's probably herself then."

"What about this Paul Cook?" he said.

"I don't think there's much doubt, do you? He fits the description."

"He's the one I'm gonna kill."

"We'll talk about it." I made him promise to stay at his

hotel, which was safely north of the financial district and the chance of encounters with "Missy" or Charlie Fentress. I told him, "If we locate Fentress, it's time to visit the FBI."

He mumbled and cursed but was just as happy to let them handle it. He had a business to tend to and, at least somewhere in the back of his mind, concern for a family.

For practical purposes, I had neither.

Ulrich hadn't made any headway on Pixter, Kerwin-Jones and Philiponis. "Are you certain you gave me the right names? Nobody I called recognizes any of them as active in the City. They could be cement salesmen in Bristol for all you've got."

They weren't, I thought.

"A couple of people promised to return calls," Ulrich said. "Maybe your three will ring bells with them."

I went home early with a half-formed suspicion. If Timmy were still employed, what would he tell me the three's accounts showed when it came time to pay for Leviticus's and Mortimer's partnerships?

A sudden drawdown in the cash reserves of Pixter, Kerwin-Jones and Philiponis, I thought. Povane had been looking for the right investment for them.

I was preoccupied with the thought. Fighting the vision of Anne Hargrave striding out of the office. One day it would be like that. Out of the office and gone, but this time final.

I walked into the apartment and picked up the phone in mid-ring. "Thought I should tell you," Stu Harris said, "that girl was hanging outside the restaurant when I left."

"Did she see you?"

"Not sure. She was driving a little red sportscar, except it was parked. She may've been touchin' up her nose."

"Were you followed to your hotel?"

"No. I'm sure. I took a walking tour of half the downtown. I'm just pissed that her boyfriend may sniff the wind and skip."

I told him I would drop by the hotel that evening for dinner. Then maybe we would drive out to where Simon Povane lived. Raye Donner would get us onto the island.

Regardless of where Charlie Fentress had made his camp, he and Povane or the girl would get together sometime.

Maybe tonight if she'd told him the wind smelled bad.

I walked into the big empty kitchen, mind busy, turned on a light—and the blow was so powerful that neck, head and arms flew to pieces. Lorie Menard, I knew, throwing me into the river again, into hot, spinning depths.

21

The floor shifted gently, rhythmically, like the seat of a rocking chair. The place I lay, a couple of feet off the floor, rocked as well. My face told me that the surface was cushioned. The shoulder under me was too numb to care. I tried shifting my weight and discovered two things. The first was that any movement started a jackhammer going in the back of my head. The second was that my hands were tied behind me.

The space was small and enclosed, with damp air, a musty smell, a feeling of shabby neglect. Thin light came from oblong portholes just above my head and from the hatch boards closing the companionway.

I sat up and felt the back of my skull crumble, found I could live with the inconvenience. I stared with wobbling vision at my surroundings. A sailboat, obviously, but not a very well kept one. Piles of line and sail covers were tangled on the narrow floorboards. A cardboard box held a cargo of empty beer cans and fast-food cartons. Judging by the size of the main salon, where I had been stretched out on a moldy divan, she was about a thirty-footer. From the feel of the deck's slow rocking, she lay at anchor in a place that was exposed to the tide.

Twisting on the berth, I tried to see out the nearest porthole. That was when I understood why the light was feeble: a folded sail, draped over the cabin, cut most of the direct light. The fit wasn't tight, and looking at an angle I could see strong sunlight slipping along the inside of the fabric. But that was all. The angle was too sharp to afford any glimpse of water, land or sky.

When I tried to stand up, a snug line kept my ankles together. Tripping, I sat back down.

The next time up, I kept a precarious balance and hopped to the opposite berth. The porthole was just as effectively shrouded.

I hobbled over to the companionway and tried using a shoulder to nudge the hatch covers up through their slides. As there was nothing to get a shoulder under, it was a matter of friction. I got the boards to lift a fraction of an inch. They met resistance. I tried harder and produced a rattle overhead. The hatch covers had been padlocked. Exertion had raised a sweat. I hopped back to the berth and sat down.

I heard the deep, low-RPM throb of an engine a few hours later. The sound brought me out of a panicky nap. The light creeping through the dacron shroud was duller. The cabin was stuffier. I had been sweating as I slept, struggling against constraints that became more intensely frustrating upon waking.

The engine's phlegmy gurgle stayed in the same position, somewhere behind my head on the starboard side. He hadn't been there long.

I sat up and tried to prepare myself for a visitor. With no weapon at hand and no free hand to use one, it was a short-lived effort.

So I waited for the bump of fendered hulls, and it didn't come.

The throbbing rose in pitch, and the visitor crept around to somewhere off the bow and drifted to port. As his shadow covered portholes on that side, I got the sense that something large was circling.

He couldn't be worried that I'd gotten loose.

The rumbling moved off, then became a baritone purr as the boat picked up speed.

Belatedly I wondered if a potential rescuer hadn't just inspected the oddly draped sailboat, then shrugged off his curiosity and headed back to his course.

The sun lay about forty-five degrees off the bow to port. That way was west.

I stood up, finding it easier from practice, and worked my hands to try to keep circulation alive. Sore wrists gave me something to think about.

Charlie Fentress—or Paul Cook—showed up at dusk. He came aboard with no dithering at all: less than a minute after I heard the approach of a motor there were footsteps on deck. He undid the padlocked hasp and lifted the top hatch board free. Here he displayed reasonable caution, pointing the barrels of a shotgun into the cabin and saying, "Stand up and turn around."

I got up and shuffled in a circle, letting him inspect the rope holding my wrists and ankles.

"Sit down."

I sat.

"Lie on your face."

I rolled face down. He pulled the four other boards up along the frame, stacked them on the cabin roof. When he stepped down into the cabin, the shotgun was held forward.

"When did you figure it out?" he asked conversationally. The heavy jaw was cloaked in several additional days' growth of beard. His face and arms were dark from half a summer spent outdoors.

"I haven't figured it out," I said.

The shotgun's stock banged my temple, probably not that hard, but it filled the cabin with a flash as bright as lightning.

"When did you figure it out," he said.

This time I thought before answering. I said, "When I saw you in the car."

Wham!

My stomach turned over. I tried to speak and couldn't get air.

"Come on, buddy." His voice was soft, cajoling. "You don't understand me. I don't tolerate some things. Deception is high on the list. Someone who tries to deceive me is saying he's smarter than me, and *no one* is that. The standard tests they did on me came out at 146 for IQ, and I think they missed the main things. So if you spent a few years at Yale and learned to talk, you don't want to think it closes the gap. When I ask a question and you give an answer that says you're smarter than me, I'm gonna prove why you're not. Your education may take a while. That's okay, because I like to teach. How long it takes depends on how smart you really are."

"I'm smart," I wheezed.

"Good. We'll try again. When did you figure it out?"

When the knot of fear cleared my throat, I said, "The day I met you."

Wham.

I lost consciousness.

It was dark in the cabin, still warm, still rocking. A wave of nausea swelled and crashed down on me like an ocean breaker that turned a beach ball inside out and then set it spinning, ass over tits if beach balls had such things. When the bunk stopped turning over for a few moments, I retched an empty stomach onto the floor. If you were disposed to seasickness, a few slaps in the head made pitching and yawing seem inconsequential. Our direction had shifted as the tide receded, turning the boat on the bow anchor line like the hour hand of a clock.

He had left the hatch boards off. Above my knees a rectangle of stars was visible, tilting to the rocking of a child's cradle. I rolled my legs off the berth, tried to sit up as the darkness swam with jagged bright shafts of light. The fireworks were silent, not even a hiss and pop, no booms at all. It wasn't surprising I couldn't hear them. Someone was whimpering and gasping. I closed my eyes and the fireworks went on. An energetic bastard kept time with the explosions by driving nails into my skull.

If I waited until I felt like standing, I would still be sitting when the bay froze over in January.

I got my feet back and my knees forward and levered the rest of me off the berth. The fireworks soared toward one of those bang-up crescendos that goes *bup-bup-bup-bup-BLAM.*

I crossed in baby steps over to the stairway that led to the deck, leaned against the worn treads and breathed cautiously. Past the raised threshold I could see that the cockpit was unoccupied. It was as cluttered as the cabin with scattered gear and garbage. Among his other deficiencies, Charlie Fentress was a shitty housekeeper.

I could reach the deck by hopping up a step at a time. Not much use in that. Once I got up there, I couldn't do much except stumble overboard and drown.

If Fentress was a slob, I wondered if he had left anything useful in the lockers.

I shuffled a few feet away from the ladder, past the snug galley. On either side, hip-high dividers reached into the cabin from the bulkhead, each with a pair of stacked drawers opening on its end. I squatted, hands behind me, and tugged at the top handle on the starboard side. Nautical drawers are designed not to fly open every time the boat rolls. Once I remembered to lift the drawer over its protective lip as I pulled, it slid out heavily. I turned and peered down.

Charts, compass, protractor, sail ties, canned air horn. I couldn't tell what lay deeper. Twisting to get my hands onto the job again, I yanked the compartment the rest of the way out, dumped it onto the floor. Now I could count other useless artifacts: a winch crank, a flashlight without a bulb or glass, a pack of tissue.

The next drawer gave up only coils of rope.

I was working on the port side when it occurred to me that if I was looking for cutting tools, the galley might be more productive.

Was that what I was looking for?

The knocks on the skull hadn't left me very bright. My best

bet—never mind cutting tools—would be bolted just above the counter near my smelly berth. I hobbled over, leaned forward in the darkness and tried to use the tip of my nose to find the switch on the front of the boat's marine radio. It was a short metal stub, resistant to the pressure of a nose. I wrapped the end of my tongue around the tiny post and flipped it to its other position.

Nothing happened.

I waited for the hiss of electricity, an imperceptible warming, the glow of telltales.

None of them came.

Shit! I still wasn't thinking. If this was Charlie Fentress's boat, why would I expect it to have a working radio? It probably didn't have a bilge pump that worked.

I shuffled back to the galley. It was only about a three-foot trip, but it took time.

Then I tried opening drawers and groping through them without turning to face what I was doing. That didn't take much time. Fentress kept a poorly equipped kitchen. There was nothing in the galley drawers but a spoon in one and a bottle cap in another.

Nothing to help.

The trembling started in my shoulders. When my legs began shaking, I heard myself whimper and couldn't do anything to make the sound stop.

I concentrated on something else. My face ached from the shotgun. The pain didn't take my mind off the main thing.

I didn't want to be there when Fentress came back.

The water was more appealing. Even with hands and feet tied, it was better than meeting Fentress again.

22

I hadn't got up the nerve to try it when the boat rocked. They came aboard on the port side, at least two, one heavy-footed. Legs appeared in the cockpit. Wide, muscular, hairy legs below khaki shorts. Feet clad in tasseled leather slippers. A bulk that shut off the moonlight as it filled the companionway. The darkness vanished as he shined a flashlight beam in my eyes.

"He's awake. Made a goddamned mess." With surprising speed, Simon Povane flowed down the steps into the cabin, forcing me back onto the berth. "What did you hope to find, Richard?"

"Where are we?" I said.

"On a boat, of course. The *Magnolia Honey* if that makes a difference."

"But *where?*"

He shook his boulder-sized head and said softly, with what I chose to hear as regret, "It doesn't matter. Believe me it doesn't. . . . Tell me, Richard, wouldn't you like to make this easier for everyone?"

I said, "Very much."

"Some things, by their nature, just aren't terrifically easy, are they? My young friend is prepared to give up on asking you questions and let nature take its course. His nature being what it is, the thought repels me."

I didn't say anything.

A voice from the companionway said, "You're wasting *everybody's* time!"

Laurel came below, wrapped an arm over the big man's shoulder. She was wearing dark slacks and a red off-the-shoulder blouse. She peered at me with analytical detachment and said, "He won't tell you anything. And if he did, you wouldn't be able to trust it."

Even in the cabin's gloom, I could see Povane's stubble-toothed grin. He said, "Your reputation for deviousness is catching up with you, Richard."

"I wasn't devious with Fentress," I said. "He just wouldn't believe me."

He opened a steel panel left of the ladder, flicked switches. The cabin lights came on, dimly, draining weak batteries.

Povane stared at me. His expression wasn't particularly brutal or threatening. If he had broken heads in the trucking business in England, there was no evidence on his face that he had derived sadistic pleasure from damaging bones and flesh. Delivering the pet dog's head to a reluctant banker wouldn't be his handiwork. But he would let Charlie do it.

"No," he said. "You haven't been candid. You've been sniffing around Laurel and me from the day word got out about Leviticus's partnership. You latched on right away to what we had done to Harris Marine. Nobody could have made the connection without help. Somebody told you at least enough to get you started."

Wiggling back on the berth, I tried to get the weight off my arms, which were going numb.

"I didn't make the connection," I said. "I just sized you and your daughter up as frauds and went from there."

Hard, relentless intelligence worked behind his eyes. He tried for a moment to do the impossible—to see his act through someone else's eyes and judge its transparency. He catalogued his accomplishments: Simon Povane, a patron of the arts, cultivated man, international investor, sportsman, fond father, soft touch for old employees. He added up those images and decided I couldn't have seen through them.

I didn't tell him about sitting in the gravel and listening to Laurel taunt him.

Add a fracturing detail to Povane's image: *Fellow who sends his daughter out to bed the opposition.*

He watched me with unwavering curiosity. I thought idiotically that the ability to focus on a problem was an advantage in business. In his case more so than most. He bought distress. He created distress. Ambrose & Welles one day. Harris Marine another. A well-rounded investor.

And I wondered, *Who does he think told me something? How had they known we had a client ripe for plucking down on the Gulf Coast?*

How?

Or who?

Povane sighed. "You're right, my dear. He won't tell us anything we can credit."

"I could get him to tell me," Laurel said.

He looked over his shoulder at her. "Where our friend has failed?"

She tilted her head. Girlish sunshine spilled across the cabin. Lilacs bloomed, rose petals caught the rain. She smiled, as brightly as she had done over lunch, and I guessed maybe I had always seen her without the mask, that Laurel's smile was real, that she would have beamed it at her father while asking where she should sleep next, that she would have thrown it like an armful of flowers at Stu Harris as she and Charlie looted his company, that she would splash it over me as she held my head underwater and sang a pretty song as the bubbles rose.

"I'll bet Richard will talk to me," she said.

Povane's voice rose plaintively. "Why bother, sweetheart? We know where the leak must have come."

"Because I *want* to! Because he's a shit. Because he's got it coming." There was no edge in her voice, just the singsong of a little English schoolgirl asking Daddy to let her kill a pet rabbit. "Charlie's had *his* fun. Now I deserve a turn."

"I won't watch this time."

"Do what you like. Go away."

No, don't! I thought. I leaned forward, told Povane: "There was one more thing that made me wonder about you. You had your daughter sleeping with Pat to get information about the firm. Gentlemen don't do that."

"Your brother told you this?"

"Not the reason. He thought she couldn't resist his charm."

Povane leaned against the divider. "I could say, 'And why not?' We both would find that implausible, wouldn't we? Is it simply your low opinion of your brother that tells you Laurel had another motive, or do you really know something?"

"I know my brother wouldn't send a daughter out to screw for profit." Not necessarily true. White lies didn't count.

His broad, lined face twitched. His hand found the girl's shoulder, rested there like a bird expecting to be scared away soon. "Laurel makes her own decisions."

Her up-from-under look at him was a mockery of adoration. "Yes, Daddy."

"Don't say that."

"You're so weak, Daddy."

"I'm *not.* . . ." He seemed to have lost the energy to say more.

"If you don't want to watch me talk to Richard, you'd better leave. Go on. I'll come make you happy later."

He turned away from her and clambered up the ladder. His feet slipped and thumped on the cabin roof. As he climbed across to whatever was tied up alongside the *Magnolia Honey,* the boat rocked and lines creaked.

I lay watching her.

Their relationship, whatever it was, eroticized fingernail-pulling. *I'm not.* . . . , he'd begun. Not what? Not weak, or not your father? They played father and daughter even when the audience was out of sight. I wondered whether she left Pat's bed and hurried home to tell Povane the firm's gossip spiced with details from the bed.

I said, "I never guessed you weren't his daughter."

She paced the cabin, inspecting bins and lockers. "And you think you understand people."

"You're too good an actress. Were you on stage?"

She gave me a sharp, loathing look.

I said, "You had the people from Harris Marine thinking you were from Texas."

She put her hands on her thighs, bent forward. "Why, now, honey, I *ahm* from Tek-sas. How'd you figger otherwise?" It was a burlesque of a cotton queen accent, but she'd had time to get out of practice.

I'd made a mistake in having Ulrich check out Povane. I should have put him on Laurel.

A blast of music erupted as Povane cranked up the sound on the other boat. For all his modernism, he was playing a big, showy, pots-and-pans and breaking-glass sonata of Liszt. He didn't want to watch or hear.

I said, "Why did you go after Harris Marine?"

"I found out they had a gob of loose cash. Your brother talked about it. He's good at talk." Her glance was level. "He was jealous, y'see, that you'd gone an' done Harris Marine's financing. He thought you needed to be brung down a peg or two."

Not Pat, I thought. He wouldn't do that. "I don't believe you," I said.

"Simon had the contacts to find a fleet of boats for sale along the Gulf where the title could get confused," she said, no longer either Texan or English. "Some of his friends had played a game like that with railroad cars in Belgium, I think. People get careless when you show them a bargain."

"Were the friends named Philiponis, Pixter, and Kerwin-Jones?" I said. The investors-in-waiting.

"So you know that much?"

Not stockbrokers, I thought. Just basic crooks. Ulrich had been asking in the wrong circles.

"You're a very clever shit," she said.

"Where did Charlie Fentress come in?"

"What do you care? Johnny Kerwin-Jones knew him from California. They did something together years ago." She stopped her rummaging. She held a length of line in her slim hands. As she twisted the rope, her eyes got sleepy. The summer was out of her. I wondered what bughouse Simon had recruited her from, recognized I would never find out.

I brought my knees up. *Richard reverts to the fetal position.*

I tried telling her to stay away, but my mouth was dry.

She came for me. "Firstwise, honey, I want to know where Mr. Harris is. . . ."

She was hovering over the berth when I snapped my legs straight and kicked her with both feet just above the belt. Her eyes bulged as she flew back. The electrical panel door was ajar. Her head clipped the steel edge, after which she went down with less fuss than a bag of laundry hitting the floor.

I made sure she was out. Spatters of blood smeared the back of her neck. Above her left ear a patch of fine hair was matted and dark. She lay mostly on her face, breath puffing lightly between dry lips.

With the lights on, my hobbling tour of junk stashes was faster. Also more productive. In the lower bin on the port side I found a pair of scissors. It took a half hour of cursing and bloody nicks before I found a way to wedge one handle in the gap between the propane stove and the sink so a rusty blade was exposed. Hands behind me, I sawed on the dull edge while trying to keep the other blade from jabbing my back.

When the strands loosened, I shook free. The feet took only a minute. I pried the line from Laurel's hands and tied her wrists.

Next door the music went up-tempo as someone spun the dial to a heavy-rock station. I crept up the ladder and sneaked a look across the cockpit. Tied against us, creaking at the fenders, loomed a Bayliner cruiser with a high bridge and no running lights. Povane's myth-evoking *Alcyone,* I supposed. A dim glow slipped past the curtains of a forward lounge, which seemed to be the source of the music. Nobody was visible on deck. I looked away, held my eyes shut, then with a little night vision tried to get a bead on where we might be. The light from below washed away the fainter stars. Looking up, I could tell north from south, nothing more. We were somewhere in the two-hundred-mile length of the Chesapeake, apparently at one of the wider points. There were long stretches where a boat never left the sight of land on either side. Here the eastern horizon lay empty. Either we were out to sea—which I knew we weren't by the absence of serious roll—or we were somewhere near the bay's western shore. Craning out of the hatch, I looked over the cabin and picked out a darker band in the west that edged the phosphorescent surface of the bay. Above that strip hovered a muddy glow denoting distant urban life. Open water was deceptive, but I didn't think the land lay more than a couple of miles west. We weren't in midchannel. On the other hand, we weren't close enough to shore to be sitting as we were without lights.

My impulse was to slip overboard and head for shore.

Instead I ducked below.

If Povane came back aboard to see what his blonde had left of me, I wanted to be prepared. I kicked through the junk from the bins. The chrome-plated winch handle weighed a good two pounds and was the best thing at hand. On a well-kept boat there would have been a flare, possibly even a flare gun that fired charges the size of shotgun shells. Whoever owned the *Magnolia Honey* didn't bother. I tucked the winch handle into a back pocket. Found a restaurant's box of matches in an otherwise empty larder and pocketed it.

Laurel hadn't come to. I used one of the sail ties and a handkerchief to bind a gag in place, which left her breathing raggedly through her nose.

I hoisted her onto my old berth, went about stowing gear and garbage indiscriminately in the same compartments, collected a couple more sail ties and rigged a snare on the ladder. Then I went forward and unfastened the hatch cover in front of the mast. Slipping onto the roof, I crouched and watched for any sign of movement on the cruiser. I knew Povane was over there. Charlie Fentress could be. Or he might have taken off in a runabout to make sure Mrs. Povane went to bed on time. His "fun" that Laurel mentioned? No way of knowing.

There was a line cleated to the *Magnolia Honey* at the bow, another reaching aft. I edged forward and untied the bow line. As I retreated to the cabin roof, the amplifiers next door thundered, *"We are gonna ROCK you!"*

I heard a voice rising in complaint.

The boom subsided. It thumped, kicked and pounded the air and still left bruises.

I crawled down the hatch, ran aft and scuttled into the cockpit, keeping low. The line was wrapped sloppily around the cleat next to the mainsail winch. Two turns loosened its grip, and I let the frayed end slip into the water.

Putting space between myself and the cabin cruiser was a tougher and more delicate order. There was enough current that we had already pulled away several feet at the bow, and the stern was creeping sideways. Given time, the tide would carry the lighter sailing craft away. But I couldn't count on time.

The gap had widened enough as I stood up in the cockpit that I doubted even Fentress would try leaping across. But it wouldn't get much wider until I got the *Magnolia Honey*'s forward anchor up. And that posed a dilemma. If I started hauling it, my neighbors might hear. On the other hand, an anchor line was too heavy to be cut by rusty scissors.

I went forward, got a grip on the anchor line, and began tugging. The line didn't move—the anchor's fins were dug in somewhere on the muddy bottom—but the boat did, creeping ahead on the long baseline of a sail-shaped angle that was formed thirty feet ahead, where the anchor rope entered the water.

By the time we reached that spot, we had a little headway, and as the boat passed over, the anchor turned and pulled free. I hauled up the rest of the line, the slimy metal lead, and left the aluminum wedge on the prow. This time I stayed above decks as I headed aft. I pulled free the sail that had been draped over the cabin roof and dumped it overboard. If anybody came after me, it might foul a propeller.

The mainsail was lashed to the boom, dirty, damp and grit-filled, without a cover. I unfastened the ties, cleared the lines and ran the old thing up the mast under a shower of dead leaves. A little air came from the shore. I set us crawling westward on a starboard tack and turned my attention to seeing if I could have an engine as well. The fuel indicator said the diesel tank was half full. I ducked below to turn off the lights. Whatever juice the batteries had I wanted for cranking an engine that was almost certainly badly maintained and abused.

When I came up, the cruiser had fallen a hundred yards behind, reducing the music to a tinny wail over the slussing of water on the hull. With the lights off, the stars had brightened to a dusty sweep that flung its arms from horizon to horizon.

I pulled the power feed, then held off starting the engine. If Povane or Fentress heard the diesel turn over, the cabin cruiser had enough horsepower to catch up with me in minutes. It would be better to get more of a lead.

Ten minutes later, when I looked back, the cruiser had shrunk to a pale gray wedge. I had the engine going by then and was making six or eight knots, closing in on a spit of land that had separated itself from the indigo line of the shore. I was hoping I had lined up the channel markers right. The *Magnolia Honey* was coming in awfully close to a clump of rocks that caught glimmers of starlight. If I got around the finger of land that joined the rocks to the shore, Povane could scour the water all night and not spot the sailboat.

They turned on a searchlight while I was still a quarter mile from cover.

23

If Laurel hadn't been aboard they'd have rammed me.

For a while the Bayliner powered along twenty feet off my starboard side, matching courses. None of its cabin lights were on and no running lights. Only the spot that had picked me out, which held steady on the cockpit. I stole glances from the cruiser to the channel ahead of me. I could appreciate his thinking. If we made land at about the same time and place, he might be able to overpower me. If Charlie Fentress was aboard, I wouldn't be a match for the two of them. He abandoned that strategy when lights appeared a mile down the cove. He didn't want witnesses. I looked to the right across the calm black water as Fentress appeared at the railing with a rifle.

When he raised it to aim, I spun the wheel hard, losing the wind, and crouched low in the cockpit.

The boom swung across the deck and for a moment the canvas hid me from the Bayliner. The sail rippled, and I raised my head and caught a glimpse of Fentress, searching through the sights for a shot. I reached back to the wheel post and pushed the gear level into neutral. As the sailboat slowed, the bigger yacht began pulling ahead until someone on the bridge—Povane—reversed engines and cut the power.

I responded by slipping the diesel into gear again. The Bayliner had swung around a few degrees and for a while Fentress was out of sight. I spun the wheel to port and began heading for the shallow water outside the marked channel.

I had only made about ten yards when wood splintered from the hatch frame. I threw myself flat as the rifle cracked again.

It was time to swim.

If I could get a little closer to shore. . . .

No more shots came. The light-footed sailboat sputtered toward the shore lights, rolling as the cruiser's wake swept past.

Just another few yards and I would go over the side. . . .

I was counting off the distance when the *Magnolia Honey* rammed the submerged rocks with a ripping, shuddering, splintering finality and all forward motion ceased. The boat was heeled over at almost forty-five degrees as if we were sailing into a stiff wind. But the deck no longer moved.

I pulled myself off the bottom of the cockpit. My forehead was wet, and an exploring hand came away bloody.

Povane had reversed engines and hovered ten feet off my stern. The spotlight bathed the cockpit, blinded me, gave Charlie Fentress as clear a target as he could hope for.

The *Magnolia Honey* showed no sign of wanting to do anything. I cut the engine and felt the silence underfoot. We weren't floating. We weren't sinking. The abused little craft had suffered its greatest indignity and probably its last. She was solidly hung up.

"No—no! She's still aboard!"

Shielding my eyes I could see two figures at the cabin cruiser's rail, Povane's bulk leaning over the water as if by willpower he could close the distance between us.

"Richard! Richard! Throw us a line!" Povane tried to command in a voice that pleaded. "You're sinking. We'll pull you free."

Odd that he thought I wanted to be rescued by them.

"He won't throw a line," Fentress said.

"I could get closer."

"Don't risk it."

"We've got to get her!" Povane's voice rose in panic.

"We will," Fentress said in a detached tone, "if he didn't put her over the side. Me, I'd have done that first thing. Hey Welles! Where's Missy?"

I went below, sat her upright in the galley, untied the gag. "Can you swim?"

She didn't answer. She looked shrunken, robbed of elegance, as humiliated as if I had stripped her and done a body search. She tried to reach the back of her head with the bound hands, gave up. "Charlie will get you for this," she announced. The accent was neither British nor Texan. I couldn't place it. I wondered if she had been with Povane since his New Zealand days.

"Charlie's come to rescue you. But you'll have to swim. We're aground. Can you swim?"

"Not with my hands tied."

"They're going to stay that way for a while. Can you stand up? I want you to go up on deck so they can see you."

She didn't move.

"It's in your interest, I said. "If Charlie starts using his rifle again, he's as likely to hit you as me."

That made sense to her. She got to her feet, wobbly and pale. "What'd you do to my head? It feels funny."

"You banged it on something, Missy. It bled a little."

She started up the ladder, stopped and looked back. "How do you know my name?"

"Charlie called you that at your house. And you were Missy in New Orleans."

She said in a small voice, "You figured it all out from that?"

Not really. But I nodded. "You're a crook. But you're not clever."

"Charlie is."

I shook my head. "He's a lightweight. Otherwise he wouldn't have let that slip."

She stuck her head out of the hatchway with the caution of a rabbit knowing a weasel is nearby. Charlie might be smart but she wasn't confident of his shooting reflexes. I set about uncoupling the feeder line to the propane stove. If the pressurized tanks weren't empty. . . .

"Whose boat is this?" I called.

However irrelevant the question struck her, she answered. "Simon's. It came with the house."

I could live with that.

I left the line open and stuck my head above deck level. Ungallantly, I kept Laurel between me and Fentress's rifle. As far as I could tell, we weren't any lower in the water than we'd been two minutes ago. If the *Magnolia Honey* ended up underwater, it would be from the tide.

I called, "Charlie, maybe we can work something out! Laurel goes her way. I go mine."

Charlie Fentress leaned on the railing in a reflective pose. He even rolled the big jaw before grinning. "That sounds fair. There's always another day. Might be I'll catch up with you and that fat clown Stuart at the same time."

I looked up at Laurel. "Can I trust him?"

"Charlie always keeps his word."

"That's good enough for me. Wait here." I came back from below with the rusty scissors, had her turn toward me while I sawed through the sail ties. I turned her around with a shove. "On your way."

She stepped over the lifeline and dove, fully clothed, from the high end of the boat. I stayed in sight as Fentress and Povane watched her churn across the few yards of water. When they hauled her aboard, I dropped most of the way down the ladder.

They didn't surprise me entirely when Povane and Fentress disappeared toward the stern of the cabin cruiser and returned in less than a minute carrying an inflated dinghy. They dropped it over the side. Fentress lowered himself into the bottom, and Povane handed him a single oar and then the rifle. He set out paddling, side to side, coming fast for my refuge.

It promised a less raucous solution than shooting apart the boat until he hit something. If he cornered me in the boat, one shot muffled below deck would do the trick. If I started swimming for it, the dinghy would catch me before I reached the shore.

I went below. The roof hatch in the forward cabin was still undogged. Trusting the boat's mast and lines to hide the movement, I lifted the lid, confirmed that Fentress was headed for the stern, dropped back.

He came aboard with the confidence of a superior hunter, a fellow who could go up against a family's sheepdog and come back strutting with its head. He poked the rifle down the companionway and came after it. I lighted one of the matches from the galley, inverted the box with just the heads exposed, felt them blaze, and tossed the box into the cabin.

I saw him raising the rifle as I slammed shut the forward cabin door and flung open the hatch cover.

Even so I barely made it out.

The cabin exploded and the door blew. As I climbed through the hatch a blast of withering heat reached my legs.

I pulled myself onto the roof as the flames lapped from blown-out portholes.

I heard a scream and Fentress came up the companionway, stumbling out the cockpit, the front of his shirt ablaze. He plunged over the side, less in a dive than in a cartwheel.

Holding the lifeline, I eased over the opposite side, sliding down the fiberglass hull till water slapped my knees. Then I let go. It was warm and deep enough for swimming. I set off, bashing submerged rocks with every third or fourth stroke.

Grass poked up through the shallows, hemming muddy banks strewn with bay trash and shore trash. When I reached the first trees, I knelt and looked back. Flames had taken over the entire cabin of the *Magnolia Honey* and were eating at whatever wood they could find on the decks. The fire lighted the water and the shore, but from where I huddled the flames hid what was happening in the cabin cruiser. Fentress was injured—at least injured—and his fate from here depended on how Povane treated damaged employees.

Fifty feet down the shore, people from nearby houses clustered on a wooden pier watching the sailboat's death. Two men were pulling a rowboat across the grass with the urgency of would-be rescuers. I intercepted them at the water's edge. Both were black, middle-aged, dressed in khakis and T-shirts. "Can I use somebody's telephone?" I said.

"Are you from that boat?"

"Yes. Nobody else is aboard."

"What happened?" The taller man let the painter slip from his hand and assumed a relaxed stance.

"The stove exploded."

"You're lucky you got off. Maisey here thought he heard shots. Were you shootin' at someone?"

"No."

"I know shootin' when I hear it," the other man said.

"He says it wasn't him."

George Preston, the taller man, walked me back to his house where his wife brought half a tumbler full of bourbon to warm me. The telephone was in the living room. I held the receiver and wondered where I was calling from.

"Those people in the cabin cruiser—you know them?" George asked.

"No."

"So you weren't shooting at them—or them at you?"

"No. I ran aground and opened up the bottom. Maisey must have heard that."

Hands in his pockets, he watched me, neither believing nor disbelieving. "The channel doesn't go over that far."

"I lost track of the markers. I'm not a nighttime sailor. I was coming across from St. Michaels and got lost—couldn't find Annapolis in the dark. Your light drew me—yours and that cabin cruiser's. Are we south of Annapolis?"

"Just a little. This is Miller's Bridge." It was a tobacco country community twenty miles down the bay.

I dialed a number I had known by heart until a few months ago.

When Raye Donner answered, I told her I was aground in Miller's Bridge and asked if she could come get me.

"Do you know what time it is?"

"No."

"It was midnight an hour ago."

"Sorry. . . ." What day?

"Never mind that. How could *you* run aground?"

"I'll tell you when I see you."

"You're awfully cocksure." She laughed, more delighted with herself than embarrassed. "My daughter would never forgive that Freudian slip. Give me ninety minutes. More if I get lost."

George Preston's wife brought me a blanket and took the whiskey glass from my fingers. "You better sit down. And don't drip on my carpet. Your forehead's bleeding."

24

Raye showed up in less than ninety minutes. She made a joke to the Prestons about rescuing a daughter's ex—beyond the call of duty, outrageously presumptuous of him and so forth. They warmed to her and regarded me with slightly less suspicion.

I'd had trouble keeping my eyes open as the bourbon spread to the brain, turning off motor centers and shutting down the too familiar roads of methodical thought. In Raye's station wagon, I left the window down and leaned into the slipstream of warm evening air.

"So you ran aground," she said. "Wait until I tell Mary-Alice. Richard isn't infallible! How did it happen?"

I started telling her, and her driving became erratic as she tried to watch my face. Finally she pulled into a convenience store's lot.

"You knew some of this before—about Simon being crooked and didn't tell me when I invited his wife over. Into *my* house!" Her tone was accusatory with a last-straw pitch.

She was ready to throw open the door and let me walk back. I didn't want that.

"I didn't know any of it," I said. "And what I suspected was nothing like the truth. I thought he was an opportunist. No more predatory than anyone with a little extra money to invest." Sitting back, I tried to picture Povane as I had seen him a few weeks ago. An interloper—disturbing to a comfortable family business. I had seen the pattern too often to take my own hostility at face value. At least half the clients I shepherded into the public financial markets were selling stock to avoid a Simon Povane. Despite Harvey Breton's best intentions, Ambrose & Welles was rudderless, drifting dangerously, as Harvey and my father fought for dominance. If the firm remained independent, at best we would flounder along, weakening as partners like Leviticus withdrew capital, until one of the large financial services conglomerates bought out the exhausted survivors. At worst we would hit a stretch of rough weather and perish with two commanders shouting conflicting orders. Those who had salable talents would jump to stabler decks. Others would find reality outside the sheltering routine of tradition harsh and unwelcoming. Which group I belonged to wasn't certain, which contributed to my wariness of the man threatening to disturb our comfortable disarray.

"I wonder if he does beat her," Raye said.

"What?"

"Carlotta."

"I don't know."

"Are you going to the police?"

"Yes."

"Simon and his man will have a story of their own. I'd say you stole my boat and made the rest up."

"They'll have left town." I yawned, fought sleep, and added, "Stu Harris will back me—at least about Fentress and Laurel . . . or Missy." I reached for a thought that slipped past, as fluid as a breeze. Couldn't retrieve it. All that remained was vague apprehension—the nameless dreads, my mother had called them when I was barely old enough to imagine she might have moments of regret that couldn't or dared not be named.

I woke up in dim light in a bed that was familiar yet incongruous because it lacked the energetic presence of Raye Donner's daughter. When Raye and her husband were off the island last summer, Mary-Alice and I had tied ourselves into figure eights on that doughy mattress, surrounded by relics of her adolescence and the outer silence of the island. As a teenager she had found it stifling. As an adult she accepted the house as a refuge whenever her life in the city blew up.

I got up and dressed. The robot's march from Raye's car I remembered only as a hazy scene from a bad dream. Looking into a bureau mirror, I saw myself for the first time in days. Forehead and right cheek were swollen purple. My upper lip was crusted; I didn't remember Charlie Fentress's attentions there. Bleeding, wet and wild-eyed, I must have been a harrowing sight last night. It was generous of the Prestons to let the creature sit in their living room.

I walked into the kitchen and saw the pottery clock above the sink. It was almost three in the afternoon. Which day? I thought Friday. Two days after my lunch with Laurel.

Raye was in the backyard, a sketching table open and ignored as she sat with a paperback.

"Thanks for your help," I said.

"There's coffee on the stove. Don't expect me to wait on you."

I retreated inside and tried phoning Stu Harris at the hotel. They rang the room without getting an answer. I hung the phone up.

I went back to Raye, head thudding with each step. Fentress's backhand had left me foggy. "Do you mind making a phone call for me?"

She looked up.

"Two, actually," I said.

She sat at the kitchen counter and dialed. A dulled voice answered, Carlotta Povane. Raye hung up.

"Either the bastard's left her behind or he's bolder than you think," she said.

"Let's see which it is."

After I'd briefed her, she tried the office of Overseas Asset Managers. The receptionist said that Miss Povane wasn't in and Mr. Povane was tied up in conference.

With salesmanship precision, Raye said, "Tell him Mrs. Miller called. I'm with Investment Research Distributors, and we had several products focusing on international portfolios that I would like to show him." She couldn't leave a number because she was on the road but would call again tomorrow afternoon.

She hung up the telephone and looked at me. "What did I just say?"

"You said you sold things that might help him manage money better."

"He's still around because he knows it's his word against yours."

Maybe his and my father's, I thought. It was already pretty well established that young Richard was an unreliable fellow with a grudge against Simon Povane. If Fentress was nowhere to be found, Povane had a reasonable chance of bluffing down any inquiry. The tone of British outrage would soar convincingly: *My God, the young man stole my boat! And burned it yet! Why are the police questioning me?*

Even if I had Stu Harris along to accuse Fentress and Laurel, they had a chance. Mr. Harris had suffered a terrible business reversal—certainly not the fault of Miss Povane—and was grasping like Richard to find a scapegoat. Paul Cook? Mr. Povane is sorry but he knows no one of that name.

Simon Povane could pull in a half-dozen prominent figures in town to testify to his generosity, civic-mindedness and integrity.

I would call on a horny German who might be drunk and on Harvey Breton, who might equivocate.

"Try my office," I told her. "Ask if I'm in or whether anyone has been looking for me."

She held the phone aside. "Do you want to talk to yourself if you're there?"

A secretary said that Mr. Welles hadn't been in for two days and she didn't know when he was expected. Her tone implied heavily that Mr. Welles's return was among her least pressing concerns.

"Has Mr. Wombat reached Mr. Welles?" Raye asked.

"Mr. Who?"

"Tyler Wombat. I believe he dropped by the office looking for Richard."

"Nobody's dropped by that I'm aware."

I whispered and Raye said, "Is Ms. Hargrave available?"

"She's not at her desk. Would you care to leave a message?"

There weren't a lot of people in the department who had become my friends. My fault, not theirs, that I couldn't think of another name for Raye to try. She hung up and said, "What would it matter if someone had been looking for you? *They* wouldn't dare show their faces."

"Povane has had all day to dig me a hole. I was thinking of someone with a warrant for a boat-burner."

"If it happened, it didn't seem to alarm the young lady I spoke to. Perhaps she knows you and has always expected it."

While I pondered that thought, she said, "Who is Ms. Hargrave? A friend?"

"Trusted colleague."

"Mary-Alice's successor?"

"No."

"Do you want me to make another call?"

I shook my head.

"Good. Now you can do me a favor. Tell me what you did to my daughter last weekend."

She wouldn't want an uncensored account. What then? "Nothing," I said.

"I got too much of an earful of what a shithead you are to believe it was nothing."

"Mary-Alice didn't say why I'm a shithead?"

"No, *dammit*. That's why I'm asking."

It would have hurt my battered face too much to laugh. I said, "I let your daughter dump me. Again. I would be less of a shithead if I'd fussed about it."

Nodding, Raye said, "It's only decent to make a fuss—or protest just a little, and I imagine you didn't do that either."

"There didn't seem much point," I said.

"You should have anyway, dear. It's a sign the other person's absence would matter to you, which means the person's presence matters. But you—I guess you've got Mary-Alice so thoroughly analyzed, so booked and printed and pigeon-holed that the girl can come or go and you can live with it, because you've got her figured out."

I withheld the thought that analyzing her daughter wasn't much of a chore. Mary-Alice's approach to life was as pure and uncluttered as Ulrich Lenz's. "It matters," I said feebly. Just not as much as Mary-Alice wished. "She's better off with Spencer. He responds the way she wants."

"He takes orders."

We looked at each other and laughed, to my immediate regret. She went outdoors to her book, and I poured coffee. In the next hour I tried Stu's hotel twice and Ulrich's office once before imposing on Raye to drive me into town. She eased out of the rush-hour traffic and dropped me on Light Street, at the door to my apartment building. We'd agreed I wasn't presentable for the office. My shoes were warped, my pants wrung-out, my shirt torn in a couple of places and stained most everywhere else, my face an ape's finger painting of bruises and scabs. Your everyday investment banker after a rough morning of haggling. The security people let me into the apartment and promised to send a man up to change the locks. I said I'd lost the keys, didn't mention an intruder.

"What happened to you, Mr. Welles?" the guard ventured.

"Boating accident," I said, and kept him from looking into the apartment. "The idiot who was steering ran aground."

He left and I closed the door and glanced through the room. There hadn't been anything going on here for months. The orderliness proved that—no abductions, no searches, no evidence of a life lived here.

The bedroom was a little different. My keys lay beside the bed, where my inaccurate toss had left them. The jacket I had thrown onto the bed was gone—not hanging in one of the closets, I discovered, just gone, with my wallet, replacement credit cards, driver's license and whatever else I'd been carrying. If Charlie Fentress had spotted the keys on the floor, those would have been gone too, along with Rich Welles, a reclusive young man who had trouble adjusting to his firm's new order.

Only after I had gone through the place did I think of unpleasant surprises left behind. They fitted Fentress's style but would have clashed with the illusion of a willing absence.

I made sure the bolt was thrown, took a shower, dressed in respectable gray worsted and trashed my tattered clothes. Five minutes later the maintenance man arrived to change the locks.

I told him to close up when he was done and crossed the few blocks to the office. My appearance drew several stares among the after-hours staff but no comments. I picked up my messages from an empty secretarial desk, sat down and shuffled them. Ulrich had called just an hour ago. Two clients. One prospective client. My mother at noon. Ulrich at eleven-forty. Mr. Harris at eleven-thirty with scribbles indicating twelve-fifteen and one o'clock as well. And at eight-thirty, before the markets opened, when the early birds were chasing business and the trading desk was turning on lights, while I slept safely at Raye's, a call had come in and an early shift secretary had duly recorded it. The message said:

Don't be rash. Call me.
Simon.

25

He was affable, courteous—sounding relieved as if apprehension had dogged him through the day. Still at the office, he picked up the phone himself on the first ring. "I wondered if I would hear from you, Richard. I had the pleasure this afternoon of talking to a friend of yours. Do you know Mr. Harris?"

My stomach turned over.

The deep baritone glided on. "He said he had this absolutely extraordinary notion—my description, not his—that I had injured his business. What truly shocked me is that he said you shared this belief. I just wanted to say that I think I've put Mr. Harris's mind at ease, and I hope you'll come see me some time so we can discuss matters."

"Where's Stu?"

"He had to rush home. Mr. Harris had a very brief conversation with his wife and then caught this afternoon's flight."

"What did you do?"

"If you're accusing me of things, Richard, I don't think we should continue this conversation."

He was being careful, talking for other listeners I might have with me. I said nothing.

He went on in a placating tone. "As I understand it, a small matter had come up. I believe one of his children wandered away ever so briefly. Those things happen. It usually works out for the best."

It would have taken a potent threat to drive Stu to flight.

"I understand," I said.

"Most things work out," he said conversationally. "People pursue conflicting interests, but if no one behaves rashly the differences can be resolved. Business goes on. Men continue to prosper."

It was like being propositioned by a scorpion. *Come sit beside me. Let us see if our conflicts can be resolved.*

Then the lethal strike.

You see, that was easy.

Povane said, "I was thinking of inviting your colleague Miss Hargrave to dinner on my boat one of these weekends. Given her dedication to the city's musical life, I'm certain she will accept. I've a young employee named Charlie who's a bit of an artistic buff as well. They'll no doubt have much to talk about. Charlie, by the way, is eager to meet you again. He's a bit under the weather today."

"We're even then," I said.

"He doesn't see it that way. Fortunately, my views prevail."

I set the receiver down with an unsteady hand. He could have threatened family, old friends, could have assumed that no civilized son could be indifferent to a father's good health; could have guessed that push come to shove, I might even care about Pat's safety.

Why mention Anne Hargrave?

That he had seen us together on one occasion wasn't enough. The answer, I knew suddenly, was that I had given him that lever when I told Laurel of the date who stood me up. Wishful thinking about a relationship on my part, instant certainty on his. A period of courtship or tentativeness wouldn't fit into the world he and Laurel shared.

His threat didn't depend on her walking willingly onto his

yacht. If Simon could reach Ellis Samuels, he could reach Stu or Stu's wife or kids or my pretty colleague.

I looked up from the telephone and saw my brother. He struggled across the suite, half-dragging a nervous and anemic-looking redhead who clung to his arm as bonelessly as Raggedy Ann. He detached her a half-dozen desks away, left her playing with a quotation terminal. He scowled at my bruises, couldn't remember inflicting them himself, and pointed. "You've been fighting off the ladies again. What happened?"

"Sailing accident. Ran aground."

"You? Run aground! That's a hoot!"

"Thank you."

"I think I'll contribute an item to the Annapolis Squadron's newsletter. You know, how a sailor's never too experienced to make beginners' mistakes. What do you think of my date?"

"Lovely."

"Dimmer than a watch dial. She thinks she was born to be a party person. You know, if you did just the smallest amount of ass-kissing, the old man might keep you on. I could put in a word. Convince him all the screwups were Harvey's fault. He might be coming around to the idea that he'll need all the Welles votes he can muster."

He let that half-finished thought dangle, and I didn't pick it up. I sat and said nothing. I'd discovered the trick at age twelve. He could never stand it. Pat said, "Simon's made it clear to the old man that our money management business should be sold to his company."

For a moment I couldn't answer, stunned by Povane's audacity. Give or take a few six-digit chunks, three hundred million dollars rested in the managed accounts at Ambrose & Welles. Much of the money belonged to pension plans ranging from corporate pools covering a thousand employees down to one-man TV repair shops, whose owners might have eaten forty years of lunches at the desk to save for their retirement. So much toil, so easily misspent.

So quickly shifted from its new home at Overseas Asset Managers to the Jerome T. Willard Company.

All plausible, reputable.

I looked at Pat, whose attention was wandering from the firm's new pecking order to his redhead. I said, "How does our father feel about the sale?"

"Doesn't like anything slipping from his clutches. But it makes sense. Consolidate the money-managing business under one roof, let Ambrose & Welles spend more of its efforts on investment banking and stockbroking. It makes sense, but he doesn't like it."

"Does he know he'll soon be working for Povane?"

"Not yet. He regards Simon as a supporting vote. The old man's a great judge of character." There was no bitterness in the mockery, instead a current of fondness that might have been real. The old man had gotten him out of scrapes, had overlooked office escapades, and had left no doubt that if another Welles ever headed the firm it would be Pat. My brother wouldn't deliberately undermine the old man, wouldn't knowingly let a predator crawl under the tent flap.

I had to be right about that.

"Have you ever met a friend of Povane's named Charlie— or Paul?" I asked. "Young guy, heavy jaw, short black hair, six-two—"

"Sure, but only once or twice. Paul Cook."

"Does he work for Povane?"

"Sort of. Laurel told me about him. He's the son of a friend of Simon's. Simon's sort of given him jobs—you know, running his boat, yard work." He chuckled. "He's a rough-hewn intellectual. Laurel and I came in once, and he was at the house, in Simon's library reading Kierkegaard. Couldn't shut him up on the subject. We want to screw and he wants to talk philosophy. Your kind of fellow, bro'."

"So which did you do?" I asked.

"Couldn't keep up with him on the highbrow shit. Took Laurel back to my place and discussed our own philosophies. Too hot for you."

I wondered what Fentress had discovered in Kierkegaard about torture and murder.

Pat reclaimed his prize of the evening and left. I collected my car and drove up the expressway at the tail end of the evening rush.

My mother opened the door with an expression that shifted from perplexity (it wasn't Sunday) to delight (Richard was here anyway) to dismay (he'd been fighting again).

"Hello," I said. And for the fourth time: "I ran aground."

She stared for a moment and then said, more or less aptly, "Well, it does one good to be reckless now and then."

My father was in his game room, sitting under the head of a deer slain fairly by his rules, his slippered feet up on a brocaded ottoman, his attention absorbed in a green ledger that I had watched him study from my first memory. The ledger held a life's record of personal investments, all balanced by an immutable calculus he applied to everything: value expended, value received, gain or loss. It was a formula I would never ridicule, however cold the equations seemed, because I'd inherited a genetic respect for measuring success or failure. The risk in keeping your own accounts lay in the temptation to fudge the numbers. He would no more consult his wife on his estimate of his contributions to her life than he would ask my view. By his record-keeping, their life together was a triumph.

He kept his place with a finger. His expression was self-consciously stern. "Come to grovel for your job back?"

I sat on the corner of a battered sofa. "Didn't know it was lost, but in any case, no."

He shrugged. What else could we talk about then? He examined my bruises with distaste. "Is that from fighting, or did you wreck your car?"

"Mostly it's from the butt of a shotgun which belongs to Charlie Fentress, who looted Harris Marine."

"What are you talking about?"

"He calls himself Paul Cook sometimes."

"So what?"

"He works for Simon Povane."

He stared at me in silence for a moment, then exploded, "You've told enough lies! God damn you, get out of here."

"What do you think will happen to the managed money that goes to Overseas Asset Managers?"

"How do you know about that?"

"What do you think Povane will do with the money?"

"Manage it better than you would!"

"Siphon it off."

"That's slanderous!"

"But true. He has a friend——"

"Stop it. If these accusations came from anyone responsible, they would be outrageous. From you, they're contemptible. What can you hope to gain?"

"So you're going along with it?"

"That's none of your concern."

"Pat thought you had reservations."

He sighed, leaned back, the hard face tired. Mentioning Pat softened him. "I don't know why I should tell you, but yes, at first I felt uneasy about shrinking the firm. The money management arm has been a steady source of profits. Less volatile than underwriting or trading or retail. But it hasn't been very dynamic. In Simon's hands that will change. We'll retain a thirty percent interest in the division's earnings. Looked at that way, the deal makes sense."

"What's Povane paying for the other seventy percent?"

"A little more than four million."

"Cash?"

He didn't answer.

I said, "If not in cash, then I guess it's his IOU for four million."

"He's still at risk," my father said. "If he can't make the payments, we reclaim the assets."

"If you can find them."

As he stared at me, I saw far back in the cold gray eyes a wiggle of fear. He scowled but it didn't go away. On some level Simon Povane didn't add up to him. And on some level he had decided to ignore his misgivings, which were shapeless, and accept the benefit of having Povane as an ally, which was clearcut and immediate. Once again Patrick Welles would command the firm with no challengers, especially no Harvey Breton.

You've sold out everyone, I thought. *Even yourself, for a short-lived daydream.*

He stood up. "Richard, you've caused enough trouble for

the firm. Enough for this family. It would be better if you didn't come here again."

"That's not your decision."

"Oh!" His face widened into a laugh. "That's right, you're a mother's boy."

I couldn't reach him, I thought, because he already knew. He knew the truth about himself and Pat as surely as he knew the truth about Povane; not all the details, but enough to convince him he didn't dare understand more. He couldn't ask his wife about one thing, couldn't ask Stu Harris about another. He had built a world that would turn to dust in the daylight of another person's reason.

I got up and headed for the door.

"What are you going to do?" he demanded.

"Sink another boat," I said.

From a service station just off the Jones Falls Expressway, I telephoned Ulrich. He was almost sober, and he had found out more about Simon Povane's three obscure investors.

26

We met at a boater's hangout downtown. Ulrich showed up in a tank top and shorts, rolling his backside at most of the women between the door and our table and taking in a few of their escorts. He dropped onto a chair and glanced back to see what effect he'd had. A teenage girl with short hair leaned from a booth and brought her hands together in exaggerated applause. Ulrich nodded. "She wants me," he said.

"She thinks I'm your date," I said.

He managed to look horrified. "Then let us put our heads together while I tell you about Philiponis, Pixter and Kerwin-Jones. They are not familiar to my friends in London for a reason. Two reasons. They do no business in the U.K. financial markets, not as brokers, or dealers, or traders, or so far as anyone knows as investors. Second, they are not English. I finally found somebody who had known Povane in his early days. The name Pixter he recognized. Mr. Warfield Pixter was a partner in Povane's transport business, and like our Simon he had come over from New Zealand. Well, you will be happy. When I lived in London there was this petite subeditor on the *Financial Times* and she remains in love with me. She called a colleague in Auckland who went through their clipping files. What do you know? Pixter, Philiponis and Kerwin-no-Jones—as he called himself then—were arrested in Christchurch in 1978 for fraud involving forged securities. Apparently proving the case was difficult because of the hesitance of a certain witness. After they were released, Pixter emigrated, first to Rhodesia and then to the U.K., while the others stayed behind conducting their investments offshore."

He paused to let me express appreciation. I said, "Perhaps they went straight?"

"Perhaps." He found that funny. Three quarters of his own countrymen claimed to have gone straight. He said, "You do not seem surprised."

"You've told me they're old hands at crime. I'd already learned that about Povane. So it fits." When I gave him a stripped-down version of my whereabouts of the last forty-eight hours, he tried to conceal the dismay in his expression.

"My friend, I should have worried more. Your brother assured me yesterday that you must be off drinking to mourn your dismissal."

I shrugged. He'd heard. I hadn't.

"So now you go to the police. They round up Mr. Povane and his friends." Less questions than commands.

"No, I don't go to the police. Would you believe my story—remembering it comes from a man who's lost his job and blames Povane. If you were a policeman, would you arrest an important businessman on that?"

"I would investigate," he said.

"That's not good enough. Povane and Fentress both believe in reprisals. Ellis Samuels and his wife weren't a threat. But Fentress got to them. Stu's boats weren't a threat. But Lorie Menard sank them. They were striking back against Stu, and it worked, he remembered. All Povane had to do today was whisper something to Stu Harris about his children and he left town. Povane gave me a message too. I'm not to be rash. If I go to the authorities, they'll investigate—methodically, cautiously; they'll visit him for a chat—maybe on a pretext not involving me, but it won't matter. He'll know I've been rash. Even if they took him into custody, a mammoth if, I suspect Charlie Fentress wouldn't be scooped up at the same time."

He gave me a look that the dueling club members save for weaklings lacking scars. "So you are afraid of Charlie Fentress." Not an accusation, not a question, just a statement of observed fact.

"He didn't intend to let me go. You don't hammer somebody with a shotgun if you plan to let him walk away." A vivid gray and blue image jumped into my mind, a body twisting on the bottom of the warm Chesapeake, feet attached to anchors, arms turning and face bloating, brown hair blowing—an image not of me but someone else, if I made the error of underestimating Charlie Fentress.

"He is not another Englishman from New Zealand?"

I shook my head.

"Then from where?"

"Texas, maybe California," I began, then admitting how little I really knew added, "Nebraska, North Dakota—who knows? If they're under control, they work for trash haulers in New Jersey or linen suppliers in Atlantic City, doing jobs that require inflicting pain."

"That is outside your experience," Ulrich said.

"Not completely." I had worked on a company called Morristown Aggregates that wanted to sell stock a year earlier. They had a cocktail party for road-building contractors who were steady customers, and one fellow put away too many seven-and-sevens and opened up to me, just a little. His name was Augustus Gallagher, mid-fifties, round like a medicine ball, with arms and legs lost in the whole. He'd done business with my client for ten or fifteen years. He wasn't especially subtle in telling me what he thought. When one of my client's hired hands came within range, Augustus Gallagher would lift his glass to his lips, indicating the employee, and tell me what a damn shame it was how some town council member had gotten hurt a few years ago when there was a zoning dispute about a quarry that maybe abutted protected town land. As to whether my clients had a stake in the quarry, he couldn't remember for sure. Or how it was a pity about what happened to so-and-so's daughter last summer and how it took the guy's mind off bidding aggregates to Augustus's company, though Augustus couldn't recall just who had gotten the contract instead. He allowed as how he was forgetting many more things every year and supposed it was age, and he walked away with his drink. He'd pointed out just two of my client's people. Neither guy looked like a thug. Both were middle-aged, wore average suits; one had more hair than the other. They were the kind of men who vanish into the background of a company. Unless you have to talk to one of them about something, you're not sure if he works in shipping or in accounting.

"Or in expediting," Ulrich said. "Was Mr. Gallagher giving you the truth?"

"Close enough, I think. He was telling me what he knew about my clients but in a way that didn't entail a big risk to himself; it was a disconnected ramble and I could choose to hear or not hear the message. If I had approved of the way Morristown Aggregates did business, he hadn't given me anything I could take to the president and have one of the leg-busters sent out to see Augustus. If I didn't like what I heard, I could look at the company a little closer and make my own decision. Which I did. I kept them on the hook for a few weeks and found a piece of industry research from Salomon Brothers that said sand and gravel companies might not do too well if governments in the Middle Atlantic region had to cut their budgets because of taxpayer revolts. I told the president of Morristown Aggregates that we couldn't sell stock for him until the outlook improved, which might be a couple of years. He didn't want to wait that long. They had some very large environmental problems that they were hiding and they needed to do a deal before the bad news got out. So he went to a famous junk bond house, now defunct, and got the money that way."

"Other firms would have taken the business," Ulrich said. "Imagine preppy investment bankers screwing something up and getting a visit from your expediters." His smile faded. "What do you do about Simon Povane?"

When I didn't answer, he prodded: "You are out of the firm, Richard. It is not really your concern who your father goes to bed with."

"True," I agreed.

"Well then."

A tempting thought. Let nature take its course.

Let money take its course, flowing from the trusting to the ruthless.

Povane couldn't count on me to do that.

Ulrich gave a loud sigh. *"Look!* It is very simple. I am owed three weeks' vacation. I will take one week now. We will charter the *Dunuthin'* and start south. Pick up only essential provisions—it would be essential that the provisions be young and eager to indulge hungry sailors—and we shall head out into the Atlantic. During the first day I will explain to you the essentials of trading so that you may join our firm. In fact, I can explain the essentials right now: Do not fall in love with any of your stocks. Treat them like you treat a woman—take your profit or pleasure and throw her out. They all look like hell the next morning."

I smiled. Ulrich's first rule of games: sentimentality is for losers. Given that starting point, would my friend Ulrich trade the safety of a woman he scarcely knew—or of anyone else— to put Simon Povane out of business?

"Hire the boat," I said.

"That is the right decision." Was it my imagination that he sounded disappointed?

"Bring it up here. I'll have a passenger for you."

He blinked in surprise. "What do you have in mind?"

"Just hire the boat," I said.

Ulrich loved it when someone else was being forceful.

27

It was too early to try reaching Stu Harris at home. Hearing Povane's exact threat probably didn't matter, but it might tell me whether he expected Charlie Fentress to be up and around soon.

When Anne Hargrave opened the door of her apartment, I said, "Would you reconsider a boat ride with Ulrich?"

"Where have you *been?*" She ran on without a breath. "When you didn't show up for work yesterday I tried calling your apartment. Then someone came through, Robby, that smug little twerp from the bond department, and said you'd been sacked. . . ." She backed up and made *come-in come-in* gestures. It was eight-thirty, and the open collar of her terry cloth robe showed a black T-shirt underneath. One pocket of the robe sagged from the weight of a paperback. Her hair was a mop of damp curls, her face unmadeup and drowsy.

"Robby's gossip is usually good," I said.

"He said Mr. Breton was fired by the partners that morning. But your desk wasn't emptied so I . . ."

"Still isn't," I said. "I was there a couple of hours ago." It was a fitting epitaph for a half-hearted presence that nobody leaves word when the presence no longer is wanted.

"So where've you been?" she asked softly.

She wasn't certain how much to commiserate. Richard was still the boss's son. How do you tell the boss's son you're sorry he lost his job? She finally said, "Is this because of Simon? If it is, I might be able to help."

"Appeal to Simon's better side?" I asked.

"Something like that. He may just be following your father's line. I mean . . ."

"Offer me a cup of coffee and I'll tell you about me and Mr. Povane."

"C'mon then." She led me into a tiny kitchen. It was an older building, the rent probably low, the appliances well-broken-in. She started a coffeemaker, pulled a package of wheat biscuits from an overhead cupboard. "Here—help yourself. You know, I saw Simon this afternoon. He called and invited me over to his office at the Harbour Court. I went because I wanted to get a line on what other shake-ups might be coming at the firm."

"Did you?"

"He was selling peace and tranquility. Until you showed up, I think I'd bought it." She smiled on one side. "You look like hell and you want to talk about Simon." Something struck her. "What did you say about a boat ride with Ulrich?"

"Skip that for a moment. . . ."

"Why don't you come along and we'll toss Ulrich overboard. Let him 'fornicate' the fish."

Catch Ulrich on the right day and he might agree. I said, "The environmentalists wouldn't approve. Tell me what Povane had to say."

She pulled a bamboo stool from under the counter, hitched herself onto it with minimal fussing about the robe. "He asked after you, first on the phone, then when we were at his office. Had I heard from you? If you'd decided to get away for a few days, did I know where you might be?"

My neck crawled. If Povane had asked early and had

found a source who guessed right, Raye Donner and I wouldn't have slept undisturbed.

"I said I hadn't the slightest idea," she went on. "I had the oddest feeling that he didn't believe me."

"He didn't. He thinks we're an item."

She shook her head. "He should know that Richard Welles doesn't go for tawdry office romances—or me either, by gum. I should've punched his lights out for such a slur on my character."

"Okay, okay. You're enjoying yourself enough."

"Another character flaw. You're closer to the coffee, you pour."

There were mugs on the counter, milk in the refrigerator. I handed her a mug and poured.

"What else did he say?"

"Well, he implied you were a little stressed out—really it was like you were a few feet off the deep end. I said you'd had a bad experience down south, and he was really sympathetic. And then he chatted about the firm, its grand reputation, its terrific prospects. He asked if I liked the investment banking side and did I plan to stay? And then he talked for a little about the symphony and how a community defines itself by its commitment to culture." Her tone was quiet, neither enthusiastic for Simon Povane nor ridiculing him.

"Did he get into Kierkegaard?"

"What?"

"Nothing." I wondered if Povane had picked up his love of culture from his pet psychopath. "How did he act towards you?"

She frowned into her coffee. "Weird, now that you mention it. At first, he was edgy—teeth set, talking through them, eyes almost suspicious, especially when I said I didn't know where you were. Then he seemed to accept that and relaxed a little."

"Be glad that he believed you." Starting more or less at the beginning, I told her what I knew about Simon Povane. Her calm faded—whether from my description of Povane and

"Laurel" or because she'd decided that this ranting madman across from her might be dangerous.

When I was finished, she said, "I don't think I've seen Charlie Fentress—or whatever else you called him. But the rest—it's hard to accept."

"I don't blame you."

"No—no! I believe you! It's just—a *lot*. But there was definitely something funny about Simon this afternoon. Now I know why." She sat for a moment, coffee mug resting on a bare knee, eyes thoughtful. "Have you talked to Stuart Harris?"

"No. Where's your phone?"

"Living room."

Noel Harris answered, sounding closer than the Gulf, and said her husband wasn't home yet. "He called from the airport—they got stuck in Atlanta 'cause of thunderstorms."

"I was surprised he flew home so suddenly," I said.

"Oh really?" Her voice was taut. "I guess he felt he'd been away too long. You'll have to excuse me."

She hung up.

"Scared lady," said Anne, who had listened in. She moved to the arm of the sofa. "So what does that have to do with my taking a boat ride with Ulrich?"

If I said, *It would put you out of reach,* she would never consent. So I said, "I want someone to keep an eye on Povane's place on the island for a few days."

"From a sailboat?"

"Right."

"With that gorgeous Prussian hunk?"

"That's a drawback," I admitted.

She tilted her head. "Who knows? After a few days at sea, I might decide he's cute. And if I don't, I'll swim for it."

"Ulrich won't bother you if he thinks you're spoken for." At least, I thought, not much.

Her look was direct. "You shouldn't deceive a friend. We should decide if I'm spoken for."

Those empty rooms that held nothing but missed opportunities beckoned, comfortable and familiar. Closing one door, I opened others. I said, "You're spoken for."

"Good. You took your time."

* * *

A muffled voice said, "I'm glad we waited till you were unemployed. No one can say I'm trying to screw my way up the corporate ladder."

Later she told me she'd almost gotten married in New York. "He was cute as hell and worked at First Boston. Made money, lots of money, lots and lots. . . ." She drifted into a sigh. "What do you do after you've made the first lots?"

"What does a poet do after he's made one poem?"

"Yeah, that's pretty much what Davy said. Different metaphor, same idea. He liked going to the symphony with me though. Said it was a good place to be seen. After about a year, he decided I wouldn't be a good investment banker's wife because I really didn't give a fuck about anything. His description."

"I'm sorry," I said.

"No, no—say something like 'Davy's loss, my gain.' "

"Davy missed the boat."

"I hope you think so a year from now."

"I will," I promised, not really knowing. She was asleep before I answered in any case. There was a lot I didn't know about the person beside me. Pieces of the Anne puzzle would come day by day, and if they added up to something like the picture my mind had already shaped, there was a chance my word might be good. It was a large burden to impose on anyone, meeting expectations they hadn't created. How she would feel when she knew Richard Welles better was a matter I didn't want to explore tonight, nor next week. Plenty of time later to worry, when one glance understood the other too well.

I stretched in the darkness and found a cool hip, pulled it close, and she came half awake and murmured something that sounded like sighs and grunts but was, "Good fit, friend."

28

We ignored the daylight until anxiety finally drove me out of bed. Ulrich was at the trading desk and answered on the first ring. "Yes, Richard. I pick up the *Dunuthin'* at eleven and will be in Baltimore by late afternoon."

I said I would meet him at a pier in an older part of town known as Fells Point. In the next thirty minutes, I tried Stu's number four times and got busy signals. Finally an operator said the phone seemed to be off the hook. As I hung up, arms came around my neck, and bare girl pressed against my back. "So you're still going to toss me to Ulrich."

"No, we're going to toss Ulrich to the sharks."

That pleased her. While she called in sick—having decided that one of us should keep a job—I nibbled here and there, first teasing, then becoming absorbed in the moment. A little before noon I scrambled eggs and broiled a frozen steak, which we ate at a dinette table looking down on a bleak stretch of warehouses. "Why does Simon do it?" she asked. "He's smart, forceful, capable of better things."

"I suppose because crime feels more comfortable to him."
I sat wondering. "Or maybe he's not really that good at better
things. Doing business honestly does take ability, especially if
you want to be both honest and successful. Think of some of
our clients—haven't you met a couple who couldn't get along
without cutting corners?"

"We're supposed to weed those fellows out," she said.

"But we don't always, because we don't discover the corners they've been cutting until it's too late. That's not my
point, though. Some of them couldn't operate any other way.
It would go against all their instincts; they could never be
comfortable without holding some little undisclosed edge
over everyone else."

"Like Robby."

"Robby?"

"He could never work anywhere without collecting all the
office gossip. That's his edge, knowing everybody else's business."

"Okay, but this is—"

"More serious, I know." She folded her hands across a
knee, leaned forward. "What makes it more serious? Isn't it
just that the stakes are higher? Robby is basically a devious
little soul but we tolerate him. Simon Povane is a devious little
soul whom we don't tolerate. Robby plays office politics.
Simon plays for other people's money, and his methods are
rougher."

"I'm not sure you've made your case."

"I certainly have. They're similar personalities."

"You're being too generous to Povane, or too tough on
Robby."

She smiled. "You're just sympathetic to Robby because
you like having your own edge. What would you do if a client
ever got the better of Rich Welles?"

"It's happened," I said.

"Not often, I'll bet."

We boarded the *Dunuthin'* at the bottom of Thames Street in
the motionless late-afternoon heat. Ulrich took her under
power away from the pier and followed the channel as it bent

around empty-windowed factories and skirted the glitter of the main harbor's retail neighborhood. We headed out into the widening estuary that formed the great freshwater bay that straddled two states.

With little to say, Ulrich stayed at the wheel while I brought up beers. The inboard throbbed at high throttle, pushing us at a steady five or six knots down a bay undisturbed by any trace of moving air. When I sat at the back of the cockpit, I could watch Anne and appreciate her the way I would admire a nicely built boat, with very little fear of emotional complications or conflicts. I didn't know her well enough to be in love, and muddling sex and sentiment made no one happy. She sat on the roof, scanning the receding skyline with the enthusiasm of one seeing familiar sights from a new perspective. Catching my glance, she called, "This is wonderful!"

Ulrich frowned. "We have no wind!"

She shrugged.

To take my mind off her, I worried about Stu and Noey Harris, whose phone had stayed off the hook all day. *Povane might not have believed he'd scared Stu off.*

He couldn't count on scaring Stu or me.

Couldn't afford to leave things to chance with either of us.

I felt a stalking dread. If Povane had taken steps to make sure of Stu, I knew it was my fault. I could have gone to the FBI, could have stirred enough unrest that Stu would have had time to get his family into hiding. . . .

And then what? Asked the bureau's methodical investigators to provide round-the-clock protection for me, all the Welles clan, Anne, Ulrich, anybody else that Povane might strike at?

An impossible task, protecting people with lives to lead, even if they are willing to be protected.

When we were a mile from Povane's expensive lair, I went below and dug out the cellular telephone I had lifted from Anne's car. From the same duffle, I pulled a compact boom box, set it on the foldaway galley table and tuned in a classical station. It was better background noise than the hull's shushing or the rumble of the engine.

Carlotta Povane answered at the house, sounding as if she'd had an early supper of Quaaludes. I made my pitch, and she responded, "I'm sorry—Dr. Rugsdale. My husband is still at the office."

"How late may we reach him there with vital news?" I asked.

"I—imagine—seven-thirty. . . ."

"Thank you, madam."

"You're very convincing," Anne said, slipping down the companionway. Her frown was disapproving. In one corner of her person, she was a freewheeling hedonist, in another, a fussbudgety perfectionist. If the lover didn't exhaust a regular companion, the school mistress might.

We put in at the Yacht Squadron and were welcomed curtly. Ulrich leapt for the pier and complained to a dour young woman in a captain's hat that the engine was overheating. Anne and I followed, looking for soft drinks. I went into the frame building, wandered with no seeming purpose from window to window, taking in the floating ramps and, farther out on the bay, the moorings crowded with boats ranging from small day sailers to ocean-worthy yachts.

Motoring in, I hadn't been able to spot Simon's heavy cabin cruiser and hadn't wanted to make a production of the hunt. Now I could see that the approaching view had been blocked by a long, steel yacht flying a French flag. The decks of Simon's lunky *Alcyone* were empty, and although dusk was settling in neither the ports nor the bridge showed lights.

A woman lugging a tote and cushions stepped nimbly off the bow of a catamaran at the end of one of the ramps. I went out and intercepted her. Her sun hat was tilted at a rakish angle, and dark glasses hung by a halyard against a sunken chest. She was in her seventies, well-weathered. She wore a high-hipped single-piece swimsuit that Anne might have looked good in.

She was going to pass but I nodded and said, "I'm told there's a Bayliner for sale. Do you happen to know if it's that one out there?"

She sized me up. On a good day I looked waspy enough

for Gibson Island. This wasn't a good day. Wasps didn't have their faces kicked except at the lacrosse field.

She said, "Which one?"

I pointed. "Mr. Povane's," I said.

Marina people live as much for gossip as for fair weather. "Oh, *him*. I wouldn't be surprised. All any of them do is sit on the deck and sip daiquiris."

"Doesn't look like anyone's there now. Actually I was looking for Simon's assistant, a young guy. . . ."

She shook her head, jiggling her pillows. "I know who you mean, but I haven't seen him today. No loss. Good luck."

Ulrich met me at the top of the pier. We walked back to the *Dunuthin'*, which was tied to the westernmost ramp. "What are you up to, Richard?" He hadn't asked before, being stoic.

"Visiting a friend. Why don't you and Anne shove off? Take a run down to Annapolis, or better yet over to St. Michaels."

"I am not a baby-sitter," he said.

"This time be one. And keep your hands off the lady. She's involved."

"What are you going to do?"

"Surveillance."

"I could help."

"This is helping." If only we could load the *Dunuthin'* with a brother, a mother, an evil-tempered SOB—and how many other targets might Povane have chosen? "I'll meet the two of you down in Annapolis for dinner," I said.

We agreed on nine o'clock at Middleton's, and Ulrich climbed aboard the *Dunuthin'*. Anne was sitting on the roof and admiring the sixty-footers owned by islanders who didn't believe in ostentation. I called out: "See you in a couple of hours!"

She sprang up. "What?"

"Povane's down there. You and Ulrich are going to tail him." Men lied to women all the time, usually from worse motives. I watched Ulrich back the *Dunuthin'* away from the ramp, the diesel miraculously recovered and well-behaved. He sent Anne to the bow to push the hull away from a piling in the event he was less than the usual perfect helmsman. She was too busy to wave, and I walked up to the road and across the island to Raye's.

Jack Donner opened the door. He was tall and bald, solid from climbing around his construction sites. As a father who knew his daughter was being had six ways for Sunday, he had always been diplomatic. After a few mutual efforts at friendliness had fallen flat, we had given that up. All we had in common was his daughter, and our interests there were different. Raye carried the burden of friendship.

"Well, Richard! What a surprise!" He held out a wide hand, sort of pulled me in the door. "You've gotten on our neighbor's wrong side, huh?" His blond brows rose as if to add, *Been fooling around with* his *daughter, too?* But Raye had filled him in, and he took me into the living room, handed me a Scotch I hadn't asked for, and watched the road from the shuttered window as Raye came in from the backyard, knees and fingers grubby.

"I thought I was rid of you," she said.

"Bad penny. Have you seen any of Povane's crew today?"

"No. And I'm not inviting Carlotta to tea again. What have the police done? You *have* gone to the police—or the FBI—or someone, haven't you?"

"Uhm. Povane and I have a *modus vivendi* as long as nothing becomes official. He suggested that if things become official, someone will get hurt."

"Threats wouldn't normally deter you," she said.

"I'm not the one who would get hurt."

"Still—if they picked him up—"

Hands in his pockets, Jack Donner came away from the window. "If the police picked up Povane, sweetheart, there would still be a couple of thugs on the loose to even the score. Right, Richard?"

"At least one."

"If I went to the police every time someone tried to shake me down on a job, I'd be in bankruptcy court. You know—subcontractors would have accidents, suppliers would be late, some little official guy who's a friend of a friend would shut me down for a couple days for safety violations."

She looked at her husband with alarm. "So you pay?"

"Sometimes I pay. Sometimes I make them see it isn't worth the trouble."

"That's vague."

"Meant to be. What have you got in mind, Richard?"

"If I can find out where Povane's main arm-twister sleeps, the FBI might put him out of circulation first. He runs Povane's cabin cruiser, but it doesn't look like he's there now. He could be at the house." I sighed, thinking how vague Pat's impression had been: the athletic gofer reading philosophy in Simon's library. Did he belong there or not? My own first glimpse of Fentress was no help: driving Laurel up to the house in the red sports car, he had appeared to be dropping her off and heading back to his own berth. But if Ulrich and I hadn't been there, might he have parked the car and stayed? Outside the restaurant in Baltimore, Stu had seen Laurel behind the wheel of the same car. I said lamely, "If he's not at the boat or the house, then I don't know."

"You wouldn't expect Povane to leave him in sight if there's a chance you've gone to the police," Jack said.

"No. . . ."

"I could take a walk past the place. Maybe knock on the door and ask about my stray springer spaniel."

"No," Raye said. "They'll be suspicious of everything. I don't want Povane thinking too much about who invited his wife to meet Richard."

"She's right," I said.

"I'll just take the walk then. No funny business."

He put on crepe-soled shoes and a porkpie hat, stuffed a briar pipe, kissed his wife, and walked out to the road. We were five minutes from Povane's house. He was gone twenty minutes before I got edgy enough to go out onto the porch, another five minutes before I followed the path to the road and looked for a sign of him.

It was close to dusk, and the road was shiny with fading light.

Raye came down to the newspaper box. "I'm going to kill him."

We watched the empty road for another five minutes

before I started toward the corner. Raye came along. No point in telling her not to.

We found him because of the smoke.

He was a few steps off the road, ankle deep in chicory— not really noticeable against the trees unless you started looking for the source of sweet cherry tobacco smoke. When we were close, he waved two fingers.

He met Raye's angry gaze meekly and asked, "Is that sleek blonde we see at the club Povane's daughter?"

"Sort of," I said.

"She's been loading a van with suitcases. Sweaty work all by herself. I'm waiting to see if she leaves."

He had walked past once and caught a glimpse of her, had come back a few minutes later and had seen no sign that she was getting any help.

"I'd say she, at least, is clearing out."

His wife said, "I'll take the walk this time." Before we could object she was on the blacktopped road striding along the wall of hibiscus and mock orange, glancing discreetly up the driveway as she passed Povane's house.

She reached the top of the road, turned and waved. In the dusk she could have been someone I didn't know, congratulating herself for something I didn't understand.

Then she started back.

As she reached the driveway a sound came that I couldn't identify. Raye's head turned and I heard it again.

She'd heard it too and was moving toward the source—up the driveway.

"Jesus Christ," Jack said and broke from the weeds. He ran uphill, stumbled on the overgrown shoulder. I reached the driveway two steps ahead of him, saw a deep maroon van parked near the house in the bright light of a house lamp. The van's sliding door was open. Raye pressed against it, arm stained wet and black, trying to retreat from the woman facing her.

It was Laurel and she had a knife. Another figure huddled on the ground, head half-hidden in her arms. I recognized Carlotta. One knee was scraped raw, and her cheek was bloody.

Laurel chewed her lip and edged closer to Raye, blade jumping side to side.

I called out cheerfully, "Hello, Laurel!"

As she turned, Raye slipped away. The girl glanced back, grimacing annoyance, then fixed her attention on me. Wisps of hair stuck to her forehead and neck, and sweat had cut streaks down her shirt. Her feet moved as compulsively as the knife, getting ready to attack. There was no elegance in her, just the instincts of a street fighter. She tried to sound like the gentleman's daughter. "You've caused a bit of trouble, dear Richard." It was a cracked parody. *Where the hell had he recruited her?*

"There's more trouble to come," I said.

"Oh?" She tried to stop her jitterbugging, hoping I'd come closer. "What kind of trouble?"

"Well—" I began, but she wasn't waiting. She flung herself forward at the same instant Raye, coming from behind, swung a full-laden suitcase like a flyswatter. The sidearm blow knocked the girl against the van with a sound like steel doors slamming.

She bounced off still planning to get me. But her reflexes were dull, and I caught a thin wrist and twisted until the knife dropped. She slumped against the van, eyes out of focus, arms limp.

Jack tore a strip off his shirt and tied it around his wife's arm. "What were you trying to do?" he demanded.

"She was pulling Carlotta by the hair, toward the van. The woman was making this pathetic sound. . . ."

"We heard," Jack said.

"I didn't think enough about it," his wife said. "I figured I was bigger than the slut . . . didn't suspect the knife."

I wished they would quit talking. If someone else was in the house, I wanted them—*him*—to stay there. The fact that Laurel wasn't yelling made me hope she had been alone.

Jack Donner swished the remains of his shirt at mosquitoes that had noticed his back. I pointed. "Can I have a strip of that?"

He ripped the back open, peeled off a piece that was long

enough to tie the girl's hands. I did the job thoroughly, snugly, behind her back.

She called me a name they probably didn't use at English girls' schools. I edged past the propped screen door into a vestibule, where other bags and boxes left a tight path to a swinging door that led to the kitchen. It was empty and felt that way. I didn't have much appetite for going through the house. If Fentress was lurking behind a door, I didn't want to open it.

When I went outside, Raye was kneeling beside Carlotta Povane. The older woman's arms embraced her head, closing off the world. Raye whispered, "Carlotta?"

Carlotta snuggled deeper into hiding.

I asked Laurel, "Where's Charlie?"

She sniggered at me. "You'll find out."

"Not in the house?"

She shrugged.

"With Simon?"

She smiled.

"On the boat, then?"

She didn't react.

I took Jack aside. "Call the police."

"Don't you think of running off."

"I'm not going far, just the yacht club."

"Charlie sounds like more than you can handle."

"I'm not going to try to handle him," I said. "But I want to know if he's at the boat."

29

The sporty convertible was in the marina's parking lot. I checked the back and saw a mound of fast-food bags and wrappers, which settled whose car it was. I walked up to the Yacht Squadron's headquarters, where a half-dozen sunburned men and women were complaining about the damn calm weather. I picked a likely customer, a guy about thirty standing a little outside the circle. "Do you know if Mr. Fentress is here?" I said. "I'm supposed to see him about a boat."

"I don't know any Fentress. Anyone know someone called Fentress?"

Shrugs and indifferent stares answered him. He was enough of an outsider in that group that no one bothered to speak.

"Thanks anyway," I said.

"What kind of boat?" he asked for the sake of talking to someone.

"A twin-diesel Bayliner, forty-five-footer. It's called the *Alcyone,* he said."

"The *Alcyone?* The guy that owns that is a stockbroker or something. But his name isn't Fentress." He frowned at an inner core of doubt. "At least I don't think so."

"Fentress works for the owner."

"That could be then. Let's see. . . ." He stepped outside, looked around for the right section of moorings. "There it is, out that way. You see the white bridge? Looks like nobody's home. What's Fentress look like?"

"Big jaw, small head."

"That could fit half the island." It wasn't true, but he was ticked off.

"Maybe I'll row out and have a look."

It was his turn to shrug, dismissing an off-islander who, it had occurred to him, was even more outside the group than he was.

No one complained as I rowed the marina's tender out to the wide-hipped cruiser. On closer inspection, Povane's boat had the same signs of shabby upkeep as the late *Magnolia Honey*: frayed unraveling of lines, blistering on the hull, tarnish on the brightwork. The neglect hadn't had time to become serious but in another year it would be expensive to set right.

I read things into the decay from what I knew about the owner and the handyman. Such inferences didn't work in reverse. I'd known a doctor who said he viewed his little day sailer the way he viewed a screwdriver, as a tool, and would no more polish the sailboat's brass than he would polish a screwdriver. He said a person couldn't hold off his own decay by preserving boats, houses, cars or old postage stamps—though a lot of dwindling time could be misspent on the symbolic effort.

But there was a difference between unfeeling neglect and the laziness of philosophical resignation. My resigned doctor friend still managed little acts of tenderness toward his boat, giving it the due of a hopeless patient.

If Povane had been a doctor, he'd have specialized in pressing pillows on sleeping faces. Charlie Fentress's remedies would have been more direct.

Even from below her, the *Alcyone* had a feel of utter emptiness. Wherever Fentress had holed up, it wasn't here.

I swung the little tender around. Off to the right was the massive steel yacht of the visiting Frenchman. As I drew across the bows of the ocean-goer, a single-masted sailboat crept into view. There were a couple of empty moorings between the yacht and the sloop, sixty feet or so. Each stroke of the oars brought more of her into sight, furled sail, closed hatch.

There was nothing distinctive about her. She slept quietly at the mooring can, thirty undistinguished feet of fiberglass. . . .

Even in the distance and the darkness, I knew that up close she would look a bit worse for hire.

Even in the distance and darkness, I knew it was the *Dunuthin'*.

30

I sat and the bay's tiny waves clucked at the tender's slats.

The ports of the *Dunuthin'* were as dark as those of the cabin cruiser. I breathed silently, listened to nothing, and cursed my dumb-assed stupidity.

There were innocent explanations.

Ulrich could have decided to hang around.

He and Anne could have sacked out early, very early, and turned off the lights. Or they could have come ashore. Right now they could be hanging out on Raye Donner's front step, wondering what mischief I was up to.

Or I could be wrong about the sloop. It wasn't the *Dunuthin'*. One Newport 30 didn't look much different from another. The lines were the same; a white hull was a white hull, a wrapped sail a wrapped sail.

Unless you had taken her out often. Then she was as recognizable as the warty-nosed friend in a crowd.

It took every shred of my will not to row over to her.

Unshipping the oars, I gave what I hoped was a convincing final inspection of Povane's cruiser and stroked back toward the shore.

There were innocent explanations for the *Dunuthin's* presence.

I knew none of the innocent ones was true. Knew it at the primal level that tells a mouse when it has blundered onto a cat's dinner plate, the level that told me sometimes when a slick operator was trying to put one over on Ambrose & Welles, told me too late when the slickest ones had succeeded.

Charlie said he was smarter than the rest of us.

To get aboard the *Dunuthin'*, if he had been hanging around when we sailed in, wouldn't have taken much intelligence or cunning. Maybe just a swim around the flanks to the little sailboat's stern while the foolish threesome were ashore playacting.

What a surprise for the German buffoon and the girl, who'd thought they were crafty. I blocked any thought of what had happened next as I rowed around the bow of a big Catalina and brought the oars aboard. For the moment I was out of the direct line of sight for anybody aboard the sailboat. It wouldn't be good for long, because from somewhere forward on the *Dunuthin'* Charlie Fentress would have a decent view of the floating piers and the lighted building. If the tender didn't show up at the dock soon, he would notice.

But the cover gave me a moment of shaky silence to try to think of options. Clever options for a clever Charlie.

In the end there was no choice. I stroked hard to make up for idle time and came out of the shadows making a lazy pace back to land. For part of the trip the Newport's bow was in view, white and anonymous in the moonlight and seemingly empty.

I tied the tender to a piling at the top of the dock, walked up stretching and indifferent to the unpretentious Squadron headquarters where the unpretentious helmsmen and women cheered themselves on in the good life and kept a wary eye out for people who weren't entitled to share it. I got a can of Coke and came out and started off toward the car park, not making it too leisurely. Richard would be on the lookout for Simon and Charlie even if he hadn't recognized the *Dunu-thin'*.

When I was out of sight from all the boats at the far end of the moorings, I left the road and crept down to the shore. I stripped to my shorts, waded into the warm bay, and began the long and tedious swim.

A couple of the moored boats were occupied. One had a lively party under way, half on a deck strung with a yellow canopy, half in the brightly lighted lounge where figures did a musicless dance of lifted glasses and wide gestures. No one noticed the fool out for a splash among the sea nettles.

I had to hang onto the diving platform of Povane's boat for a breather. My watch said it had taken me fifteen minutes to circle the flotilla of moored vessels and arrive from behind the boats at the place I wanted. If it hadn't been for the need to be quiet, I could have done it in less time.

Being quiet would be possible for only so long. Sucking in the gummy August air, I held my position with slow kicks against the tug of an incoming tide, sized up the next stretch I had to cross as less inviting than the first even if it was only a tenth the distance. There was no way, once I reached the *Dunuthin'*, of coming aboard without alerting anyone who was there.

His warning would be shorter than if I'd rowed up and called for permission—*Bring out your shotgun, Charlie!*—but any warning would make him more than I could handle.

I didn't see any choice.

I set out swimming strongly around the *Alcyone*'s broad behind, switched to a breaststroke once I'd gotten past the French yacht and faced twenty yards of open water and the *Dunuthin'*. As far as I could see from a frog's vantage point, the sailboat's decks were empty. From thirty feet, I could make out the familiar name in blue script on the Newport's stern, patchy but legible. I kept on paddling, around to the starboard side. It wasn't a random choice. When Ulrich and I were sailing, we kept the boat hook on that side, lying against the cabin rail. It wasn't much of a club: a five-and-a-half-foot fiberglass pole, not more than a few pounds, but it had a cast aluminum K-shaped head. If Charlie came bolting out of the companionway, I might have a chance at him.

The long swim had left me trembling. I stayed in the water, trying to think buoyancy while gathering the energy to come over the side, across the lifeline and onto the roof in one surge. I wasn't certain I could hitch a foot over the side, never mind surging.

I was no match at all for Charlie.

Moving against the hull, I tried to listen for sounds aboard the *Dunuthin'*, but my ragged breathing could have drowned out anyone who wasn't running a chain saw.

I grabbed the plastic-clad line and kicked up, got a heel over the bulwarks and clambered onto the side deck on face and belly. Not quite as smoothly as I'd hoped. I rolled against the cabin, got onto my knees and climbed onto the roof.

My hand groped along the rail.

There was no fiberglass pole.

No aluminum hook to bang his head.

He would be out in an instant.

I groped like a blind man across the cabin roof. Felt along the lip of the forward hatch, knowing it couldn't have rolled there. Scrambled among lines from the jib sail. . . .

I looked back to the cockpit, knowing I would see his head.

He was there, grinning.

Ready to kill me.

Only for a moment. Then he was gone and the cockpit was empty, the wheel strapped and still, the transom a patch of bare fiberglass full of blurred shadows. The hatch cover was still in place.

Inching forward, I slipped to the side deck, well away from portholes. I found the boat pole in a nest of bow lines. The K-hook was caked along one edge with something dry and black and flaky. I looked around the deck and the cabin roof. There were no large incriminating splashes.

I went aft, lightly over the roof.

He could be waiting anywhere below, cradling his shotgun, savoring the irony of a genius being stalked by an idiot.

I wondered if he was waiting alone.

Well below the surface of my attention, like a face seen through dark water, an image turned and tried to confront me, the woman's shape I had seen before caught in swirls and eddies, blindly rolling through tidal grass, lurching without purpose toward the rough meeting of bay and ocean. I looked away, not to recognize the face.

If he was alone, I would kill him.

At any cost.

Kill him and take the *Dunuthin'* out, dropping parts of Charlie in the water, clever food for the night fish, an improvement of the species, both species.

I banged the head of the boat hook on the hatch slats, raged incoherently.

Then I got just five percent smarter and crouched, holding the pole like a javelin.

He didn't respond.

The hasp and eye on the top slat were apart, the way they would be if you were inside. You padlocked the hatch upon leaving. If you were bunking down with your favorite shotgun, you left the latch undone.

I reached forward. Almost pulled the top slat up. From below, he would have a hard time nailing me with the first barrelful unless he got lucky firing through the cabin roof. He couldn't know whether the blast would carry through the layers of fiberglass.

I almost lifted the slat to give him his chance.

Then I pulled back and squatted in the silence, while sweat wriggled down my back, while the *Dunuthin'* shifted with imperceptible slowness to the changing pull of the tide, while the overcast sky hung motionless above the mast tops. I squatted and waited and listened and heard nothing.

Finally something thumped below, as soft as down pillows colliding. The vibration traveled more through the fiberglass to my feet than through the air. An instant later the sound repeated. A loose cupboard? The boat wasn't rocking.

I wasn't alone. The person below knew he wasn't alone.

But he hadn't come up to kill me.

I got on hands and knees and looked down at the oblong

ports on the side of the cabin. The glass was black, the curtains drawn. I crept to the other side and found the same situation. The forward hatch cover was one of the Lexan models. Sometimes owners equip them with shades, but the *Dunuthin'*s hadn't. If there had been lights I would have been able to see in, but the cabin was dark.

Slipping fingers under the edge of the cover, I tried lifting. It was locked inside.

Cockpit entrance accessible, front hatch locked.

If Charlie was waiting with his shotgun, it wouldn't matter which door I chose.

If he was waiting, I wouldn't have heard the thumps.

I collected the boat hook, slipped the pole under the hatch's lip and pretended I was levering a boulder out of the mud. The *Dunuthin'* was pretty solid. The hatch creaked and gave a quarter inch—that and no more, not even a second quarter inch.

I strained and sweated at it for a minute before letting the pole clatter onto the roof.

Jesus.

There was still the cockpit hatch.

I ignored the thought. The *Dunuthin'* had two anchors stowed in the lockers to the left and right of the jib halyard. Paying out line, I carried the eighteen-pound Super Hooker from the starboard locker, stood over the hatch cover and gripped the anchor chain about four feet below the straight steel lead. I swung the anchor overhand like a pick axe, jumped back as the blade rebounded near my shin. I shortened my grip and tried again. This time the Lexan cracked. It never really shattered, but by the third blow I had a large, jagged hole. I swung the anchor twice more, knelt and pried free plastic splinters, reached through and unlocked the cover.

If anyone in the neighborhood was curious about the hammering, the long black hull of the French boat hid the *Dunuthin'* from casual inspection.

I stowed the bent anchor in its locker, then came back and lifted the hatch cover. Another thump came from somewhere aft. I slipped down into the cramped forward cabin. Ulrich and I never used it for much except stowing bagged sails, and as a private place for an occasional midday screw. I switched on the light, saw nothing out of order except for a few shards of Lexan, and opened the door to the main cabin.

Nobody was waiting with a shotgun.

One person was waiting in the port berth. Mouth gagged by twisted sail ties, hands bound and out of sight, shoulders, waist and legs lashed through ventilation slats to the berth itself, ankles tied together with a line that ran taut to the base of the alcohol stove. About all that was mobile was a crewcut head, which he'd driven against the cushioned berth to produce the soft thuds. His way of warning someone not to come down. Not through the cockpit hatch.

Charlie had left a greeting for anyone who came that way.

Ulrich's eyes still bulged in raw, heart-bursting panic. Probably nothing like they'd done when he thought someone was about to lift the slats covering the companionway.

I pulled the gag free.

"He tied the bomb to the hatch boards!" Ulrich shrilled. They were his first words. He had waited a long time to say them.

I started on the ropes that held him to the berth. "Where is he?" I said.

"Don't know—gone."

"What about Anne?"

"He—I think, he took her."

"How long ago?"

"What time is it?" I told him and he tried to sit up, which was awkward with the lines still around his chest. "Two hours then. He jumped on me before we were a half mile out. Hiding below. Must have snuck aboard at the landing. Where are we?"

"Gibson Island."

"I thought so. Could hear riggings and masts."

I untied his wrists and left him to do the feet while I inspected Charlie Fentress's surprise. It consisted of a dozen or so sticks of dynamite taped together, a cocked mousetrap taped to a piece of two-by-four, that in turn taped to the dynamite, a red shotgun shell lodged through a hole in the mousetrap, a string running from the trap's trigger to an eyelet in the back of the second hatch board from the top. It looked effective. A visitor started lifting hatch boards. The first one was easy. The second sprang the mousetrap, which discharged the shotgun shell into the dynamite, and for a minute or so it rained boat pieces on Gibson Island.

If you didn't blow yourself up setting it, you could chuckle at the crafty design.

It looked extremely unstable. How often did mousetraps fire on their own?

Ulrich stood up, wobbled. In the pale cabin light, he looked green, mouth drawn, cheeks sunken. The side of his head was swollen from the ear to the jaw. He held his chest delicately. "I believe I have broken ribs. Winch handle."

I laced my fingers for a step, and he climbed through the forward hatch, silent except for one loud gasp. When I came up, he was on his side choking. His skin was damp and cold.

"We're going to have to swim," I said.

"You swim. I will make sure the *Dunuthin'* does not drift away."

"We'd better both swim."

"I will lie here very quietly." His voice was fuzzy.

"Come on—or I'll tell your friends that a broken rib puts you out of action. Mimi, Sue-Sue, all of them."

His teeth clenched when we got to the edge of the deck. There was no gradual way to get into the water. He jumped first. I waited until I saw his head on the surface, then went in beside him. The French yacht was twenty yards away, and there would be nothing to hold onto there except an anchor chain. Far around its graceful stern, we would face another ten yards to Povane's Bayliner. Not far on my own. Too far for Ulrich. He tried a few strokes and began sinking.

"On your back," I said.

He rolled over and I slid a hand under his chin. Forty yards all the long, angled way around. Forty yards to the Bayliner's diving platform. I knew I couldn't keep us both clinging there.

The water was warm. I tried to avoid bumping Ulrich's ribs with one-armed strokes that cut under him.

The warmth felt good even as my arms got heavy. It was the kind of evening to float and stare at clouds.

Water washed across my chin, pressed my lips.

I shook my head.

Kicked and stroked.

Started counting the strokes, reached ten and counted backwards.

It would be nice if Ulrich helped.

Always I got stuck pulling someone else's load.

Water pushed into my nose.

I dog-paddled, coughing. It would have been easier if my legs hadn't grown fat and weak.

The dark steel hull was lost in a haze. I wondered if I had swum past it and was struggling toward the open bay. Except that I wasn't struggling much. And at the pace I'd been setting, I couldn't have covered half the distance to the yacht's stern. Now I was making no headway.

Ulrich had been an unbearable drag. Suddenly he had gotten lighter.

As easily moved as the water itself.

And I knew with little interest that my hand was empty. I had lost him.

Too bad.

Might as well rest, close the eyes.

The water spread across my face. It wasn't a problem.

Something bumped my shoulder. On the second nudge I tried to turn and look for the source.

"You may as well stop swimming," a voice said. A familiar voice.

That sounded good. I'd never make it anywhere pulling Ulrich.

And the familiar voice said, "Come on aboard, Richard. Join your friends." From the prow of the Yacht Squadron's tender, Jack Donner stretched a hand toward me. Behind him another man I recognized was ministering to Ulrich, who looked over the rocking bulwark at me with a sickly grin. The man tending him was grim-faced as he spared me a glance.

"Hiya, buddy," Stu Harris said. "I came back."

"Thanks," I said.

He hunched his shoulders, embarrassed twice—that I'd thought he was gone for good and that I had to thank him for not being. "I got as far as Atlanta; wanted 'em to know I'd boarded my flight, just in case. Took damn near two hours to get a plane back, and it had to be first-class."

"I'll reimburse Harris Marine."

"You just give me an hour alone with Charlie or your Mr. Povane. I think the boy likes his work, likes hurting, and that kind of animal you shoot and drop in the swamp. But Povane, for him it's business. He sends somebody to kill your kids, it's business."

"He threatened that?"

"He convinced me."

"Thanks for coming back," I said again. I wasn't sure that in his position I'd have risked Povane's anger. Wished I hadn't in my own circumstances.

Stu had driven onto the island with two FBI agents in tow. They had come across the lurid scene at Povane's house.

"I was afraid you'd gone up against Charlie on your own," Stu said.

I tried, I thought. No choice. I tried.

"I couldn't find him," I said.

31

$\mathbf{T}$he small boat rocked as Stu began rowing. I knelt beside Ulrich, vying against cracked bones and a dozen bruises for his attention. He turned his head toward me sluggishly. His eyes were losing focus. I leaned close. "Did Fentress take the *Dunuthin*'s inflatable?"

His expression remained dreamy.

"Ulrich!"

He looked for the source of the sound—frowned at my mouth. Opened broken lips. "The dinghy? . . . Will not get far in it."

No, not far. Not onto the bay in a bobbing rubber inflatable. Maybe ashore? Only if there was somewhere secluded; but how could he travel after reaching land, pulling or carrying an unwilling companion?

Not ashore, then. I knew the answer of where.

I grabbed Stu Harris's arm, breaking the stroke.

We were just coming round the prow of the French yacht. The lighted pier was visible fifty yards across the reflecting water. A half-dozen people, several in uniform, had gathered in front of the frame building looking our way.

"What now?" Jack Donner asked.

We drifted. The foreign yacht's bow slipped past. The unlighted bulk of Simon Povane's Bayliner crept into view.

Clever Charlie.

"Richard?"

Clever, dangerous Charlie.

I knew there was no chance of trying, if I thought much about it. I turned away from Ulrich, held the gunnel, rolled over the side. The shock of hitting the water brought no invigoration this time. I struggled feebly like a man who had forgotten how to swim, grabbed the tender's side to get my bearings.

"For Christ's sake, Richard! What are you doing?"

"They're on Povane's yacht," I said.

"Get back aboard," Jack commanded. "We'll tell the police."

And they'll make a quiet, underwater approach, I thought. All I said was, "Go tell them" and struck off, away from the tender.

He would be there, in the dark.

He couldn't have seen the small boat yet. None of the big Bayliner's ports had come into view. If Jack and Stu did as I'd said, a moment from now he would see men rowing harmlessly back to the pier. If he was looking at all.

Not getting an explosion from the *Dunuthin'* must have been disappointing.

I gulped water, buried my face in it.

God, I hoped Ulrich could warn about the booby trap. I hadn't thought to.

When I raised my head, the tender was fifty feet away, Stu's head and shoulders a silhouette against the shore. The *Alcyone* didn't seem much closer. My arms didn't want to move, and the water was too thick anyway. I choked out another mouthful and faced the fact that if I didn't get moving there was a good chance I would drown.

I put my face down and willed the arms to pull and the feet to kick.

On the next look I had covered a few yards.

The cruiser's stern was still an impossible distance.

Face down, more kicks.

It was something that needed no thought. Just repetition. A truck driver could unload a hundred cases of beer. Lift, swing, lower. Lift, swing, lower. A hundred repetitions. My arms didn't have to think about the task. They only had to empty the beer truck. Lift, swing, lower.

Thirty-five repetitions brought me abreast of the stern.

Eleven more and I grazed the diving platform.

I clung and choked and knew there was no way to go farther. The arms wouldn't respond. The legs were dead weights.

In a few minutes Stu and Jack would reach the pier and tell the waiting policemen about their foolish friend. And the policemen would head out to see whether the idiot had drowned . . . or been killed by Charlie Fentress. They would come noisily—aggressive, rough.

I looked overhead. The transom was an impossible distance away. I heaved myself onto the diving platform.

The Bayliner had a big lounge on the main deck. Another level up, and forward, an enclosed bridge swayed gently against the clouds. I stayed low and peered through the long windows into the lounge. It was impossible to make out most objects inside except for chairs that stood in profile against the opposite windows. There was no silhouette of a waiting man.

I opened the door and went through in a crab-walk, got a bulkhead behind me, and tried to pick out shapes. The tall chairs were beside a bar at the front of the lounge. Long, low sofas hunkered along the back wall. The center of the room was open, inviting me to cross it if I dared.

As I crouched I smelled something besides my own body. It was a high primitive odor, the pungency of a deer shot at close range, of blood in wet grass. . . . I scrambled up and nothing happened.

I backed to the doorway, found a light switch.

The lounge had recessed overheads that cast a shadowless glare on everything: on the heavily shellacked bar, on the pale blue sofas, on the plush tan carpet, on the syrupy wet splashes that lay atop the pile, on the pale shape hunched beside the farthest wall, on the narrow shaft of the boning knife. . . .

And I stumbled out onto the deck, shivering, in the emptiness of the tight bay under impenetrable clouds, skin prickling in the silence that no air reached. When I turned back to the lounge, the deck felt remote and unreal. My feet moved between the islands of tarry brownness. They stopped at the smeared bare hips.

I knelt. She was facing the wall, knees pulled up, an instinctive huddling to protect the vital areas. It hadn't saved her.

I couldn't touch her.

The bright lights found every flaw, the small puckering of the buttocks, the long pale birthmark along the ribs that I hadn't known her well enough or long enough to discover. The ribs trembled as the light flickered. On her back the light was steady and constant.

I put my hand on her back, felt the cringing of flesh, the intake of breath. A small hand crept from under her face and stretched toward the boning knife.

I gripped her wrist, pulled her around.

The mad wide eyes focused and bruised lips opened. "You. . . . Where were you?"

I couldn't answer. I stroked her head. Not where I should have been. Off playing a foolish game at other people's risk.

"Are you . . . ?" All right? No, not all right.

She shook her head, said "Yes," closed her eyes. "Better than I was."

"Can you get up?"

She said sleepily, "Why don't you carry me?"

I carried her to the end of the sofa nearest the door, set her down. I walked through the blood, not caring.

It wasn't hers.

She wanted to keep my hands close. When I broke away, her face turned ugly. "You weren't there. . . ."

"Where's Charlie?"

She jolted upright, looked around desperately. "Please give me my knife."

"Did you use it before?"

Sliding back, she covered her eyes with her arms. The voice that slipped out was rational. "Yes."

I held her for a few moments, told her she didn't need the knife. The master stateroom was forward. From the windows, I saw the bobbing shape of the tender, Stu at the oars, two men in white shirts at the bow. At the foot of the bed was a plaid blanket, neatly folded. I took it back and wrapped it around Anne.

I switched on the deck lights, went out and caught a line Stu Harris threw. Two middle-aged men wearing dark slacks and polished shoes came aboard, took a look in the lounge and radioed to hold the ambulance when it arrived.

"Have you looked where the blood leads?" one of them asked.

"No."

It led through the door I had entered, along the starboard deck, the gouts seemingly larger every few steps. At the forward deck he had gone to cover. Lifted the lid of a storage locker, pulled out the life vests, climbed in and closed the lid. Clever Charlie, knowing he could wait out any dull average people who came looking for him.

One agent pulled the lid back and pointed his gun in. The grinning, lantern-jawed face stared back at him. His left hand was clamped like a brown vise on his bare right thigh. He was naked, crouched and grinning, knees up at the bristled chin, eyes steady and crafty. The bottom of the locker held two inches of the blood that had spurted between his fingers, then leaked, then trickled. He'd known he could just sit there and hold it in. His grin told us so.

I spent the night in the waiting room at the Hopkin emergency center. Anne left at one, huddled against a tall white-haired woman who refused to look at me. At four-thirty a harried Eurasian girl came along looking for someone who could belong to a lewd Prussian and said Mr. Lenz was very tough. He wanted her to go sailing with him. I could drive him home if I wanted to.

32

My father came back to work two days later, implausibly jovial. He flashed grins at secretaries he hadn't noticed in years. He gave a thumbs-up to the head of the trading desk. He chatted with the partner in charge of syndication and took the two senior retail men to lunch.

He didn't slap any backs, but a smile from Patrick Welles, Sr. was almost as unthinkable.

He didn't slap my back. Didn't offer a grin or a thumbs-up.

We came face to face in the hall near my office. He recoiled, then brushed past, face hard, eyes hot, color high.

Over his shoulder he said, "You think you've won, don't you, you little bastard?"

Would that it were so: the part about being a little bastard. I saw enough glimmers of myself in Patrick Welles to know that it wasn't. I met his meanness with detachment, which was another kind of meanness. Detachment said that the person behind the behavior didn't matter. Raye Donner understood what I was doing when I put her daughter in a pigeonhole.

I told myself you couldn't choose the temper you inherited.

Pat came to my desk, wearing an expression of fear that was prepared to become anger. "Whatever you heard, you'd better keep your mouth shut."

"All right."

He didn't trust my answer. "No one will believe you."

"No."

His lips pulled back. But he had run out of things to say. He left, and I tried to concentrate on papers that didn't matter.

Robby breezed through and quashed a rumor that Harvey was coming back. A position with Morgan Stanley in New York had been offered, the partners at Ambrose & Welles had dithered, and Harvey accepted. The partners looked around after the fact, found no one else to take charge, and the internal inertia of the firm left Patrick Welles there.

He couldn't have been expected to know that Simon Povane was a criminal. No one else knew.

Even Peter Eckland told friends that he was shocked and mildly disbelieving. I overheard him at the Center Club. "The government indulges in these persecutions, you know. It justifies minor officials' existence." He turned from the faltering real estate tycoon he had been addressing, saw me, and raised his nose two inches. "So you eavesdrop as well as dissemble," he said.

"Every day," I agreed.

"People in this town know better than to trust you." He turned and walked stiffly toward the dining room.

If they didn't know, he would tell them.

He had dropped Simon Povane as a client two hours after getting the midnight call summoning him to the federal building where his friend awaited a magistrate's hearing. *So terribly sorry! The firm doesn't handle criminal matters. Wish we could accommodate you, old boy! And by the way, here's your retainer back.*

Stu Harris met me late the next morning, red-eyed, yawning and cheerful, and described Povane's arrest. The New Zealander was still at his office, faxing account records to a destination in London. His computer screens were full of bank and brokerage statements. His satchel was packed with client checks and securities. Last-minute looting was a chore that demanded hours. Povane spread his hands and pleaded puzzlement. Accounts were asking for European exposure. This was an age of international markets. What could he have done wrong?

An FBI agent said they wanted to discuss, among other things, the death of an agent named Fertig.

Simon shook his large head and said that—well, it was absurd, of course, but he had better consult a lawyer. The senior agent put handcuffs on him and offered to dial any number.

It was indeed an age of international markets, and internationally minded cops went with them. Financially astute sleuths from New Scotland Yard swooped down on the offices of Jerome T. Willard Company in the late afternoon, London time, and froze every dollar and pound in place. Their efficiency gave a second chance to American investors who had been careless. Handling other people's money, they would grow careless again.

I went up to see Anne. Her mother lived a few minutes off the expressway on a shaded street of old houses where porches were perfectly painted and lawns freshly trimmed, as if the owners feared the neighborhood might go down. Other disasters caught them unprepared.

Her mother saw me and cried, "How could you?"

Unanswerable.

"She trusted you."

A mistake, I thought. Hoped not.

The stern woman went away with her anger, and the young one came to the door.